A
KILLER SEASON

*Gambling Gets Tough
When You Bet Your Life*

PAUL SEKULICH

Novel

This book is a work of fiction. Names, characters, businesses, organizations, places, events, and incidents either are the product of the author's imagination or are used fictitiously. Any resemblance to actual persons, living or dead, events, or locales is entirely coincidental.

Copyright © 2014 by Paul Sekulich

All rights reserved.

Published by Omnibus Productions

and

Printed in the United States by

CreateSpace,
a DBA of On-Demand Publishing, LLC

ISBN-13: 978-0991559466
ISBN-10: 0991559460
BISAC: Fiction / Thrillers

DEDICATION

To my wife and muse, Joyce. With love, a kiss, and a snifter of Gran Marnier.

Acknowledgements

My thanks to Jessica Page Morrell for her professional guidance, expert editing, and advice on fiction writing. And for caring about writers.

A special thanks to Detective Jan Ryan and Detective Mike Pachkoski of the Criminal Investigation Division of the Harford County Sheriff's Department for taking their valuable time to show me the technical inside to real police and forensic work.

A grateful bow to all the members of The Panera Writers' Group for their diligence, time and critical comments that make writing so much less a lonely business, and novels so much better.

To Lois Woodward for her keen eye for things the author should've caught, changed, or removed. She's the real detective in my books.

To John C. Rehmert for always being in my corner all these years.

Chapter 1

The hole in the jerry can was more oval than round, as if the bullet had struck at an angle. Coll Nolan studied it with his finger as he lay behind the object that may have saved his life, and might need to again.

He was amazed at how many people were trying to kill him, but he'd made plans for his life that didn't feature dying. More than two dozen men had fired death at him that day, and all of them got to visit their ancestors sooner than most young men plan. Plans don't always work out for average folks, but Coll Nolan was no average person. An average person would've been dead by now.

All he wanted out of life was to be able to bet on baseball, so what was he doing shot up in Southeast Asia where survival was a far more pressing need? *Good question*, he thought, but, should he survive, a more worrisome one kept spinning in his head: What changes and challenges would be awaiting him back home?

"You hit anywhere important?" Coll said to the marine next to him. The man immediately checked his belly and groin.

"Nope, my stuff's okay."

"They got us about everywhere else."

"Only hurts when I breathe."

"You can breathe?"

The battle between the advancing North Vietnamese Army and the U. S. Marines had raged on for almost an hour, but the heaviest exchange of gunfire was beginning to subside as the sun dipped to the horizon. Lifeless bodies and the crawling dead were strewn everywhere across the wide grassy expanse. Coll and the marine next to him seemed to be the last men standing. They were both separated from their units, wounded, bloody, and exhausted. Coll's weary eyes searched the area for a suitable place to retreat, patch themselves up, and try to make it through the oncoming night. He scanned the smoke-laden terrain where he stood. Nowhere his vision took him offered protection.

Coll plodded south for several minutes, and came upon a muddy swale near the village of Thanh Phu, about five miles northeast of Saigon. It wasn't a fortified bunker, but at its edge were a few trees and tall shrubs for cover. He grabbed his buddy by the arm and limped over to the spot with him in tow, where they welcomed the chance to sit down. The smells of burning palms and spent explosives filled the humid air. He stared out at the killing field from his hunkered down position at the base of a hibiscus bush and thought about the number of the enemy he'd killed. It was a large number. Way more than John Wayne had whacked in *Sands of Iwo Jima*, and it saddened him to think about it, but they were trying their best to kill him, so he'd done his duty and stopped them.

He looked down at himself and saw blood everywhere on his battle uniform, and he could feel sharp pains in his leg and shoulder. The noises of staccato gunfire, explosions, and approaching helicopters still thundered in the distance and in his head. Crouched next to him was the other young marine in camouflage face makeup with deep-set, tired eyes. Coll had dragged him out of a losing firefight after the guy had spent what was left of his energy in a hand-to-hand match-up with a tough NVA soldier, who took a long time to kill. Coll was dog-tired, but grateful for a chance to catch his breath and for the moment of non-combat.

Coll's eyes closed and the weariness made his real time thoughts ebb in and out, but he was fully aware of one thing: the man next to him was a fellow marine. He thought that if he had to die today, it was a comfort to know that another marine would be there with him.

"I'm sorry... I'm fading a bit on you," Coll said.

"You take it easy, buddy. You saved my ass out there and Eddie Menning don't forget things like that. What's your name, sergeant?"

"Coll Nolan."

Eddie shifted around to better face Coll and slapped his hands on his helmet.

"You're shittin' me. I'm sittin' here with Gunnery Sergeant Collin Nolan? Jesus, everybody knows about you, gyrene," Eddie said.

"Who says crap like that?"

"Every guy in the Corps. You got enough medals comin' to weigh you to the ground."

"Horseshit."

"You hang in there, baby. Help's on the way. Hear 'em, Coll? Hear them big gyros?" Eddie said. "They're coming for us, sugar. You just stay cool."

The sounds of the approaching evac helicopters grew louder. Most of them were heading for the U. S. Embassy in Saigon, but one broke from the rest and headed toward a landing spot less than eighty meters from where Coll and Eddie sat.

"Run and catch a lift out, Eddie. I'll be okay."

"I ain't running nowhere, baby. They either save us both or they leave us."

The helicopter's exhaust bursts became deafening as it settled on the wildly whipping grass.

"I think our ride to the prom is here," Eddie shouted. "Choppers scare the crap out of me, but if it can get us out of here, I'm in."

Eddie jumped up in jubilation, but Coll saw something far more dangerous than a helicopter ride heading for them, a mere baseball pitch away.

Chapter 2

Two Viet Cong soldiers clambered out from behind the remains of a hut in the dense kudzu less than twenty meters west, as the horizon rose to hide the last sliver of the sun. Coll saw the black-clad, VC soldiers raise AK-47 assault rifles toward Eddie, who spotted them in time to dive to the ground. Eddie aimed his M-16 in their direction, but when he pulled the trigger nothing happened.

Two shots rang out. The Viet Cong soldiers stared at the two marines for a moment, then crumbled to the ground. Eddie checked himself for fresh wounds. Finding none, he snapped his head to Coll, who sat with his .45 caliber pistol perched on his knee, smoke rising from its barrel.

"You got them bad boys, partner. We don't let no black pajamas in Dodge."

A pair of shadowed figures rushed toward the two marines in the twilight. Before Eddie could draw his sidearm, they were on top of him, restraining him from getting his pistol out and doing them any damage. Eddie's eyes filled with terror, but Coll realized who they were and lowered his .45. One of the two U.S. Army corpsmen shined a flashlight in their own faces to assuage the men's fear. One man was a black man, the other was white.

"We're the good guys, marine," the white corpsman said.

"Jesus wept," Eddie said.

"We're going to put you in our brand new Rolls Royce limo out there with that big propeller on top and get you gents out of here," the white corpsman said.

Both medics helped Eddie to his feet. The white corpsman then hefted Coll up, put Coll's arm over his shoulder and helped get him walking to the Bell UH-1E helicopter. Eddie and the black corpsman led the way across the open field.

"Take care of him, doc. He's got a lot of medals coming. That's the Audie Murphy of the seventies," Eddie yelled back to the corpsman supporting Coll.

"What's his name?" the black corpsman asked.

"Sergeant Coll Nolan, to you and me, but the NVA call him c*on ác mong*."

"*Con ác mong?*" the corpsman said.

"Means nightmare," Eddie said.

"Shut up and move, Eddie," Coll said.

"A bad motor scooter, eh?" the black corpsman said and glanced at Coll.

"He just shot up about thirty belligerents out there in that field, and he saved my butt today," Eddie said. "I'll tell you something, doc, if he was after me, I'd shoot myself."

"Do you know you're wounded, marine?"

"Your ass. They missed me."

"No, *your* ass. It's bleeding," the black corpsman said.

Eddie contorted and checked his behind. It was covered in red. He patted himself on the area of the wound.

"Sonofabitch. My own damn juice. Popped me in the fuckin' can. I didn't even feel it. Must've ricocheted off something," Eddie said.

"I heard you jarheads were butt-tough, but I'd still put a couple of band-aids on that," the black corpsman said.

"You got them nice flesh-colored ones?"

"Right on, brother."

The black corpsman pulled up the sleeve on his forearm to reveal a "flesh-colored" band-aid, apparently intended for Caucasian application, on his very dark-complected wrist. "See? One color fits all," he said with a grin.

"You know, truthfully, I ain't never seen nobody yet with skin that sick-pink, band-aid color. But gimme a couple anyways,"

The four men boarded the helicopter and took off into the night sky.

* * *

"Got a little rough out there today," Eddie said, over the copter noise.

"Saigon's ready to fall," the black corpsman said. "We're pulling people out."

"Shit," Eddie said.

"You'll be somewhere safe soon," the white corpsman said.

Coll somehow knew that their helicopter was not just rescuing them and taking them to temporary safety, it was taking them out of there for good. After eighteen brutal months, Coll felt an eerie feeling in his gut that he and Eddie were going home.

"Eddie, do you think the Orioles won today?" Coll asked.

Eddie looked puzzled.

"The Orioles? The baseball Orioles? Yeah, sure," Eddie said. "What did you expect with that nitwit Steinbrenner runnin' the show? They beat my slacker Yankees 26 to 3. Palmer pitched. Killed their ass. Brooks Robinson hit two grand slams. They was bombing the Yanks so bad they tried to find that dickhead Billy Martin to pinch hit."

"Where'd you hear all that crap?"

"Got one of them shortwave pocket radios. Picks up everything but money and chicks."

Coll brightened for a moment. "You're full of bravo sierra," Coll said, then looked at the date on his wristwatch. "My God, it's the end of April. The season's running away from me. What I wouldn't give to place a bet on a game back in Baltimore."

"What I wouldn't give to place one at Aqueduct," Eddie said. "Mainly because I'd be in New York and not in this shakin' sonofabitch."

"We both need to spend some time in a marine hospital before we do much," Coll said testing the tenderness of the blood-soaked wound on his thigh.

"Yeah," Eddie said. "Can you believe one of those monkeys got me in the can?"

"Be thankful that's all he got."

"You got plans when you get home?"

"Yeah. I want to be the biggest money winner in the history of Las Vegas."

"What? At poker?"

"Baseball."

"Baseball. You are nuts, you know?"

"Maybe. We'll see."

"What're your plans for the near future," Eddie asked. "For money now. Not for when you're broke in Vegas from betting on the Orioles."

"Like for work?"

"No, for bank heists. Yeah, like work."

"Haven't thought that far ahead."

"Well, look, when you heal up and get back on your feet, give me a call. Now I want you to understand that I don't do this for just any old combat hero, but since you pulled my bacon out of the fire, I'm gonna make an exception and put you onto a sweet paying job that'll beat the beans out of doin' actual work."

"Does it have to do with a bank heist?"

"Keep your voice down. We don't want every jamoke on this chopper wantin' in," Eddie said, looking around like his head was on a lazy susan. "Look, my uncle is a big diamond merchant, among other things he does to make money and, brother, let me tell you, he makes a ton of it."

"Why would he want me to work for him?" Coll said.

"Because you're my buddy and he loves me like a son. Trust me, I'll get you something cushy to do for decent bread."

"How do I call you?"

"Look up Vandermeer Diamond Brokers in Manhattan. They'll tell you how to get in touch with me."

"Okay, but I was really up for boosting a couple of banks," Coll said.

"No joking around, hear? Call me. I mean it."

Coll had contemplated going home someday, but he wondered to what. He had his dreams and his list of future aims like most young men, but occupationally the only thing he knew how to do was soldiering. What he yearned to do, and had a modicum of talent for, was figuring out professional baseball game outcomes. And, in the American job market, he wasn't sure there was a huge demand for that limited skill.

They were going home, and they'd had heard about the anti-war movement and the angry protests. His sister had written him about returning soldiers being spat on as they got off the planes. He had fought the good fight and done his best to honor his country and his uniform. Now he was going home.

Coll had never feared the enemy as much as he did that thought.

Chapter 3

Finding work in Baltimore was tough. At least work above minimum wage that didn't require entry level cooking. He found that a soldier returning from Vietnam received little or no praise outside of family, and many of one's own relatives harbored bad attitudes about the justification of war in general. It wasn't restricted to the hippies and the love-thy-neighbor Christians either. Coll saw it becoming the mindset of the majority of 1970s America, weary of seeing the body counts and the flag-draped caskets, which the media played up every day on television and with bold headlines in the newspapers.

Coll Nolan soon realized that he wasn't going to be able to build up the bank he wanted to take to Las Vegas to pursue his dream. Not in Baltimore, anyway.

* * *

Coll was impressed by the bustling activity at JFK after he deplaned from the U. S. Navy transport, and took a moment to survey the open concourse below from the upper level of the terminal.

Eddie Menning intercepted Coll as he stepped off the escalator lugging a jumbo suitcase and a military duffel bag slung from his shoulder

"Was the chicken cordon bleu in first class as good as it used to be?" Eddie said.

"Tasted a lot like peanuts," Coll said.

"I'll speak to the chef."

Coll and Eddie came out one of the door gangs of the terminal and hit a wall of steamy July air and city exhaust fumes. They queued up and got a Yellow Cab.

"Where to?" the cabbie said.

"Where's the nearest bar?" Eddie asked.

"There's a nice place I know in Queens," the driver said.

"Maybe somewhere a little closer," Eddie said.

"Got one in a few blocks, but the one in Queens is nicer."

"We'll take the one that ain't so nice," Eddie said.

A short ride later, the cab pulled to the curb in front of a narrow doorway jammed between two storefronts. A rusty, paint-chipped, neon sign hung out from the building with the succinct wording: "BAR." The rusty chains supporting the sign might have anchored the Mayflower. A filthy window held a sun-parched, corrugated cut-out of a faded, Canadian Club whiskey bottle about six times life size. Several hundred insects and one brown mouse had made the window their final resting place beneath a bare, flickering fluorescent tube.

It was a basic kind of place, nothing fancy, booze and a bartender, all that was required. The mahogany bar surface had a patina and smell like it had been mildew-rag wiped for decades. Varnish long gone, it had been swabbed down to expose a raised grain you could feel. The air fresheners hanging from the fan cords had lost their battle with the overwhelming atmosphere of stale beer and ancient cigarette smoke that may have gone back to Sir Walter Raleigh.

Coll and Eddie sat at the end of the bar and ordered beers. Eddie tossed a twenty down on the bar while Coll gave the well-worn place the once-over.

"I bet the one in Queens was nicer," Coll said.

"Yeah, and cost us a hundred bucks to get to."

The bartender set up their drinks, took the money, and stopped to stack some spotty bar glasses on his way to the cash register.

Eddie looked Coll over.

"Last time I saw you you looked like you'd been in a war," Eddie said.

"A couple of months in Ocean City and I clean up nice. Looks like they pasted your fanny back together okay."

"Being back in civilization fixes a lot of things."

"When are we supposed to meet your uncle?"

"Saturday. His place, around ten."

"*His* place?"

"Owns a bar and restaurant in the city."

"Is it a *nice* place?" Coll said, studying at the antique ceiling fans, and taking in the outdated TV above the bar, layered with years of brown smoke tar.

Coll felt Eddie's stern stare. The bartender placed the change from the twenty on the bar and moved several feet down to the television set and turned it on. Coll waited until he was out of earshot and turned to Eddie.

"I don't want this to sound ungrateful, but I have to ask," Coll said.

"Ask what?"

"This uncle of yours. Is he, you know, connected?"

"Connected? What?"

"To the... mob?" Coll said.

"What? For Christ's sake, he owns a restaurant and operates an import business. That don't make him Al Capone."

"Okay. I don't want to get involved with anything illegal."

"Look, he's a proud Dutch-American who loves that his decorated nephew and hero buddy are goin' to work for him. Everything he does is above-board. He's my mother's brother, for crying out loud. *He* should be concerned about *you* --- half mick and half paisan."

"All right, already. So we'll see him next week. What's the job?"

"Manager for one of his import houses. That'd be me. And he needs a driver to go around town to his job sites. He hates to drive in the city, and his regular guy married some chick and's movin' to Kansas. *Kansas.* Can you believe it? Whatever happens in *Kansas*? Oh, yeah, I remember now: Nothin'."

"I don't feature being a chauffeur the rest of my life."

"Bartel Vandermeer pays his people very well. So you might wanna rethink those plans after your first paycheck. And it's not only chaufferin'. He brings in foreign cars you'll get to drive every month. Very nice rides guys like you and me don't get to wheel around in often."

Coll took a sip of his beer.

"I'll try it," Coll said. "We'll see."

"Like we got skills to peddle to the highest bidder. 'What is it that you boys can do?' Well, we can sleep in a rice paddy, shit on a dead run, and shoot coconuts out of palm trees with an M-16. That'll oughta rate a corner office on Wall Street."

"You left out getting three straight weeks out of a pair of socks."

"Is this that baseball thing?" Eddie said. "This why nothing's a good enough life for you?"

"It's not all about money. If I had a million dollars I wouldn't know what to do with it except bet on ball games, but winning money is how success is measured."

"Damned if I wouldn't know what to do with it," Eddie said. "So what's your big plan?"

"I want to be the biggest money winner in Las Vegas history. And I'm going to do it betting on baseball."

"Oh, man, here we go again," Eddie said.

"Eddie, you like playing the horses. You bet on maybe seven of nine races, you win on three. When I bet baseball it's like betting on the horses every day, every race, for seven straight months. And I'll win at an eighty percent clip."

"You're out of your goddamn mind. Nobody does that. Nobody wins like that. It don't happen, Coll."

"If it was easy, anybody could do it."

"And I suppose you ain't just anybody," Eddie said.

"Some people can run a mile in under four minutes. Some guys can climb Mount Everest, or win gold medals at the Olympics. No one achieves anything believing they can't. I believe I can do what I say I can."

Eddie shook his head, took a pull on his beer, and stared at Coll. Coll knew the look. It was the one you get when telling someone you could sail around the world in a sixteen-foot boat, or go to the moon in a homemade rocket, or eat a hundred hot dogs in ten minutes. He knew Eddie's look said: *Who wins real money on baseball games? -- Nobody.*

Chapter 4

There were people Coll had read about who had an aura of such authority that just hearing of their exploits caused one to be a bit awestruck. There were men like the legendary Marine Corps General Lewis B. "Chesty" Puller, who was the most decorated U. S. Marine in history, and the recipient of five Navy Crosses. There were giant people like George Washington, Abraham Lincoln, and Babe Ruth. He remembered meeting President Gerald Ford in a medal presentation and recalled how the hair had bristled on the back of his neck at the ceremony. During a political rally in Atlanta he had shaken the hand of Coretta King and had never forgotten the electricity of that moment. There was something about these people with their huge accomplishments and their historical place in the world that made most folks at once humble and even obedient.

Bartel Vandermeer was not one of them, but he was close.

He was tall, tan, with razor-sharp features, and sported a full head of gray-blond hair that belonged in a L'Oreal ad. His clothes were from the finest haberdasheries, even though Coll believed Bartel could wear a muumuu and still be equally respected. His eyes were pale blue, cold, and piercing when he stared at those in his presence, which he did often. Bartel was a paternal man around whom those in his employ did what they were told.

Coll and Eddie worked for almost two years for Vandermeer, who was a large player in the diamond district of New York and in the international market. Eddie had been right. The man paid his help well. So well, in fact, that Coll's plans to make baseball betting his full-time profession got put on hold. He placed a few weekly bets through a local bookmaker and let that be enough to satisfy his drive to be the greatest baseball gambler ever. He rationalized that if he socked away a lot of his money now, when the time to go west arrived, he'd have enough to last him. Being the greatest Vegas money-winner was going to require a healthy pile of seed funds.

New cars arrived at the port every few weeks and Coll drove some of them to the people he presumed had bought them. Vandermeer's empire wasn't solely dependent on South African diamonds and Amsterdam jewel auctions. He also had his hand in foreign cars purchased directly from their factories in several major European cities. Coll wasn't sure about the reason for Vandermeer's foreign car interests, but he knew enough to sense that Bartel was a major player wherever he had investments. Coll might be able to out-bet him in baseball, but he damn-sure wouldn't play *Monopoly* with the man with real money.

Coll had only seen the diamond side of the business once, when he had to take a car to West 47th Street where Eddie worked. The diamond district there was a booming place and inside Eddie's building Coll saw more diamonds than he thought existed in the world. He described it as the place where blings came to show off, and where the rich came to shell out.

Coll had reached a comfort level in New York that temporarily deterred him from going for his life's goal: to go to Las Vegas and bet on every major league baseball game, every day, through the conclusion of the World Series. He was only twenty-three and there was plenty of time for that, he figured. For now, he was loving life. He had an easy job, got paid great money, and was working for a man who liked and welcomed Vietnam vets at a time when a large segment of America treated soldiers returning home like murderers. What would be wrong with staying a while, building up a bundle of cash, and heading west later? In Eddie's estimation: Nothin'.

One thing, though, bothered Coll a little. Each time he went to the port to pick up the car he was to drive to its new owner or dealer, it was always one particular car among the football field of cars in that same shipment. He had to procure a single, special car with a particular vehicle identification number. It struck him as peculiar, but he figured the car with that VIN must have included certain extras, and perhaps a specific paint combination custom-ordered by the buyer, even though many other models at the port appeared to be identical. He allayed his curiosity and went about the job of delivering the cars without much more thought.

On one particular delivery to a dealer he had driven cars to often, he stopped to have lunch at a diner en route. When he returned to the car, he noticed that the something behind the rocker panel beneath the driver's door was hanging down. Coll lay on his back and scrunched under the car enough to tug on the piece and re-align its fasteners with holes in the frame. While it was pulled downward, a thin stream of a pale powdery substance fell to the asphalt of the parking lot. It was coming from one of the holes in the frame where a fastener pin belonged. He pushed the part back flush against the frame and checked to assure it was securely in place.

Coll swept some of the powder onto piece of paper, folded it into a small envelope, and tucked it in his jacket pocket. The car was a red Ferrari 308 GTS, imported directly from Maranello, Italy.

He hoped what was in his makeshift packet was pizza dough flour.

Chapter 5

Bad news can come in many forms. On this particular night, it arrived in a long black automobile carrying two large, darkly dressed and heavily armed men.

Behind the wheel of the shiny new, 1978 Cadillac limousine was Big Al Marko, a huge Serbian man with a jaw and mouth like that of a giant grouper. Next to him, in the passenger seat, was the even larger Theodoor de Groot, known by his close friends and distant enemies as Two Ton Teddy. Both men appeared to be older and more shopworn than most forty-year-olds, but they could still intimidate the fittest of young men. Perhaps their accelerated aging was because of their super-size frames, or because of their almost permanent, grim facial expressions, but more likely it was because they both looked like guys who would just as soon kill you as tell you where to get good goulash.

The long black limo raced down 67th Street, then screeched to a halt in front of Albrecht's Restaurant on New York's west side and parked in front of a fire hydrant, even though ample, legal curbside parking was available.

The two men struggled out of the limo and headed into the restaurant. A neon sign in the window tersely touted the establishment as "Authentic Dutch."

A poster in the window below the sign advertised the musical *A Chorus Line* at the Shubert Theatre.

Inside, the entire place appeared deserted of patrons. A bartender was putting away a tray of bar glasses as the two big men entered. The bartender smiled at their arrival.

"Well, ain't my night complete," the bartender said. "Big Al and Two Ton Teddy just in time for last call. What's up, fellas?"

"My blood pressure and Teddy's weight," Al said.

"Like he's on a crash diet. His ass cheeks have separate climates," Teddy said. "Gimme a little espresso and an Alka-Seltzer."

"No Heineken, Al? What, big doin's tonight?" the bartender asked.

Al shook his head.

"Yeah, big doin's," Teddy said. "Bad doin's. Gimme the seltzer first."

Big Al clomped toward the back of the bar and disappeared down a long, dimly-lit hallway.

"I'll be right in," Teddy yelled after him. The bartender set up the fizzing glass of seltzer on the bar and prepared the espresso.

"Big poker game going on in the back. You and Big Al sitting in?" the bartender said as Teddy belted down the seltzer.

"Naw, we got family business to take care of."

"Anybody I know?" the bartender said.

"I tell you and then maybe we take you along on the ride," Teddy said.

The bartender served Teddy his espresso. "No thanks. Don't need to know that bad,"

"Smart decision," Teddy said as he picked up the hot espresso and sipped it carefully.

The bartender wiped his forehead with a bar napkin, then poured himself a double shot of Jack Daniel's and downed it like he'd just survived a plane crash.

Teddy smiled as he marched down the hall toward the back. He knew prying into the Vandermeer family business was not good for one trying to make it to Medicare, and going "along on the ride" with Big Al and him could be riskier than going on a ride with a hopped-up kamikaze pilot.

Chapter 6

Big Al stepped into the back room of Albrecht's, a smoke-filled, card players' paradise. He stood near the large poker table and looked over the game and studied the players. Several men sat around an octagon table puffing on every variety of tobacco-burning pleasure. The dominant smell in the air was a mixture of smoldering cigars of decent pedigree, and varied aromas from the restaurant's adjacent kitchen, which this night was strongest from fresh-from-the-oven parmesan cheese bread. If one wished to get a heady nicotine rush in a bakery, this was the place to do it.

Kyler Rotermund, a six-foot-two, broad-faced man in his late twenties, dealt the remainder of the cards for the current hand of draw poker. He dressed like an Izod Lacoste model, a man that central casting might describe as a "bad boy" type that married women in a supermarket stared at for a moment and wondered: *What if* . . .

Al knew a genuine, happy smile was a stranger to Kyler's face, and imagined his teeth were only exposed when he brushed them. He also knew Rotermund was also a fellow with whom, on first sight, smart men wouldn't pick for a fight.

By contrast, across the table from him sat Coll Nolan, an athletic-looking fellow with boyish good looks and a bit of mischief attached to smiling teal blue eyes. Perhaps because of his mixed Celtic-Italo heritage, some described him as a young Irishman with an Italian face, whatever that meant. Others described him as a northern Italian, whatever that meant. His auburn hair and adobe tan had a lot to do with those impressions, but the eyes were definitely once sported by a Viking ancestor.

A stack of paper money sat in front of him. He studied his cards and took out a Zippo lighter and lit an unfiltered cigarette dangling from his lip. He placed the lighter on the table with its engraved side up. The lighter contained the U.S. Marine Corps emblem and the inscription:

To: Coll "Nightmare" Nolan
USMC
Vietnam 1973-1975

"Your open, Nolan," Kyler said.

"Open for twenty," Coll said.

"What bullshit," Kyler said to the others. "He's got nothing."

The men at the table tossed in cash to match the opening bet of twenty dollars.

"I never know with you whether I'm playing against Irish sheep dip luck or guinea grease," Kyler said.

"I got a little of each in me, Kyler, so why don't you stop whining and deal. I'll take two cards."

Kyler dealt Coll's two cards and, then dealt to the others as they tossed their discards into the center of the table. Kyler put down the deck and looked intently at his hand, made a tight-lipped grin at Coll, and placed his hand face-down on the table.

Two Ton Teddy brushed both jambs of the door as he pushed into the room with his espresso cup. He stood near Big Al and slurped down the last of his high octane brew and set the empty cup on the card table.

"I'll play these," Kyler said.

"Ah, got a pair, eh, Kyler?" Coll said. "Well, if you want to see the shepherd's pie and spaghetti I got in this hand, it's going to cost you a yard, boys." Coll placed a hundred dollar bill in the pot and looked over at Kyler. The other players, except Kyler, showed their dismay, folded, and tossed in their cards.

"I wouldn't pay a hundred bucks to see Venus DeMilo in the buff," a gray-haired player stated with disdain.

"Who'd want a broad with no arms and sealed lips?" another player said.

"You might want to think about that," the gray-haired man said.

Kyler looked hard at Coll, then drummed his fingers on his down-turned cards.

"See the hundred, and raise your McWop ass three more," Kyler said tossing a stack of bills in the center of the table.

Coll studied his cards, then stared at the pot.

"Three Benjies. That's a lot of money," Coll said.

"Probably take you a week of pimping to make that much, right, Nolan?" Kyler said.

"Two days, if your sister was better looking."

"One day I'm going to shut that mouth of yours for good, you miserable mick dick."

"Your three hundred and five more on top. In the immortal words of Sherlock Holmes, 'the game's afoot.'"

There was dead silence in the room. Kyler and Coll stared at each other like two prizefighters facing each other down as they awaited being told the ring rules.

"You know what, Nolan?" Kyler said. "This is poker, not that baseball bullshit you bet on."

"And your point would be?" Coll said.

"You may do okay betting on baseball, but this is my game. You're nothing but a tourist here in

Pokerville. Your five hundred and a G on top," Kyler said and slammed down a large pile of bills on the pot.

Coll thumbed and riffed the bills in front of him as he stared at his cards. Every eye was on locked on him. Then, as in a ritual, he flicked each card in his hand by snapping his middle finger off the ball of his thumb.

"I win at baseball because I've got a thing with the game." Coll said. "A MacGuffin they call it. I've got no MacGuffin with cards. I'll just see the thousand, Kyler."

"Right, because you're scared, and you're beat and you know it," Kyler said and turned over his cards revealing a mixed-suit straight from an eight to a queen. "Five cards, all straight from the lady."

A long moment passed before Coll spoke.

"All I got is two pair . . ."

Kyler grinned and reached for the pot.

". . . of kings," Coll continued, putting down his cards and exposing a hand that contained four kings and an off card.

Kyler's grin disappeared and his expression turned to shock. His face flushed red with rage.

"You sonofabitch!" he shouted.

Kyler rose from his chair and lunged for Coll who made no move to avoid his attacker. Al and Teddy grabbed Kyler and forced him back into his seat. The two big men stood nearby, ready to restrain him further, if necessary.

"None of this now, Kyler," Big Al said. "The boss wants you to pick him up in twenty minutes."

"And he wants you to go too, Coll," Teddy added.

"Me? What's up?" Coll asked.

"What's he want us for?" Kyler said.

"The boss don't need no reason. Just do it," Big Al said. "Wear gloves tonight, and you two put on some jackets and ties. The boss wants to go eat somewhere special tonight, so don't be lookin' like the Village People."

Coll got up from the table, picked up his winnings and stuffed them into his sport coat pockets. He picked up a newspaper from the table and started for the door with Big Al and Teddy.

"This ain't over, Nolan," Kyler said.

Coll turned back and stared at Kyler. "With guys like you, Rotermund, nothing's ever over, is it?"

Coll picked up his beer from the poker table and moved into the center of the room. He faced Kyler and raised his glass as in a toast.

"Here's to a long life and a merry one. A quick death and an easy one. A pretty girl and an honest one. A cold pint and another one."

Coll tossed down his drink, then placed the glass back on the table, smiled at Kyler, and left the room with the two big men.

* * *

Kyler snatched his drink and downed a big swig of it as the other players at the table got up and filed out of the room in silence. Kyler sat alone, seething about his loss, especially since it was a loss to Coll, a man he saw gaining favor with his boss every day, a man who wasn't even of Dutch descent like he, Bartel, and Teddy were. He despised the guy and his marine buddy Eddie, who had brought Coll into the family business. But Kyler had already laid the groundwork for getting rid of Eddie.

	Coll Nolan was next on his hit list.

Chapter 7

Kyler Rotermund knew he was a man with resolve, an attribute that went way back to Amsterdam. People didn't get in his way for long. Like his Simon Legree of a stepfather, a Brit named Freddie Thompson, whose strict and sadistic rule over Kyler and his siblings ran unchecked by his financially dependant mother, who chose appeasement as the safest course in dealing with her bread-winning spouse. Kyler hated his mother for being so spineless, and never forgave her for allowing her lout of a husband to administer his cruelty upon him and his blood family. Kyler longed for the time when he would not have to take orders from people who had power just because they were bigger or older. He went through his early years trying to find a way to get his own power, power over others, and attain his own twisted version of respect.

Later on, when his brother and sister cowered in the presence of the stepfather, twelve-year-old Kyler was defiant and stood up to the tyrant. It was a tack that took attention off the other family members, but often cost him heavily in severe corporal punishment.

Freddie owned a small fleet of commercial fishing boats in Amsterdam and forced Kyler to work with him on his personal boat, even though the boy was not of teen age. On one late fall outing, Kyler and Freddie went to sea without any of the usual crew members. The plan was to rod-fish for cod, rather than use the deep, trawling nets that required a fully-manned boat. It was to be, more or less, a rare fun day on the water, but Kyler feared that there was another reason for Freddie's charitable disposition.

Freddie shut down the boat's engines about twenty miles out, removed his fisherman's vest and gave it to Kyler to hang up, and went forward to the point of the bow to set the anchor for a windward drift. Kyler soon followed, and when his stepfather leaned over the gunwale, laboring to free a fouled anchor chain, he shoved him overboard into the frigid water of the North Sea with the butt end of a gaff. At first, Freddie yelled angry curses and demands at what he thought was the bungling youngster, but his stepson just looked on and did nothing to help him.

Freddie's curses turned to clawing at the hull, and later to pleading as he realized the boat's freeboard was too high to pull himself back aboard. The cold water was already having its hypothermic effect on Freddie as his shivering body made his pleas for help come out in stuttering phrases. Soon, the supplications ceased. Kyler watched his stepfather's feeble struggling with stone-faced detachment until the blue-black water swallowed him slowly into the depths and out of sight.

At that moment, Kyler, for the first time in his life, felt powerful and secure. It was the best feeling he'd ever had.

When Kyler returned to the marina he was consoled and embraced by all for having endured such a tragic maritime accident, and because he had been so brave and had tried everything a young lad could do to save his beloved parent. A soaked and punctured fisherman's vest twisted around the gaff hook proved to everyone how heroically little Kyler had tried to pull Freddie from the icy sea. It was an Academy Award performance by the young man, and the happiest day of Kyler's life.

Trouble followed Kyler's new-found bravado and encouraged a life of crime. Freddie had willed his fishing business to his mother back in England, who immediately sold it to the highest bidder and kept the money for herself. The selfish move left Kyler and his family destitute. Stealing for a living cost Kyler many of his youthful years of freedom and put him in several juvenile institutions, and later, an adult prison.

When Kyler was freed from jail at twenty-one, Bartel Vandermeer entered his life, provided security for his family, and offered him a job in his growing diamond business in New York. Bartel told Kyler he had a real future in his new American empire, and that he wanted people around him who were tough and loyal. Kyler liked what Bartel said. He saw his new boss as strong, but kind and respectful to those around him. Kyler soon found his regard for Bartel transforming into hero worship and, for the first time in his life, he vowed his allegiance to another man.

Kyler knew that people were afraid of him and he liked things that way. He'd heard what they said about him, that he was prejudiced against all women and non-Dutch men. He even had his last name changed back to his Dutch name instead of the English one that Freddie had saddled his family with. He was particularly fond of the description a prison psychiatrist had applied to him: That he was "a man to whom contempt and hate were skills he honed and polished like van Gogh worked his brushes and oils." He always smiled at that one, but deep down he knew the shrink was right. He knew killing and violence were in his blood, in his inner being, and those upon whom he plied his arty craft didn't end up in a painting. They ended up screaming until death drowned them, and restored power and security to his life.

Chapter 8

Coll had heard that going out for a ride with the Vandermeer gang in the family car was not ever going to be a fun trip like driving to Ocean City when he was a kid in Maryland. Eddie had told him that it usually meant that someone was going to the ocean all right, but only the beach blanket was coming back.

That fact irked Coll to no end, since Eddie had been so adamant in defending the notion that his uncle was in any way on the opposing side of the law. In a way, Eddie had been correct in that Bartel Vandermeer was not mob-connected, rather, he was in his own, very special, elitist mob operating well outside of the traditional interpretation of the term. Coll needed to know if Vandermeer was legit and not a criminal. It turned out he wasn't and was. And soon Coll knew he'd have to decide what to do about it.

The black Bentley motored down several deserted streets of dark row homes in a downscale section of the city. Kyler was at the wheel with Big Al up front riding shotgun. Teddy sat in the jump seat in the center of the car, facing the back window. Coll leaned against the window on the rear passenger side, poring over the sports section of the *Times* in the intermittent light from the passing street lamps. Bartel Vandermeer, sharkskin-suited and looking like he'd just left a personal groomer, sat stone-faced at Coll's left. A long silence was broken as he turned to Coll, who buried his attention in his newspaper.

"You know we got trouble with Eddie," Bartel said.

Coll lowered his paper.

"What kind of trouble?" Coll asked.

"The kind there isn't any cure for."

"What'd he do?"

"He's a traitor. Turned over family business secrets to our competitors and we caught him stealing,"

"Your nephew? A thief?"

"Coll, the worst crimes in the world are committed by people in the same family. In school, didn't you read Oedipus? Hamlet? King Lear? Look, I know you and Eddie were tight back in the service, and I know he's the reason you're with this organization today, and for that I'm grateful to him. You've been a big asset to us these past couple of years, but your loyalty is especially important to me now. I got it cleared with people to bend some very long-standing traditions to let you become a member of a very special inside group. We've got big plans for you, Coll. Very big plans. Tonight you get a chance to show your loyalty and rid the organization of a dangerous enemy."

Coll stared out the window at the passing houses. He was riding in the back of Bartel Vandermeer's posh limousine with a TV, a full bar, and the softest leather seats a body ever dropped a butt on, but he wished he could be on a hard bleacher seat at Yankee Stadium at a game, or on a sticky bar stool making bets with a bookie, or just about anywhere but where he sat.

Chapter 9

The Bentley pulled up to the curb at a boarded-up, three-story tenement and stopped. The entire street was made up of run-down, uninhabited buildings, cheap, post-World War II housing that, after more than three decades, had outlived any practical usefulness.

The car's motor was turned off. Construction equipment sat idly about near the building and a sign advertised:

Vandermeer Contracting, Inc.

Coll looked at the sign in silent amazement. *God,* he thought, *is there anything this guy isn't into?*

The five men in the car got out and headed into the desolate building. A bare, low wattage light bulb hung from the ceiling over each stairway landing. The men went up the three flights of dark, creaking stairs to the roof. There, two uniformed cops greeted Bartel and his entourage. They led the group to a pair of men tied to a tall vent pipe.

"Your guy was a real pain in the ass. Had to quiet him down," one of the officers said to Bartel. "I doubt that Nolan here will get a government medal for his work here tonight, but I might pin one on him."

The bound men were back-to-back, on their knees with their heads bent down as if unconscious, their shirts bloody like POWs who had been beaten half to death during harsh interrogations.

Bartel gave a subtle signal to Kyler who took two envelopes from his jacket pocket and handed them to the policemen and bade them leave by a head gesture he made toward the exit door. Bartel then beckoned Coll and the others to come over to the bound men. As they approached the captives, one of them raised his bloodied face and looked directly at Coll. It was a much worse-for-wear Eddie Menning. Coll summoned every disciplined nerve in his body not to react in overt repugnance.

"These guys think they're smarter than we are," Bartel said. "They don't think we pay them enough, so they steal from us and sell out family secrets to people who can hurt us and put us out of business. There's only one punishment for such treachery."

Kyler stood next to Coll and drew a small caliber, semi-automatic pistol from his coat pocket and screwed a silencer into the barrel with gloved hands.

"I sentence you to death," Bartel said coldly as he glared at the two captive men. Kyler grinned, then aimed the pistol at the tied man next to Eddie and shot him in both of his knees. The man screamed through his gagged mouth and writhed in horrific pain.

Coll's head snapped back from the violent reaction of the shot man. Kyler gave out a raucous laugh and shot the man in each of his shoulders. More muffled screams came from the victim as he twisted in torment for several moments. Kyler finally shot him in the head. The man's body jolted for an instant, then went limp. Kyler smiled, then turned and handed the gun to Bartel.

Bartel nodded at Kyler and his other two sumo-sized henchmen. They untied the dead man and took his bloody body to the edge of the roof. Bartel followed his men to the wall and peered over the edge.

"Coll, come over here," Bartel said. "You need to see this."

Coll reluctantly steeped to the wall next to Bartel. The henchmen hoisted up the dead man to the top of the low wall, and looked down. Bartel and Coll followed their gaze to a large, open construction Dumpster against the building some twenty-five feet below.

The men lifted the dead man off the wall, swung him out a couple of feet, and let him drop. The body landed inside the near edge of the long steel roll-off. The men congratulated themselves on their body-tossing marksmanship like Olympic gymnasts whose team just scored a perfect ten.

Coll tensed his jaw, reached inside his jacket, and pulled out his Walther 9-millimeter pistol as Bartel turned to face him.

"No, Coll. It'll be better to use this one," Bartel said and indicated the small, automatic in his hand. "It's a throw-down, not traceable." He extended the gun to Coll who pocketed his own piece and took the one from Bartel, noting that its grip was wrapped with black friction tape. It was a guess as to how many bullets were left in the gun, but smart money was on only one. Coll put the gun in his left hand and slid his right hand into his pocket and cozied his fingers around his own piece that had a full magazine with seven rounds, plus one in the chamber. If things went bad he was going to make sure that he got in a preemptive strike.

"He was your friend so, as a personal favor to you, I'm going to let you handle it instead of Kyler," Bartel said. "Give you a little time to say good-bye. Just so his body is in that Dumpster in the alley in ten minutes. Understood?"

Coll looked at his pathetic friend. He had seen tortured POWs overseas who looked better than Eddie.

"Throw the piece in the garbage with him when you're done," Bartel said.

Coll nodded and firmed up his grip on his Walther. He stared at his bound friend. Eddie looked up at Coll like a pet Labrador about to be euthanized. Coll held the gun with the silencer in his hand and stared down at him.

Vandermeer and the other three men filed toward the roof door. As they approached it, the door swung open and one of the policemen who greeted them earlier rushed up to Bartel.

"Mr. Vandermeer, Cammy Delano's on the CB in our car," the cop said. "Says there's trouble on the east side."

Bartel strode to the roof door to leave, then paused and turned back. He nodded at Coll as a final encouragement. The four men exited the roof and closed the door.

Coll stepped close to Eddie.

Big Al Marko was the last to exit, and Coll was certain that he'd be watching the activity on the roof through a peep hole in the roof door. Coll knew well that the "trust but verify" concept was a long-standing philosophy in the Vandermeer family.

"Jesus, Coll, you gonna dust me?" Eddie said.

"What kind of jackpot did you get yourself into, Eddie?"

"Shit, I dunno. I took a couple of little stones from some of the back room stock. They weren't even primo. But then they accused me of giving important information to some of our competitors and I didn't ever do that. Anybody with half a brain would know I'd never rat out no family business secrets. Somebody's framing me?"

"Got my ideas on that," Coll said.

"Last month Bartel put me on some chicken shit allowance. I felt like Beaver Cleaver in the principal's office. So I shaved a couple of rocks off the top and sold 'em. I needed some decent bread, man."

"What for?"

"You know... I got a little thing for the ponies."

"Damn it, Eddie. Vandermeer wants me to be some kind of Dutch-style, made man."

"You'd've grabbed some of that ice just like I did. It was laying everywhere."

"I'm not the one tied to a toilet vent pipe."

"I'm not here for boostin' some ice," Eddie said. "It's somethin' else. Somebody's planting stories. It's all bullshit."

Coll looked at Eddie and shook his head. He slowly raised the throwdown pistol and pointed it at Eddie.

"Semper Fi, Nightmare," Eddie said and closed his eyes.

"This has to look good. We don't have much time."

Coll jammed the pistol in his belt, took out a snap-blade pocketknife, and cut Eddie loose from the vent pipe.

"Where we gonna run to?" Eddie asked.

"*We're* not running,"

Coll grabbed Eddie by the arm and led him stumbling to the edge of the roof where Bartel's men had thrown over the dead man.

"The only person who's going anywhere is you. Down there." Coll said, pointing to the Dumpster in the alley below. "Bartel's too smart to leave me up here with you alone. One of his stooges is behind that door's peep hole over there watching everything I do, and he'll report all he sees. Thing is, he can't see us over here, but he knows I have to get you into that big trash bin."

Coll directed Eddie to the edge and leaned him over the wall. Eddie looked down at the open metal receptacle. The dead body lay on its back atop high-piled trash, wide-eyed and staring blankly back up at Eddie.

"Are you nuts? It's three stories," Eddie said.

"And you have to hit the trash on target or else this turns into a bad exercise."

"Let me get this straight. I gotta jump over this wall, off this perfectly safe building, and land in the middle of that shit pile with that stiff staring at me all the way down."

"The secret to the benefit package is to hit the center of the shit pile, but miss the stiff," Coll said. "And if you think this building is safe, hang around until Kyler gets back up here."

"Aw, jeez, Coll, do I have to?" Eddie asked.

"It's like jump school. Hook up and do it."

Eddie started to climb up on the wall, but Coll stopped him.

"Take this," Coll said as he reached into his pocket and pulled out a wad of cash and handed it to Eddie. "Stuff it in your pocket. You're going to need it."

"Coll, I don't know how to —"

"One more thing. We need more blood. Lots of it," Coll said. "All over your head."

"Isn't this where Alfred Hitchcock yells 'Cut!'?"

"We also need a gunshot. A gunshot and blood. Where do you want it?"

"Only one place I won't feel it. Give it to me in the buns, and make sure you bang nothing but muffins."

"Bend over," Coll said.

Eddie reluctantly pushed his pants down a few inches, and bit down on his jacket collar as he bent over. Coll took careful aim at Eddie's buttocks and fired. The bullet skinned the flesh and ended up in the roofing tar a few feet away. Eddie recoiled, but restrained himself from crying out.

"How come that hurt like a sonofabitch this time?" Eddie said, massaging his bleeding rear.

"You were expecting it. Now get up there, aim, and jump."

Eddie yanked up his pants and steadied himself up on the wall.

"Rub blood all over the back of your head and above your eyes," Coll said.

Eddie smeared the blood on his hands, then onto his head, back and face.

"If I survive this, I'll be in Miami where it's warm. Look me up. You'll find me wherever thoroughbreds hang out," Eddie said.

"Under what name?"

"Joey... *Geronimo*."

Eddie jumped saying the last word and plummeted, feet-first, toward the steel receptacle below. Coll peered over the wall as Eddie landed next to the dead man's body.

"Geronimo, buddy," Coll said low and tucked the throw-down piece in his jacket pocket.

Coll looked back at the roof door and knew that once he passed through it and appeared downstairs he was going to face a test of fire against an enemy that outnumbered him and had more firepower. It was like being high up in a burning building with the choice to jump or be burned to death.

There wasn't going to be a good way out.

Chapter 10

A moment earlier, Bartel Vandermeer, Kyler, and Teddy sat in the Bentley while one of the rooftop cops hung by the open limo window.

"You tell that joker Delano we'll send some resources over there to help out, but he better not be stirring up shit over nothing," Bartel said to the cop. "The moron spooks over his own security cops checking his shop doors at night."

A muted gunshot carried down from the roof. Kyler and Teddy turned toward the sound. Bartel waved away the cop near his car window and looked up at the top of the building.

"Think he shot him in the head?" Kyler said. "Think he shot him at all?"

"I don't care where he shot the little bastard," Bartel said, "just so he's dead and in that Dumpster."

A minute later, Big Al emerged from the door of the building. He looked over at Bartel as he bee-lined for the limo and nodded his head. Bartel returned the nod, then lit a Churchill-size cigar. A few more minutes passed. Coll emerged from the building. He face was grim, his eyes downcast.

Coll trudged over to the car and got into the seat to the right of Bartel. He stared out at the darkness through his window. Vandermeer patted Coll's leg like a father giving a son assurance that all was well. But Coll's face did not reflect the gratitude of a loved and protected son. Coll felt like an orphan in an abusive and horrible foster home. He hadn't bargained that he'd be asked again to shoot people, and certainly not a friend. Maybe, he thought, it was time to run away from home.

Big Al got into the limo and rocked the car as he plopped his hulking frame onto the front seat and closed the door. Kyler started the car and drove around the block and down the alley behind the building. The twenty-foot green Dumpster loomed ahead on the driver's side of the car. Kyler pulled up to it and put the car in park. He and Bartel got out, walked over to the large steel receptacle and slid open its side access door. Inside Coll could see the bodies of Eddie and the executed man. Eddie was covered with blood from what appeared to be a gunshot wound to his head. Bartel peered inside, nodded his approval and returned to the car.

Kyler lingered by the access door and looked back at Coll in the car, then turned back to Eddie's body. He picked up a discarded mop handle and whacked Eddie with it across the midsection. There was no live reaction from Eddie, but Coll's jaw tightened so hard he could feel his tooth enamel grinding off. Kyler tossed the mop handle back into the trash, took a switchblade knife from his pocket, and flicked open the blade. Coll slid his hand into his pocket and snicked the safety off the Walther as he readied himself a second time for the bloodbath that was going to ensue should Kyler inflict further harm to Eddie. Kyler placed the point of the knife a few inches from Eddie's genitals, took dead aim and cocked his arm to make the stab at the same moment Bartel yelled from the limo.

"Kyler, knock it off and get in the car. *Now*. I want to get something to eat."

Kyler stopped his follow-through with the knife a split-second before finishing his stab into Eddie's groin, and a nanosecond before Coll started taking out every one of the thugs he could kill before they knew what hit them. He had already mapped out who would follow Kyler to hell, and in what order. *Cơn ác mộng*. Coll was a modest man, but he knew the Viet Cong had named him right.

Kyler folded up the switchblade and turned back toward the car, never knowing how close he'd come to being Coll's first real victim of the night.

"The two rats looked dead to me, boss," Kyler said as he slid shut the bin's access door, then got behind the wheel and put the Bentley in gear.

"Now get us to Four Seasons. I got a craving for lobster," Bartel said.

The limo drove off down the alley and turned onto the intersecting street. Coll flicked his pistol's safety back on and took his first easy breath of the evening. But he knew breathing was not going to come so easy in the coming days.

Chapter 11

The access door of the Dumpster scraped open and a battered Eddie Menning eased his blood-stained head out of the receptacle. He peeked carefully up and down the alley and, seeing no one, lowered himself carefully to the ground. He thought about the past twenty-four hours, in which he'd been beaten like a waif in a Dickens novel, shot again in the ass, been forced to jump off a three-story building into a narrow trash tank with a dead man who stared at him, and made to wipe his own blood over his face like he was chumming for vampires. His ribs and midsection painfully throbbed from the whack he'd received from Kyler. Eddie grimaced as he forced himself to stand straight, then plodded down the alley gripping his wounded buttocks.

A second later, a noisy garbage truck turned into the alley. Eddie ducked into the shadows as the truck rolled straight for the Dumpster, picked it up, deposited its contents into the truck's huge trash repository, and compacted it with its powerful hydraulics. Even though there were other overflowing trash receptacles in the alley, the truck made only its solitary pick-up, drove off, and disappeared into the early morning darkness.

Eddie came out from his concealment and whistled *The Marine Hymn* as he limp-marched in triumph down the alley. He was bloody and ached all over, but he was glad to be alive as he turned the corner at the end of the alley and continued down the adjacent street.

Eddie was hungry and wanted a drink, but thought better of heading for the all-night convenience store he spied across the street, since he looked like a survivor of a piranha feeding frenzy. Instead, he flagged down a cab and headed for a homeless mission he knew of on the lower east side. There would be food and fresh clothing there and, with any luck, maybe an alkie with a pint of vodka. *Any luck?* he thought. Hell, he was the luckiest bastard on the planet.

The celebration of his recent good fortune would be wind down quickly, and he would have to think about what he was going to do with his new situation. Right now, he didn't have the vaguest idea, but the wad of money in his pocket comforted him.

Once again Coll Nolan had saved his bacon.

Chapter 12

Dinner at Four Seasons was a quiet affair, almost solemn. The only difference between Bartel's dinner group and a library was that once in a while in a library somebody coughed or dropped a book. Only the most necessary conversation went on, consisting mainly of terse sentences directed at the wait staff. The awkward silences, while Coll and Bartel's men sat staring at each other and sipping their drinks, occasionally broke into pointless comments about the restaurant's décor and hearsay praises for the chef's reputed specialties. Dinner itself was slightly less talky than a pride of Serengeti lions munching on a zebra. Bartel Vandermeer finally ended the speech moratorium.

"Our family is stronger tonight because of the decisive action of its members. I'm gladdened by the confirmation of Coll here as a loyal part of our organization and business interests. We have a new comrade who has proven himself tonight to be an important asset to our future," Bartel said as he raised his wine glass. "To Coll Nolan: our new family member, our new brother."

Everyone at the table except Kyler toasted Coll. Bartel glared at Kyler, who joined in late on the toast, raised his glass and gave a Cheshire cat smile to the honoree, then put down his drink without ever putting the glass to his thin lips.

Coll tried to smile throughout the attention he was given, but being forced to execute his best friend was no reason to be festive. He knew that he was going to have to make some tough decisions, and make them sooner than later.

What do they have in store for me next?

Did his warrior past fill a niche that Vandermeer saw as a possible fix for anything that opposed him? Suppose the President of the United States and the U. S. Attorney General targeted Bartel's Dutch dynasty? Images of Jack and Bobby Kennedy formed in Coll's mind. Would Vandermeer order him to "fix" that problem like some high-powered guys did in the '60s? Or was Vandermeer shining him on until he could conveniently murder him on some future family ride or field trip?

Below the linen tablecloth, Coll fondled the Walther in his jacket pocket.

Chapter 13

Coll stood outside the entrance of a large office building in Washington, DC and dreaded what he was about to do. Written over the building's entrance were the words:

J. Edgar Hoover FBI Building

He walked away a few yards, leaned his back against a nearby light pole on Pennsylvania Avenue, stuck his hands deep into his pockets, and stared at the sidewalk beneath him. Once he walked into that building he knew there would be no turning back. All he ever wanted out of his *pro tem* life was a decent job, a job that would provide him with enough pay to indulge his passion, betting on professional baseball games. It was something he'd been pretty good at, something he loved more than Babe Ruth loved hot dogs. The job's benefits made it possible for him to save and build the bankroll he'd need to travel to Las Vegas and realize his dream. Otherwise, his dream would always be just that, only a dream.

Coll's thoughts went back to 1963, the beginning of the dream. He recalled the day his father, Dr. Michael Sligo Nolan, gave him a set of 1952 Topps baseball cards for his eleventh birthday. Michael, a professor of English literature at the University of Maryland, always gave Coll books on his birthdays because of his son's natural affection for reading classic stories. But this birthday was different, and his dad had given him those beautiful bubble gum cards published the same year Coll was born. Michael had collected them himself, and had waited to give them to his son when he was old enough to appreciate them. That was the day Coll began his love affair with major league baseball.

It wasn't to be the kind of love that typical fans of the game have, but something deeper that drove him to study every player, every trade, and each team's tendency to win or lose in streaks. He studied changes in team lineups, hitters' slumps, and pitchers' earned run averages against different opposing teams. At fourteen, he began predicting game outcomes for every team in both leagues for the season. He even picked the number of games that would play out in the World Series, and who would ultimately win. He didn't get them all right, but he had an uncanny winning average: a percentage that any major league pitcher would've liked to post as a win-loss record.

His father became concerned that his son was becoming obsessed with baseball, and thought that maybe his gift of the baseball cards had proven to be a stumbling block to the success he wanted for Coll.

Like many fathers, he envisioned his son becoming a doctor at Johns Hopkins, or an acclaimed lawyer like Clarence Darrow, or even a professor at Harvard. Michael worried that his son would never become any of those things. He saw failure for him on the horizon. An expert at betting on baseball? What would that ever do to achieve success in life and earn a decent living?

Coll's father died of a failing heart the year Coll shipped out for Vietnam, never knowing the answers to his concerns about his beloved son. Afterward, Coll's Italian mother, Maria Angelina, carried on in Baltimore for a while, but with her daughter away in college and her youngest child at war overseas, loneliness, paranoia, and deep depression ultimately institutionalized her. Coll's visits to her consisted of watching his drugged mother stare vacantly out a window, while he talked to her and read her books. The one-sided visitations began to depress him so much that he saw her less and less, and finally decided to take Eddie up on his offer of a good, money-making opportunity in New York. He planned to get her private care when he could afford it, but fate intervened while he was away. A massive stroke took her life on a snowy Christmas morning, three days shy of her fiftieth birthday.

Now at twenty-six, all Coll wanted was to be able to ply his uncertain ability into a money-making sideline. Coll wasn't attracted to it so much for the money itself, but betting money fixed a value on his skill and instincts. Playing poker for fun wouldn't prove anything. Prowess at anything wager-wise had to result in attaining something that people valued.

There was one very special, far-away hill he wanted to climb. He wanted to go to Las Vegas and bet an entire season all the way through the World Series championship and come out ahead. If he could do that, maybe he could be somebody special and be the king of that hill, if only for a season, if only to prove he was a winner at something. Maybe then his doubting father would smile down on him.

He never bargained for the killing, and that "made man" jive, on his way to being a baseball-betting guru. He didn't have to kill anyone to be a made man in the Marine Corps, although he sent quite a few enemies to the *choir invisible*, but that was war. War was different, combat against enemies bent on your destruction, with no holds barred. But killing innocents, killing defenseless people, and killing your friends, wasn't in his blood like it was for Kyler Rotermund. Having a few bucks, an occasional friendly boff, and betting some ball games was what life was all about, and he felt nothing was ever going to change that.

He looked up at the building for a long moment. He hated the idea that he was going to be a snitch and rat on those who had taken him into their confidence, because loyalty was very important to him. *Semper Fidelis* was not just a marine motto to Coll, it was a way to reference the worth of your life, and life with your buddies in uniform was a brotherhood forever. Trying to make him into a cold-blooded killer was not a line he willingly crossed, particularly when loyalty was cast out of the mix and murder was put in its place. They had forced him and had given him no choice. And now he had given himself no choice. He squared his shoulders, took a long, deep breath, and pushed his way through the revolving door of the building.

Coll immediately encountered a security check point and passed through a metal detector. An alarm sounded. A security guard suggested that he empty his keys onto a table outside of the metal detector. He did so and walked through again without setting off the alarm. He retrieved his keys, asked the guard for directions, and was sent down a wide corridor.

Coll looked through a doorway ahead and saw a large office with numerous office workers who pounded on typewriter keys and talked on phones in their symmetrical rows of desks. Past the doorway, he approached a reception desk where a dark-suited woman typed and asked him the nature of his business without missing a key on her black IBM Selectric.

"Could you direct me to an FBI agent?" he said.

She looked up from her typing, took her fingers off the keys, and stared at him blankly.

"Why do you need to see an agent?" she asked.

"I want to report some criminal activity."

"A federal crime?"

"A lot of federal crimes."

The receptionist pressed a button on an intercom.

"Agent Capberg, there's a man here at reception I think you ought to speak to."

Within moments, a prematurely balding man in a dark blue suit came out of a side office, spoke briefly with the receptionist, and then faced Coll.

"I'm Special Agent Alan Capberg," the thirty-something man said.

"Coll Nolan."

"My office is this way."

Capberg directed Coll to an office down the hall. Once there, the agent gestured for Coll to sit in one of the guaranteed-forever, aluminum government chairs across from his desk in the small, austere office.

"The receptionist said you want to talk to someone about a crime, Mr. Nolan. Is that correct?" the agent said.

"Actually, it's about a whole lot of them," Coll said.

"Well, as you may know, we only handle federal crimes here at the Bureau."

"For the moment, forget the crimes, and let's talk about people. Does the name Bartel Vandermeer mean anything to you? I mean, *federally*, of course."

Alan leaned over to his intercom and fingered a button. "Miss Dandridge, would you please come into my office? And bring two coffees, your shorthand pad, a tape recorder. And find Special Agent Murdock, while you're at it."

Capberg looked over at Coll who stared pensively out the window.

"Second thoughts?" he said.

Coll shook his head.

"I only wanted to be a good chauffeur and watch some baseball. I never bargained to be a hit man," Coll said. "Overseas, I always thought dying was the hard part, but dying's easy. I surrendered to that fact almost every day in country. It's killing that's tough. I've thought it through, Agent Capberg. No second thoughts."

Coll looked up at the FBI emblem on the wall of Alan's office. He saw the words Fidelity, Bravery, and Integrity written on the banner under the shield on its seal. He was going to need to have all of them, especially that second one when it came to dealing with the likes of Bartel Vandermeer and Kyler Rotermund.

He could already taste blood in his mouth.

Chapter 14

Coll had never imagined that doing the right thing would cost him his freedom. After several weeks of surveillance, the authorities arrested the Vandermeer bunch and charged them with an extensive list of felonies that Coll had testified to. Irrefutable documentation, drug evidence, and wired recordings of live and telephonic conversations he had helped the government obtain, put the diamond dealer in an indefensible position. To pile on more evidence, Coll led the agents to one of the cars he had delivered, dusty with heroin in its chassis. Afterward, Coll was put into protective custody in a small but posh beachfront hotel called the Sandpiper in Long Island between East Hampton and Montauk. The code name for the retreat was "The Biltmore."

The FBI men and women were three-deep around him all day, every day. The waterfront and beach areas were filled with G-Men and G-Women posing as fishermen, sunbathers, workers, and tourists. The government denied entry to the complex to real tourists, and relocated the current guests to other facilities under the guise that the Sandpiper had a tainted water problem, which required extensive plumbing repair. The vacationers transplanted from their Sandpiper residency received generous compensation for the inconvenience to lessen any newsworthy complaints. To make the ruse even more credible, trucks disguised as plumbing company vehicles, drove to and from the hotel daily, manned by federal agents. It seemed that the Bureau had thought of everything.

Coll had the expensive resort all to himself as its only real guest, except for about a hundred annoying FBI roommates who came and went in waves. The omnipresent federal army thoroughly vetted waiters, housekeeping staff, chefs, and other hotel personnel, who worked in shifts around the clock. Coast Guard and government watercrafts, posing as fishing and pleasure boats patrolled the oceanfront. An occasional, covertly-armed jet ski zipped across the shallows, and helicopters roared above the resort's waterfront at regulated intervals. Some might've seen the situation as vacationing in paradise, but Coll thought he was in Club Dead.

Coll couldn't go to the bathroom without an escort. They analyzed his meals, and making a baseball bet was about as easy as getting uranium out of Moscow. He was under arrest with invisible handcuffs and was told that the trial of the Vandermeer organization would be long and grueling. Here he was at a beautiful vacationer's dream resort where he couldn't swim in the outdoor pool or the ocean, go fishing, or walk on the beach. The little exercise he could get was in the resort's small gym facility. If being in prison differed in any way from this, he couldn't imagine how. Coll believed that even maximum security inmates got an hour of yard time every day where they could see the unobstructed sky. When he tried to look out a window, some big-ass agent with a howitzer blocked his way and directed him back to a windowless room in the center of the hotel. Coll wondered what Alan Sherman would have written home about in his stay at this *Camp Grenada*.

On the days when court was in session, agents ushered Coll into an armored truck with two SWAT officers and escorted his vehicle with specially fortified vans. The personnel charged with Coll's protection spoke little and could've passed for stunt men in the *The Longest Day*. They traveled to the courthouse where Coll delivered his testimony against the Vandermeer crew. Directly afterward, he got returned his Eden-at-the-Beach via convoluted routes taken by three or more armored vans that scattered in different directions, in case prying eyes attempted to follow.

Coll's testimony was critical for ensuring convictions for Bartel Vandermeer, and the FBI knew all too well that Coll's untimely assassination would greatly simplify the defendant's problems. The Bureau was not about to take a chance of making any mistakes with a powerful bad guy the likes of the Diamond Dutchman, or any of his far-reaching tentacles.

* * *

Coll arrived at the rear parking lot of the courthouse as he had in all the former days of the Vandermeer trial. The back door of the armored truck swung open and two SWAT men, covered in full combat gear, helped him out of the vehicle as they had routinely done before, and started to escort him to his assigned entrance to the court.

A high-velocity projectile hit the armored truck inches above Coll's head, followed by the crack of a gunshot that echoed off the adjacent buildings. Before anyone had much time to react, a second shot pierced the helmet of a SWAT officer, who had lurched to protect Coll, the bullet exiting the helmet and slamming into the vehicle. The policeman collapsed to the ground, blood flowing from the wound in his head. Coll had been made to wear a Kevlar vest, but the bullet that went through the downed man's helmet wouldn't even have been slowed by all of its layers of woven chemistry.

Smoke grenades exploded and filled the area with clouds of dense white screening against whatever was attacking Coll and his protection group. The remaining

SWAT escort hugged Coll and pushed him to the far right side of the courthouse, away from the usual walkway to the court's back door. Bedlam was breaking out all around the parking lot. Numerous voices were screaming out commands, and several police officers and FBI agents were pointing upward toward a tall building a block away. Cars scrambled to get to the location, and a large van pulled up to block Coll from the shooter as he and his SWAT escort made their hasty retreat to the back of the courthouse.

"Where are we going?" Coll asked.

"Plan B, sir," the SWAT officer said as he shoved him around the corner of the building. "Now head down those steps on the left."

Coll did as he was directed and found a door at the bottom of the cement stairway that ran down into a bulkhead next to the building. He opened the door and entered what appeared to be a basement kitchen. The SWAT officer followed closely and closed the door once they were safely inside the room. He checked the outside situation through a window in the upper part of the door, looking in all directions.

"Looks like we got away clean," the SWAT officer said.

"Lucky that door was open," Coll said. "Would've thought with the security around here everything would be zipped up tight."

"The doors beyond this room are all locked and guarded. This open kitchen is part of Plan B."

"Now what?" Coll said.

"Now I can get rid of this," the officer said as he removed his headgear and peeled off the large white dots attached to the sides of his helmet.

"Are those to show your rank?" Coll asked.

The officer laughed.

"Not hardly. They're to designate who *not* to shoot."

"Not to shoot?" Coll said as the officer placed his helmet on a table next to the door.

"Well, you saw what happened to the other guy who didn't have them, didn't you?" the officer said as he checked outside again, then turned to Coll.

Coll's military training had provided him with the ability to identify most firearms. He instantly recognized what the SWAT officer had drawn from his protective vest. It was a Sig Sauer P239 automatic pointed at him from six feet away.

Chapter 15

Coll stared in disbelief at the man paid to protect him, now threatening harm only two footsteps away. Something about the man's voice rang familiar.

"I know a slug from a .357 like this would probably go through that vest you're wearing, but a head shot seems more professional, don't you think?" the SWAT officer said.

Coll began to recognize the arrogant man as one of the uniformed cops from the dark rooftop where Eddie had been prepped for execution.

"You're one of Vandermeer's lackeys. Still doing his shit work while he directs from a cell," Coll said. "How're you going to get out of this? Lot of people out there saw you with me."

"Not that it's any of your business, Mr. Nolan, but this gun is a throw-down that's been rendered untraceable, so, after I do you, I toss it in the trash somewhere far away. The piece issued to me is still in my holster and won't match the bullet that goes through your little bean. While I checked the perimeter, some joker ran in here, popped you, and ran out. He was just too fast for me to catch. Slick as frog snot, eh?" the cop said.

"How'd you get into SWAT?"

"I'm not a SWAT officer. Never trained to be one. Bartel pulled some strings. Told them I was a close friend of yours and to suit me up."

The SWAT imposter raised the pistol level with Coll's head and took aim. Coll knew that attempting to move away in defense was futile at such close range, so he stared at his fate head-on. The window in the door crashed inward and the SWAT officer was knocked flat on the floor by the force of the shot that came from outside. Blood sprayed everywhere from his uncovered head. A few seconds later an FBI agent entered the door with an automatic pistol in his hand.

"You okay, Mr. Nolan?" the agent asked.

"Never better," Coll said as he leaned on a nearby kitchen counter to steady himself. "Wouldn't happen to have a stiff drink on you, would you?"

"Sorry, no, but after this incident is investigated I know where there's a bunch of them. The trial will be postponed today, so we can head out of here in a little bit and grab us a few," the agent said.

"That a Smith & Wesson M&P .40?" Coll asked.

"It is, indeed. You have a sharp eye, Mr. Nolan."

Several more policemen and agents began to flow through the door and check out the situation. The agent with the S&W went over to Coll and escorted him to the door and to the outside. As they passed the fallen body of the dead man, Coll held back and looked down at him for a moment.

"He would've been proud. Right in the head. Very professional," Coll said and followed the agent outside and up the stairs into the bright sunlight.

Chapter 16

When Coll got back to the "Biltmore," the pieces of the assassination attempt began to come together. The long-range shooter had positioned himself on the roof of a thirty-story building only two hundred yards from the courthouse and had used a high-power, custom rifle that had been modified to fire bullets capable of piercing one-inch steel plating.

The first bullet that hit the armored van had to be dug out of the soil under the asphalt beneath the truck's engine. It had penetrated the armor plating on the rear door, gone through the vehicle's steel floor, and then through the surface of the parking lot where it was later extracted some seven inches in the ground. It was a projectile that could disable a vehicle's engine without any problem. The second rifle bullet that killed the real SWAT officer went through the man's helmet and head, pierced the bullet-proof window in the open van door, and ended up a foot down into the court building's basement floor. The rifle was later traced to a cop named Reynolds, a man with connections to the phony SWAT officer downed by the FBI agent, and also to the Vandermeer organization.

The shooter had tried to escape from the building where he'd set up his sniper position, but in the confrontation with several lawmen on one of its upper floors he was killed in a violent exchange of gunfire. Only one police officer was wounded in the encounter, and his wounds were not life-threatening, but Reynolds was hit twelve times and further suffered a bit of dramatic irony. He died in front of the ninth floor elevator that he had summoned with the down button. He was hit by a fusillade of bullets and took his last breath the moment the elevator doors opened.

Coll would testify to the relationship of the killed SWAT imposter to Bartel Vandermeer from his earlier encounter with him in the Eddie Menning rooftop incident. The trial of the Dutch organization would now increase in complexity, but an additional nail had been hammered into Vandermeer's legal coffin.

Back in the courtroom, Coll was once again confronted by people who wanted him dead. Again, he was heavily outnumbered. The current battlefield didn't allow for guns and grenades, but hateful eyes could penetrate you as surely as any bullet or shard of shrapnel.

Bartel and his top capos sat in the courtroom and glared at Coll every chance they got. Coll answered them back with steadfast eyes, but inside he felt the intimidation. His blood pressure rose and his pulse pounded, as it had in Vietnam before a firefight, but he knew there were no good consequences to be garnered by showing weakness.

Coll wasn't afraid of the street grade bullies in Vandermeer's organization. He had always shown strength and was highly respected by all the underlings in the Vandermeer family of bodyguards, enforcers, and paid heavies. He was one guy, besides Kyler and Bartel himself, that they wanted no part of in a beef. Even tough mutts knew when to walk around a seasoned pit bull. Coll wasn't afraid of Vandermeer nor his close entourage, at least not in the usual sense of fear. What he feared about them lay in forever having to watch his back. Some enemies can ultimately resolve their differences and learn to tolerate each other. But with the Vandermeers and Rotermunds, the biblical lamb might someday lie down with the lions, but that little fellow wouldn't be getting a lot of sleep.

* * *

Ten long months had gone by and Coll was glad this day would be his last spent in that musty courthouse surrounded by a platoon of cops. He was pleased he was soon going to be able to plop into a bed without armed men peeking in his room every twenty minutes checking to see if he was still above room temperature. Today the bad guys were getting sentenced and he was going somewhere so far off the map that not even Hercule Poirot could find him.

The trials had found the entire Vandermeer bunch guilty of everything from money laundering, diamond smuggling, and racketeering, to extortion and narcotics dealing. The bitch was that they all got off on the murder charges by convenient alibis they had concocted with intimidated witnesses who would've testified to being with Christ at Golgotha if Vandermeer told them to. That unfortunate imperfection of justice was going to severely cut their time spent in their new homes in Ossining with the attractive high walls and decorative razor wire. Justice was supposed to be blind, but even a bat would know when the *stoofpot van varkenshaas* was rotten.

The judge brought the courtroom to order and pronounced the sentences for each lower echelon gang member, starting with Two Ton Teddy, Big Al, and a cadre of lesser thugs who got 15 to 20 years each. Kyler got 25 and Bartel got 30, but any of their sentences could be shortened with good behavior and some strategically placed bribes with the right people. None of them was going to do really hard time with the life sentences they deserved, but they were all going to do some prison time, nonetheless. That thought made Coll feel a little relief and smiled inside, that and the thought that the whole courtroom ordeal was at last over. He felt like he'd just given birth to sextuplets through his penis. There had been excruciating pain, but afterward, such blessed relief.

Coll came out of the back entrance of the courtroom and descended the long flight of steps that led to the outside. He was briskly escorted by federal agents and policemen out the exterior doors of the court building and through a gamut of media people who stuck microphones and cameras in his face from every direction. The federal agents managed to get him into a waiting government car at curbside and secure the car doors. Two large men in dark suits sat on either side of Coll in the rear of the car.

Outside the car, policemen guided the handcuffed Bartel Vandermeer, Kyler Rotermund, and others into awaiting PD vans. The prisoners wore state-provided jumpsuits that looked starkly different from the Brooks Brothers and Savile Row attire Bartel and his cronies traditionally wore. Kyler paused long enough to lock eyes with Coll who watched from the side window of the government car. Kyler shot a hateful glare and nodded at Coll in a subtle but meaningful way that could only be interpreted as a portent of revenge. Coll knew that was the one thing Kyler was an expert at: getting even, and often well beyond.

Coll kept his stare on Kyler until he was forced into the police van and locked inside with the others.

Coll settled back in the rear seat of the car between the two big men as they pulled away from the courthouse and drove off. Alan Capberg, in the front passenger seat, turned back to Coll.

"Don't worry about them, Coll. They're going away for a long, long time." Alan said.

"And so am I. Makes you wonder who's getting sentenced here," Coll said.

"It's a nice town with nice people. You'll be safe there. No one will ever find you."

Coll looked out the window, but his focus wasn't on the passing countryside.

"Ever is a long, long time." Coll said.

"Take this," Capberg said, as he handed Coll a large envelope. "In this are the contact numbers you may need to get in touch with us. Only the director, my personal secretary, and myself know where you're going and what's in that envelope. Normally, you would be under the oversight of U.S. Marshals, but the director pulled some strings to place you under our bureau. When you arrive make sure you put that somewhere safe and don't share its contents with anyone. Not your best friend, your mother, and not ever with a lover."

"I've got none of those left so that'll be pretty easy."

"You know what I'm saying," Capberg said. "You call me or Elaine Dandridge if you need help. Got it?"

Coll nodded.

"Think there'll be any big league baseball games there?" he asked, posing a question whose answer he was certain of before it left his lips. He knew that finding big league baseball in Montana was right up there with finding a beef Big Mac in New Delhi.

Chapter 17

It would have been a typical summer morning in Washington for FBI executive secretary Elaine Dandridge except for the fact that, for some reason, her new 1978 Volkswagen Super Beetle wouldn't start.

Elaine thought her parking garage at the Wellington Apartments was unusually empty for a Saturday, but most of the people who lived there were active cosmopolitans, so fewer cars meant it was likely a good travel weekend for many of them. Since no one seemed to be around to ask for help, she decided to go back to her unit and call the auto club.

When she got off the elevator at the sixth floor she noticed two strange men talking down the hall a few feet past her apartment door. One was about six-foot-six, and the other was a shade over five feet tall. She didn't think much of it and proceeded to walk down the corridor, take out her key, and open the door to her unit. When the door swung open, the shorter of the two men, with reptilian quickness, muffled her mouth from behind and forced her into the living room. The taller man followed and closed the door.

Terrified, she turned to the men and noted that the tall one had a long, bony face with deep-set, black eyes. The short fellow was pudgy and reminded her of

Spanky McFarland in the old *Our Gang* movies. It was in her past FBI training to notice things about people. She automatically recorded people's faces, identifying marks, and peculiar traits. But then she noticed something else. The two men were holding large, dangerous-looking knives.

"Wha-what do you want," she said. "Money... jewelry? Take anything you want just don't hurt me. Please don't hurt me."

"We were going to break into your place and see if we could find what we want, but you coming here yourself really improves our chances for success. I think they call that a serendipity," the tall one said and smiled at his partner. "All we want, pretty lady, is a little information."

"What kind of information?"

"Where'd you guys put Coll Nolan?"

"Who?"

"We know you work for the FBI, sweetheart," the tall one said. "We also know your boss oversaw all his travel arrangements. So where'd you put him?"

"What travel arrangements? I don't know what you're talking about."

"The Witness Protection kind."

"What makes you thing I'd know that? All Witness Protection cases are sent to a different division. Only the Director himself and a government sponsor know that," Elaine said, her voice straining.

"Wrong answer, lady," the tall one said and turned to his vertically-challenged partner. "Take her into the bedroom and tie her up."

"Please ...please don't!" Elaine shrieked.

The short man covered her mouth again, shoved her into the bedroom, and threw her onto the bed. The tall one brandished his opened switch-blade knife in her face.

"No more yelling, sister, or I cut out your vocal chords right here and now," he said.

The short man tied her to the bed's slatted headboard with curtain tie-backs he yanked from the window décor. They closed the blinds and drew the curtains to further block any sightlines into the room.

"Give us what we want and we go with nobody worse off than when we started. Do you understand me?"

Elaine nodded.

"All we want is the whereabouts of this Coll Nolan guy. Look, lady, he means nothing to you, so what do you say? Give us an address. The name of the town, a couple of facts and we're outa here."

"Untie me and I'll get you what you want," Elaine said. "I have to call my boss."

"Untie her right arm," the tall one said to the short one. "You know what's going to happen if I hear anything you say I don't like. And don't tell anyone where you are, either."

"Hand me the phone," she said.

Elaine's right arm was freed and she was given the princess phone receiver with its keypad in the handset. She pressed some buttons and waited.

"Alan, some men have me under their control and want information about Coll Nolan," Elaine said into the phone and listened for almost a minute. "Yes. I can't say right now. Thanks, Alan." Elaine kept the phone to her ear and squirmed up onto one elbow to face her captors.

"He says they sent him to Florida. Belle Glade," she said.

"Under what name?"

"James...James Keller."

"He got a job there?"

"At the town's library. Does groundwork, landscaping."

"Excellent. You done good, pretty girl," the tall one said and then nodded to his partner.

The short man took the phone from Elaine, pushed a button on the receiver, and handed the phone to the tall man who listened to make sure the phone conversation was cut off. He placed the receiver back in its cradle on the night table.

The short man took his knife and stepped over to Elaine who raised her tied arm to allow him to cut her free, but instead he turned and walked out of the room with his tall accomplice.

Elaine cocked her ear toward the door and listened intently.

"Hit redial on her phone and get the person she called back on the phone. Then we need to finish up and get out of here," the tall one said, "Whoever she called will know where these calls originated."

"Think she told us the truth?" the short man asked.

"Hell no. She's FBI. But they'll be inclined to tell us the truth the next time we ask."

Chapter 18

Someone serving breakfast to Coll at a Parris Island mess hall had told him that Southern-style grits weren't for everyone. And Bozeman, Montana shared that same characteristic with that side dish. There were beautiful landscapes everywhere, scenes that made one think they were living in an Ansel Adams portfolio, only in full color. It was a place where trout fishermen came to retire and, of course, there was that "Big Sky" thing that Montanans played up everywhere. It was Eden itself to many, but early on, the Montana lifestyle began to wear thin on Coll's need to be where he could bet money on baseball, real money, not that subsistence the witness protection people had arranged for him to receive while working on the grounds of a small community center. In fact, if it came to a vote during his first week in town, Coll would probably have laid better odds on liking the grits.

After almost a month in Big Sky country, Coll, now credentialed as Robert Smith, had tried hard to acclimate to the native lifestyle and began to find himself softening a lot from his earlier prejudices. There were some things he took a shine to, such as trout fishing and horseback riding. He discovered that many of the best fishing places were only accessible by horseback, so learning how to ride became necessary if he was to become an angling hotdog and swap embellished stories with the locals down at Judson's Always Café. As a bonus, he found that he really liked trout, especially *alfresco* along with a beautiful sunset at a mountainview lake.

Coll discovered that Judson's Always Café derived its peculiar name from the fact that the original sign, high on a forty-foot pole overlooking the highway back in 1941, said, "Judson's Always Open Café," but the present owner didn't want those long hours, so he removed the word "Open" from the sign. The diner's regulars supported the change as long as the place remained *always* a café, and not some rock and roll honky-tonk. Ergo, the word "always" on the sign was preserved. They figured that old man Judson, the founder, who was buried behind the restaurant, would be okay with that even if they now closed the joint at nine every night.

Coll also discovered that Judson's was not the place to tell anyone about a great fishing hole where the area's famous cutthroat trout were biting. Within seven minutes of revealing its location, an army of fly-rodded, creel-laden bumpkins would descend on that spot and stand elbow-to-elbow on the banks and hip-deep in the water. The good news was that upon detecting the horde of mankind bantering on the shore's edge and wallowing in the stream, every fish within a half mile scooted to far away pools at flank speed, leaving the angling army with nothing but wet waders and snarled monofilament to show for their trouble. Later on, the fish would return, to the joy of the original discoverer and the endless grousing of the empty-creeled *pescadores*.

Women back east had come and gone in Coll's life and he never allowed himself to be too involved with anyone. Involvement would be counter-productive and anything like marriage would be the death of his long-range plans, so he avoided women who alluded to "nest eggs" and having children, like Tom Sawyer shied away from work. That didn't mean he eschewed women altogether. On the contrary, his libido always had its antennae up for a good clean score with any female who didn't flunk his single requirement: willingness. Eddie Menning had often described Coll's sex drive by saying that he'd jump on a mound of rocks if he thought a snake was in the pile.

The town's community center where Coll was employed held numerous public events, mostly on the weekends and in the evenings, but Coll finished his work on the grounds by afternoon and thought perhaps he should start participating in some of these activities. He also thought it might be prudent to heed the advice the FBI had given him in his going-away packet and "not become too visible too soon." He realized that the smooth handling of his public debut in town was going to be a bit of a tightrope walk.

    Most of the events held at the center were flea markets, craft and flower shows, and book club meetings, but there was one activity that he seemed to gravitate to, and that was the amateur plays the local theatre group put on a couple of times a year. If he was going to eventually become known in the comparatively small town he figured that playing a part in a theatrical production might not be such a bad way to do it. Heeding FBI warnings or not, sooner or later a lot of the people in Bozeman were going to know who he was anyway. It wasn't like Bozeman was New York where an eight-foot gibbon in a space suit could walk the streets and never get a second look. He was, if not already, going to be seen, known, and talked about. People in Bozeman got to know their residents early on, and often, intimately. Coll learned that that can happen in a town where changing the pie in the pastry keeper at the local diner was damn near front-page, above-the-fold newsworthy.

    He had always liked acting in high school and knew there was a bonus to being involved with the theatre: It was where pretty women hung out. Besides, being in a play with some good-looking gals beat the hell out of making guesses about the sex-worthy contents of a pile of rocks.

For the time being, he would content himself with some fishing trips in his free time and continue to amass money for that fine day when he would be able to head south to that place where his dream lived.

That was the plan until he went on a particular fishing outing.

Chapter 19

It was one of those perfect days for fishing. Coll recalled a short story title by J. D. Salinger, *A Perfect Day for Bananafish,* and thought this day also qualified for a title like that, except that this was a perfect day for trout, and he had no intention of killing himself like the Seymour character had done in Salinger's story. It was perfect in every way: temperature at 68 to 70 degrees, low humidity, light wind, nearly bugless, and the trout were so eager to bite that he almost had to go behind a tree to change flies on his line. There was only one small thing that might've put a caution on the day. A Native American man of about fifty, dressed in what appeared to be traditional Crow warrior garb, was staring directly at him from across the narrow river.

The Crow warrior watched Coll for almost five minutes before he waded into the gently flowing water of the river, got into a wooden canoe, and paddled across to Coll's side. Coll tried to appear busy casting his line and going about the machinations of fly fishing, but he kept his eyes on the man from behind his polarized sunglasses, his side arm at the ready on his right hip. The unsmiling warrior grounded his canoe on the shallow bank at the water's edge, got out, and walked straight up to Coll.

"Do you know these men who hunt you?" the warrior said and gestured toward the steep rise behind Coll.

"What men?" Coll said as he cautiously turned to the direction the Crow had indicated, but saw no one.

"Up there. Two men. One short, the other tall. They watched you for a long time and put together a rifle with a scope. The big one pointed it at you, then slipped and fell. They left in a hurry when they saw me watching them from across the river."

Coll wasn't sure that what he was hearing was the straight skinny, and a healthy sense of skepticism had always been a good friend when dealing with strangers in the past.

"You sure they weren't hunters out looking for game?"

"No game is in season now that needs a big rifle with a scope, and these men were dressed in street clothes. The rifle was aimed at you. Are you in season?"

"Apparently," Coll said and reeled in his fly line. He took the warrior's story as plausible, but entertained the idea that there actually were no men with a rifle, and the warrior himself might truly be the danger to him. Was Bartel Vandermeer clever and powerful enough to get a Crow native to exact his revenge? Several scenarios played out in his head as he studied the older man in the bead-decorated, buckskin shirt and moccasins who stood near him.

"Maybe you should come with me and leave here for a while."

"In the canoe?"

"We'll come back for the horse."

Coll didn't know why, but there was something genuine and trustworthy about the Crow that put his fears at ease. That and the .44 magnum Iver Johnson cannon Coll wore on his hip.

"Let's go," Coll said and took another look up at the hill behind him.

They got into the canoe and the warrior paddled from the rear seat up river for what seemed to be an hour. Coll had noted that there were no obvious weapons in the boat when he got in, and trusted that the only harm the stranger could inflict on him would likely come from a swat with a canoe paddle. He dismissed the possibility altogether and decided to enjoy the ride. Neither man spoke a word during the trip. The warrior paddled and Coll took in all that was glorious and beautiful in front of him and on both sides of the crystal-clear water. Soon they arrived at a tall, majestic waterfall that fed the river. The Crow beached the canoe at the shoreline about twenty yards from the froth and mist made by the plunging water. The two men sat and watched the falls for several minutes, spellbound by the falling water and the deep murmur it made as it cascaded down, eager to become the river.

"This is my heart place," the warrior said.

Without a word of explanation, Coll knew exactly what the Crow native meant. And he believed his warning about the pair on the hill. Men had now come for Coll, as he figured they ultimately would. The Crow's beautiful heart place was laden with fears for Coll, and drew imagess of a stranger in an unfamiliar place, being stalked by those who intended to do him harm. And here he was sitting in a canoe in a river with a Crow warrior whose name he didn't even know. He wondered what the Vegas odds on that occurrence would be. He envied that self-assured man who sat quietly behind him, and hoped one day his current fears would be over and he'd find his own heart place.

"How do you know a place is your heart place?" Coll asked, facing the falls.

"You'll know it when you see it," the Crow said as he pushed the canoe off and paddled back downstream.

Coll cast off his dark thoughts and let the natural beauty around him prevail. He watched fish darting in and out of the deep pools beneath the boat, and later, he smiled as a doe and fawn slipped out from the brush, tentatively took a drink, then disappeared. But as they distanced far from the falls, a simple statement made by the Crow warrior shook Coll from his moment of peace.

"Those men will be back."

Chapter 20

The words the warrior spoke slammed into Coll like a sniper bullet. He knew the men would return, and they wouldn't stop until they killed him. The Dutch gangsters he'd put in prison were working their power even from behind bars and inescapable walls.

The return trip didn't seem as magical as the upstream version, even though the scenery was magnificent. The thought of having to fight again took Coll's mind from the aesthetics of his surroundings and focused him on battle strategies. He would have to keep his head in the game, as the pro athletes often said, and that game was well underway.

They arrived at the place where Coll had been fishing and beached the canoe. Coll stepped out and was happy to see that his horse was still where he'd left him. He looked back at the warrior and nodded a thank you.

"You are a thoughtful man who controls his power. The men who hunt you are thoughtless and have no real power," the Crow said, shoving his canoe back into the river.

"How do you know that?"

"The men threw their lit cigarettes on the dry leaves of the forest, and left the trash from their food and drink on the land. You put your trash in your backpack. You fish with hooks that have no barbs, and release the fish you catch back into their river home."

"I'm far from perfect," Coll said. "Sometimes I keep a couple for dinner."

"So do I," the Crow said, "but only what I eat."

Coll's uphill climb to his horse was halted as the warrior spoke once more.

"There is a canyon a mile from here where the sun sets," the warrior said and pointed west. "You will know it by a tall, needle rock at its entrance. Do not go to your home tonight. Meet me there before the last light.

* * *

Coll had no trouble finding the canyon the Crow native had described, even though its opening was well hidden. It reminded Coll of the hideout of the Hole-in-the-Wall gang depicted in the movie *Butch Cassidy and the Sundance Kid*. It was closed on all sides by high, rocky cliffs, and there was only one way to enter. A small cabin had been built at the very back of the canyon against a sheer rock wall more than eighty feethigh. Smoke drifted up from the cabin's stone chimney, and an amber glow could be seen coming through the open doorway and small window in the failing sunlight.

Coll tied up his horse and approached the cabin door. He stepped inside and saw the Crow warrior standing in front of the fireplace with his back to him.

"Howdy," Coll said.

The warrior slowly turned toward Coll. A twelve-gauge shotgun lay cradled in his arms.

"I'm glad you found me," he said. "I dislike doing all my work in the field."

Chapter 21

Coll felt cold fear sweeping through his body and tightening his face. He knew he wouldn't have a chance to get out the .44 on his belt, so he managed a single phrase.

"Wouldn't want to put you out by having to go find me again."

"Very thoughtful," the Crow said and stepped toward Coll.

Coll cursed his stupidity for trusting the strange man and braced himself for the shotgun blast.

"Make yourself at home," the warrior said as he passed by Coll, propped the shotgun next to a wooden coat rack, and closed the cabin door.

Coll couldn't believe his eyes.

"It's a bit crude, but comfortable," the Crow said.

Coll released the breath he'd been holding and looked around the room. The interior of the place reflected pioneer rustic with furnishings made from rough-cut logs and sticks with the bark still attached. A welcome fire burned in the roundstone fireplace and lit the single room with a warm ambiance. He noted the gun rack above the stone mantel and the empty pegs where the shotgun had likely rested. A lever-action Winchester 30-30 hung at the bottom of the rack. Pine bunk beds with straw-filled, muslin mattresses were along the back wall, and a large bearskin rug covered the earthen floor in front of the hearth.

The warrior went over to the fire, sat cross-legged on the bearskin, and gestured for Coll to join him in front of the warmth.

"I built this place years ago when it didn't hurt so much to swing an axe and drag logs from the timberline," the warrior said. "It's not fancy, but it has always been a quiet retreat for me."

"So this is like a vacation home," Coll said.

"I come here often for the fishing, a little hunting, and the scenery, but mainly for the peace."

"But you don't live here."

"It's my home when I journey from my people on the big reservation south of Billings," the warrior said.

"I'm Coll Nolan. What is your name?"

"I am Amachee, and for you lovers of Crow name meanings, it translates to: 'the hawk with long eyes.'"

"I saw a little of that ability today." Coll said.

"Long eyes isn't just about physical vision, it extends into prophecy, I'm afraid."

"Prophecy is a wonderful gift. I wish I had it," Coll said.

"I see things at times I wish I didn't," Amachee said.

"Are you like your tribe's shaman or medicine man?"

"I am one of my tribe's chiefs, semi-retired. I let the younger men run things now so I can come here and enjoy the autumn of my life."

"You're not old. Fifty maybe?" Coll said.

"A bit more than that, but counting years will only make you tired. Count your friends, your loved ones, and your children, instead. When I do, I'm a lot younger." Amachee said. "You must be hungry. How about some havarti cheese and a glass of a nice cabernet sauvignon?"

"Cabernet? I expected something more like beef jerky and sassafras tea."

"Beef jerky? What are we? Savages?" Amachee said as he got to his feet and headed to a knapsack on a split-log table below the window. He looked out at the canyon for a moment, then placed a nearby piece of cardboard in the window, covering the single glass pane. "It's better if outsiders don't see the light."

He returned to the rug with the knapsack and squatted with Coll. He took out a bottle of wine, a corkscrew, two glasses, a loaf of crusty bread, and some cheese wrapped in wax paper. Amachee opened and decanted the wine, broke the crusty bread into chunks, and sliced the cheese with his jackknife.

"Bon appetit," Amachee said, handing wine and cheese to his guest.

"I feel like I'm at a trendy New York restaurant." Coll said, raising his glass to Amachee.

"Isn't this where you watch me pray to thank the souls of the grapes for giving up their lives to provide us with this wine?" Amachee asked.

"I guess some of us see too many Hollywood westerns."

"Yep, things are pretty modern with us these days. We even peepee in the teepee now."

They ate and drank and watched the fire dance on the logs. Coll told Amachee about his problems with the Vandermeer organization and why he was there in Montana. He also told him about his baseball dream and Amachee seemed to understand his drive to realize it. Coll felt thoroughly at home with this newly met Native American, and sensed that a much needed peace had come over him. Not since his days with Eddie had Coll felt like he was truly in the company of a trustworthy friend. If that wasn't the best feeling in the world, it was a close second.

"I'm afraid what I know about your people wouldn't fill a thimble. The cowboy movies I saw as a kid were pretty one-sided when it came to portraying the Indians, as we called them," Coll said.

"We still call them that," Amachee said. "Pisses off people from Mumbai."

"Thought you might take offense to the term."

"Hell, you should hear what my people call you whiteys," Amachee said. "References to dogs is a favorite theme."

Coll bellowed out a laugh and clinked his glass with Amachee's. The two men stared at the fire and sipped their wine. Moments passed with only the crackling sound of the burning logs.

"John Wayne, in one of his western movies, said that Indians don't cry when they're hurt. Is that true?"

"We're taught, from the time we're young, that shedding tears shows weakness, but when something truly hurts, we drop that old bullshit and scream like a stepped-on cat."

"I think my thimble's getting a little fuller," Coll said.

"More Indian lore later. Time for sleep. Tomorrow we go find those men who search for you."

"Lower bunk. I called it," Coll said.

"You sleep in the *upper* bunk or else I scalp you." Amachee said.

Coll climbed up the makeshift ladder and got into the upper bunk. Amachee added a split log to the fire and stoked the embers. He jammed a sturdy board into brackets across the middle of the door, placed his shotgun next to the bunk beds, and crawled into the lower berth. The activity of the day and the wine had taken its toll on Coll, who was already beginning to nod.

"Palefaces," Amachee said, shaking his head. "Give them a glass of wine and a warm fire and they go out like fainting goats."

"Been a long day," Coll said.

"By the way, you ought to know that I've been assigned to watch over you. I work for the FBI," Amachee said and held up his badge."

Coll bolted upright and rammed his head into the low ceiling.

Chapter 22

Amachee and Coll rose at daybreak, had some fireplace coffee, and finished off what was left of the bread and cheese. Afterward, they saddled their horses, mounted up, and set their sights for the area where had Coll fished the day before.

"I'll bet those hit men checked in town to see if I went home last night," Coll said. "I'm pretty sure they know a lot about my habits and where I live. Somehow Bartel Vandermeer obtained a good deal of intelligence on me before putting those bozos on a plane for their visit."

"Some men have evil born into them," Amachee said.

"He seemed like a great guy in the beginning," Coll said.

"My father told me when I was young that evil doesn't always look like a Gila monster, sometimes it attracts you like a puppy or a good-looking blonde."

"A blonde like Marilyn Monroe?"

"I was thinking a blonde more like General Custer."

They traveled along back trails that Amachee knew and scouted the area where Coll had been fishing. After an hour, they found hamburger wrappers, soda cups, and cigarette butts high on a ridge above the river. Later, as they moved deeper into the forest, they could smell a campfire and followed the aroma of the burning wood. Soon they could see smoke rising above the trees. They dismounted quietly and tied the horses to a low pine limb.

Coll checked his pistol for readiness and pulled a rifle from its sheath on his horse's saddle. Amachee slid out a lever-action Winchester from its beaded sleeve on his horse and chambered a round. They moved stealthily toward the source of the smoke. When they were only yards from the campfire, with just a few trees before them for concealment, they stopped and watched for any activity in and around the campsite. After several tense seconds, they determined that the area was uninhabited and moved in with guns at the ready.

What they witnessed as they entered the campsite revealed about the last thing Coll would've expected. Two men were lying face down on the ground, partially covered by a tent that had been flattened and ripped by some unknown force. Blood was everywhere on the men and the ground. Coll and Amachee pulled off the tent and rolled the men onto their backs to check for any signs of life, but there was none. One of the men had his face practically scraped off with evidence of huge claw marks running from his scalp to his neck and chest. The second man hadn't fared much better.

"Think these two are the men you saw yesterday?" Coll asked.

"They wore similar clothes—"

Amachee's words were interrupted by gunfire. Bullets were striking the trees around Coll and the Crow warrior.

Both men sprinted back the way they'd come and took cover behind large oaks. Amachee hit the ground and clawed himself to a cluster of thick brush on Coll's right. A second volley of bullets ripped into the tree branches and plowed the forest floor, spewing dirt and rock fragments. Severed leaves floated down from the branches above them.

Coll caught Amachee's eye and pointed to where he judged the shots had originated. Both men stayed silent, listened. Moments passed, then low voices wafted in from beyond the collapsed tent.

Coll and Amachee froze, barely breathing. Soon, Coll got a peek at two men slinking into the camp area, their eyes darting right, center, and left, sweep-searching with rifles at their shoulders. Amachee moved close enough to tap Coll's foot, and indicated he could see the two men approaching and that he'd take the tall one. Coll understood, since he was standing, he'd have a better angle on the shorter man.

He nodded to Amachee and turned his full attention toward the short hit man.

But when Coll looked back at the camp area, the two men were gone.

* * *

After more than twenty minutes, Coll and Amachee came out from hiding and walked back to the camp area, watchful of every bird flutter.

"Wonder why they packed it in?" Coll said.

"Smart," Amachee said, "Knew there were too many places we could be waiting for them."

"You're right. They were seconds short of getting retired."

"They'll be back."

"You say that a lot."

"Wonder who the two on the ground are."

"And what happened to them," Coll said.

Back at the tent, Amachee rolled one of the dead men over revealing a gunshot wound in the chest. The second downed man he examined shared a similar fate. He fished for credentials on the men and came up with wallets with IDs, which he opened.

"These men are federal agents," Amachee said.

"What are they doing camping up here?"

"My guess? This isn't their campsite. It belongs to the hit men. I'll file a report with the authorities," Amachee said, "and give them descriptions of the hit men."

"These two encountered a hell of a lot more than bullets."

"Bear attack," Amachee said. "Not the best way to go, but mercifully, the bear came *after* the bullets. Looks like a big one. Maybe a male establishing territory. Could have still regarded these two as a threat. Bodies aren't cold yet. Early morning attack. Both shot in the center of the chest. Never knew what hit them. Didn't have a vest on or a gun out."

"What do we do now?" Coll asked.

"Sheriff's Department will attend to them."

Amachee walked from the campsite area and back to his horse and Coll followed. They rode back to the main road and stopped their mounts.

"This is where I go back to what is loosely called civilization," Coll said.

"I'll keep an eye on you, but you're going to have to be vigilant. Your problems aren't going to go away on their own."

"How do you say 'thank you' in your native language," Coll asked.

"Aho."

"Aho, Amachee," Coll said. "You know what I want to do with my life, but what do you want out of life? Is there a dream like mine?"

"Oh, my dream would be to have a nice horse ranch near the water and the mountains, but I'll need a very large dreamcatcher for that one," Amachee said.

"To friends and dreams," Coll said and reached over and shook Amachee's hand, then rode off toward town.

After a few strides of his horse Coll looked back toward Amachee, but the Crow chief had vanished.

Chapter 23

Other than the government checks Coll received each month, there had been very little contact with Alan Capberg and the Witness Protection Program since he arrived in Montana a year earlier. The less contact with those in the program, the better, was the stance of the geniuses who dreamt up this guardians-of-the-righteous stuff. The appearance of two killers in Bozeman changed all that.

Coll went to the public phone in the community center and dialed the number he'd been given by Capberg to use in emergencies. The phone rang only once.

"Agent Capberg's office," a pleasant female voice said.

"This is Bob Smith. Is this Ms. Dandridge?" Coll said.

"This is Mrs. Tisdale."

"Is Ms. Dandridge there?" Coll asked.

"Please hold. I'll get Special Agent Capberg for you," Mrs. Tisdale said, with an evident change in her former buoyant tone.

Several moments passed and Coll swept the area near the phone booth to see who might be within earshot of his conversation. Seeing no reason for concern, he turned his wait time into an inspection of the graffiti inside the booth. Numerous phone numbers adorned the right wall, some with scribbled names and partial street addresses. Turning to his left he saw something that gave him pause. It was the name "Smith" and right below it was his address scrawled in pencil.

"Bob, it's Alan," the voice in the receiver said.

"Alan, I've been paid a visit and it wasn't from the ghost of J. Edgar Hoover."

"I've been calling you for two days. We're still trying to put things together here. Elaine Dandridge was— Are you in a secure place?" Alan said.

"I'm at the town center. As good as it gets around here."

"Okay. Elaine was accosted and threatened by some people we haven't found yet. She called me at my home and said they wanted information about your whereabouts. She wanted me to tell her what to do. She couldn't tell me where she was."

"I thought she already knew where you sent me," Coll said.

"She had access to your files, but never had any reason to review them. She knew the basics about your placement, at least the town and state."

"So she gave the thugs what they wanted?"

"To keep them from harming her, I gave her the go-ahead, but I gave her bogus information."

"They probably figured the town name was enough. Small town, everybody knows everybody and what's going on. Not a big problem to get the rest," Coll said.

"But Elaine gave them my line of crap and told them you were in Florida."

"Then how did they find me?"

"They called my office back. Said they had Elaine and didn't want to get any bullshit this time or they were going to hurt her. I gave them very little, but it was close to the truth. We didn't know if that was enough or not. I expected a second call from her, but it never came. I traced the origin of the calls. They came from her apartment. I sent agents to her place and flew men out your way to protect you, just in case."

"Where are they?"

"Still there, but they couldn't find any bad guys," Alan said. "Maybe figured the bad guys couldn't find you."

"They found me."

"You're kidding. My guys looked everywhere and never came up with any standout strangers."

"Because this burg is jumping with tourists and sportsmen year round. And because the two torpedoes were camping high up in a remote woods hunting me. No motel records to trace them."

"I haven't heard from my guys since yesterday."

Coll paused a moment before telling Capberg about the two dead federal agents.

"Alan, there's more bad news. The men you sent are dead."

"Good lord. How?"

"The hit men must have caught them sniffing around their campsite. We found them there. The local authorities will be contacting you with the details."

There was silence on the line for several seconds.

"I contacted a man we already had in that area to find you," Capberg said, his voice weary.

"Amachee?" Coll said.

"He got to you. Thank God."

"We crossed paths with the hit men."

"Where are they?" Alan said.

"In the wind."

"I'll pull up more help."

"You know Bartel Vandermeer's behind this," Coll said.

"We need to move you."

"What good will that do? All they have to do is go grab Elaine Dandridge and pump you for two minutes on the phone."

"I've removed all of your information and put it in my personal files, heavily encoded. This office gives out no information whatsoever for any reason," Alan said.

"Why not? You buckled under when you thought they had Dandridge. You'd do it again."

"That was so they'd let her go and not harm her," Alan said.

"So? How's that different now?"

There was an uncomfortable pause on the phone.

"Ms. Dandridge was found in her apartment. They raped and smothered her."

"Oh, no. I'm so sorry to hear that, Alan. Very sorry people are dying because of me."

"Elaine Dandridge and those agents died because of Bartel Vandermeer, and if I can figure a way to tie him to the murders he'll be in jail for the rest of his life. All communications to and from him are now restricted, monitored, and decoded. We have him in 23-hour a day confinement with only one hour in the exercise yard by himself. I doubt that he'll be able to give any new orders to anyone until his parole is imminent."

"He's a slick one." Coll said. "He may not be able to contact the two Boy Scouts he sent here to get me, but he's not going away."

"We can find you a nice new place."

"I know this place. I'll stay where things are familiar."

"You're sure?" Alan asked.

"I'll make my stand here."

The word "stand" reminded Coll of something Amachee had said regarding George Armstrong Custer. Coll hoped his stand turned out differently than the general's."

Chapter 24

Eddie Menning, AKA Joey Geronimo, entered the bar in the Hialeah racing complex and sat in his favorite stool at the corner of the bar, which offered a wide view of the track. The bartender set up his beverages of choice, a Dewar's White Label scotch, neat, and an ice water back.

"So, how are you hitting 'em, Joey?" the bartender said.

"Not bad this week. I can stop begging down at the intersection, and even pay my tab here," Eddie said.

"Holy shit. Maybe I can get a little subway out of you this week."

"Working for tips really stinks, doesn't it?"

"You work for tips, don't you?"

"Different kind of tips, Timmy" Eddie said. "Horse tips you can't always put in the bank."

"Damn, I almost forgot. Some gal called here for you last week. I told her you weren't here and to try back after five, but I guess she never called back."

"Get a name?"

"No, I was in the weeds, been busy as a sonofabitch here lately. Had all these old broads in here screaming for pink squirrels and strawberry daiquiris."

"You dickhead. That woman might've have been my future ex-wife."

"By the way, a letter came for you, which I did not forget, Mr. Geronimo," Timmy said and reached under the cash register drawer, extracted the letter, and handed it to Eddie. "Postmarked from Gettysburg, Pennsylvania. I didn't smell no perfume on it, so I don't think it's from one of your high-end bimbos."

"Knowing the mail service, it might be from Robert E. Lee. More likely the IRS," Eddie said as he tore off the end of the envelope and pulled out a folded sheet.

"Any porno pictures?" Timmy asked.

Eddie hopped off the stool and took the letter over to the sunny window that overlooked the grandstand and unfolded it. A check fell and fluttered to the floor. He picked it up and stared at it in disbelief. It was a cashier's check for $5,000 made out to cash from a bank in Maryland.

Eddie read the typed letter

Joey,

Sorry I haven't written more often, but you know not a day goes by that I don't think about you and wish I was there. Work here at the battlefield is hard and the hours are too long, but you have to eat, you know. I got a new job coming

up out west. When I finish working there I'll give you a shout or maybe drop by to see you.

Enjoy the dough. I took it out of your college fund.

S.F. Darkhorse

Eddie knew immediately who it was from and had trouble quelling the excitement that welled up in his chest.

"S.F. Darkhorse?" he muttered and managed a little laugh. He knew well the translation: Semper Fi - Nightmare.

His best friend was still alive and, for now, that would be all he needed to know.

* * *

The Bozeman community and Coll were quite compatible. His job was reasonably enjoyable and, thanks to an unexpected assistance increase from the Witness Protection Program, he was amassing a nice little bundle of cash to invest in what he hoped would be the next big step in his life. Apparently, his chat with Capberg had shamed the government into a raise, maybe to buy some body armor, since he'd opted to remain in Bozeman, and the enemy now knew his position.

Coll still had a stash of money he'd socked away while in New York, which, with his work pay and the government checks, added up to financial comfort. He continued to send money to his sister in Maryland, via the FBI, and she would send it on to Eddie. His friend wasn't qualified for any high-paying jobs, and wasn't the best candidate for menial work. Coll doubted that Eddie's track wagers panned out enough in winnings to constitute a living, but he dared not even think of visiting him in Florida. Eddie Menning still ranked number two on the Vandermeer hit parade.

Coll remembered the look on Bartel's face in the New York courtroom when he discovered that Eddie was not dead in that Dumpster, and that Coll had pulled off a master deception on him. Kyler had even glared at Bartel and blurted out that he should have let him do the execution instead of Coll. That was past history, but, delightful as it was to revisit, it didn't solve a current problem. If the enemy was tracking him in Montana from a New York prison, they wouldn't have any trouble tracking him to Miami if he made the trip to see Eddie. Coll wouldn't jeopardize Eddie's life by giving the thug bastards any intel as to his whereabouts. Eddie would have to dig in where he was without him.

The money he sent to Eddie shortened his bankroll a bit, but his concern about his buddy was always on his mind. If he couldn't help his best friend, he reckoned, what good was he. He had saved all the money he'd need, but it was his betting skills that worried him the most. How much more time would that take to perfect? The years were flying by. Could he ever attain the super level he knew the challenge would require?

It was time for him to dig in too.

Chapter 25

The spring of 1981 launched a new baseball season and another year for Coll to hone his betting skills, but he greeted its onset with anxiety. Successful outcomes in the past three seasons, where he had hoped to see infallibility in his formulas, had plummeted far short of his expectations. Had he wagered his bankroll in those past years, he would have ended monetarily broke and psychologically broken. And even though he hadn't lost any money, the cloud of doubt hung dark and low over his head and threatened a loser's storm. He began to think that maybe he should've gone to college and chosen a more traditional career, like sensible people did, instead of tilting at windfalls. The advice and warnings of his father played and replayed in his mind. Thoughts of failure loomed over him and portended an ugly future. It was time to retreat and regroup.

Coll knew that often spending time in a noisy place could be insulating, a place where unintelligible conversations murmured in the background, creating a "white noise" effect so doubting thoughts stopped pounding in his brain. He needed a break from the lonely hours and the frustration of experimenting with untried baseball betting formulas, and reworking the old ones. He knew just the place to offer him some relief: Judson's Always Café. It wasn't always open, but it was always noisy and diverting.

The community center was kind enough to lend Coll a vehicle whenever he needed to go somewhere distant, or do something that his horse wouldn't like or couldn't do, such as picking up gas for the power mowers or going into the business center of town. Intolerant, city-bred drivers didn't give much consideration to an appaloosa that dumped road apples on their highways and parking lots. So Coll drove the community center's blue Ford F-150 pickup down to Judson's Always and parked it in the diner's lot, which, at lunchtime, was packed two rows deep around the place.

Judson's at midday was a cross between a give-away sale at Walmart and a rock concert. Tables and booths were alive with loud storytelling and outbursts of raucous laughter, while waitresses topped everyone by yelling orders into the kitchen like boot camp drill instructors. Smells of coffee, cigarettes, and frying beef filled the air. It all combined to make the joint ideally suited for one not wanting to be alone with his thoughts. Fact was, not many there could even hear themselves think.

Coll casually knew many of the people in the restaurant that day, but other than an exchange of friendly nods to those whose glances he caught, he said nothing to anyone and positioned himself on a stool at one end of the lunch counter, which ran almost the length of the diner.

Two men, dressed in what might be described as country club golf attire, sat across from each other in a booth at the far end of the place. The man who faced Coll's direction leaned out of the booth and looked his way several times. Coll had never seen these men before, and began to wonder why anyone would come to Bozeman in its chilly April dressed as though they were ready to tee off at Pebble Beach on a warm June day.

One of the men in the booth got the attention of a busy waitress and summoned her over. Coll knew the gal, whose name was Jodi, and had even dated her. He couldn't hear what they were saying, but the waitress looked toward Coll several times as they spoke, an observation that left him uneasy. He ordered a cup of coffee from a counter server, but kept a cautious eye on the two in the Izod LaCoste links outfits.

Coll had just poured a dash of Half & Half into his coffee when a pretty woman entered the restaurant dressed in a pink jogging suit. She was dark-eyed with her black hair pulled back in a ponytail and carried a black leather purse slung over her shoulder. She stepped over to a man sorting change at the cash register and asked if he knew who owned a blue Ford pickup truck on the far side of the parking lot. Coll was close enough to hear the inquiry and rose from his stool and approached the young lady.

"There are several Ford pickups out there," Coll said to the woman. "Must be five or six of them."

"The one I hit has several red gas cans in the back," she said.

"Sounds like I'm a winner then. Let's go have a look."

Coll tossed a couple of dollars on the counter and followed the woman out onto the parking lot.

"I was trying to back into a tight space and I bumped into your truck," the woman said. "It's so crowded here today I could hardly find a space."

"Yeah, lunchtime is wild around Judson's," Coll said.

They wended their way through the parked cars and got within a few yards of Coll's truck when Coll felt strong hands gripping his arms from behind. He reacted instinctively and hurled the two men forward as he pulled backward. The tactic worked effectively at first as his assailants lost their grip on his arms and staggered out in front of him, barely keeping their balance. But Coll's freedom was short-lived. The pretty woman now leveled a snub-nosed revolver right at Coll's disbelieving eyes. Her two golf-attired accomplices followed her lead and drew pistols from their ankle holsters and took beads on Coll's body mass.

Not wanting to be their first hole-in-one, Coll raised his hands.

Chapter 26

"You guys are starting to annoy me," Coll said.

"We don't mean to annoy you, Mr. Nolan," the older of the two men said. "We mean to kill you."

"Take a number," Coll said.

"Yeah, we know a lot of people want your ass, but after today we're going to get the credit and the fame for finally doing you in," the younger man said. "We'll be like that fella who shot Liberty Valence. Practically immortal."

"No one's really sure who shot Liberty Valence," Coll said.

"Who cares who shot the sonofabitch," the pretty woman said. "Get his butt into the van and let's get this done. I want to collect my money and be on a plane to Hawaii by tonight."

"So Vandermeer's *paying* his thugs now," Coll said.

"Shut up and head for that black van by the fence," the older man said.

"If you do me here you won't get blood all over your van," Coll said as he shambled with his captors toward their vehicle several yards away.

"What part of 'shut up' don't you get?" the older man said. "I may decide to do you here if you don't zip your yap and keep moving."

"You do and everybody in that diner will hear it and see it," Coll said. "You won't get to I-90 before they scoop up you clowns like cutthroats in a net."

"Who made this into a goddamn forum?" the pretty woman said. "Tie his hands and let's roll."

The younger man secured Coll's hands behind his back with a length of clothesline.

"Move, asshole," the older man said.

The two nameless males opened the rear doors of the van and shoved Coll in. The younger man got in the back with Coll, steered him onto one of the two benches that ran along the sides of the cargo area, and closed the rear doors. Up front, Coll could see the older man taking the wheel, while the woman climbed in on the passenger side. Moments later, the van motored away from Judson's.

Coll's thoughts went back to computing his odds, but this time it had little to do with baseball.

* * *

The van drove across the countryside for more than a half hour. Coll got short glimpses of the scenery through the windshield, but his view was not wide. The longer they drove, the less he saw of buildings and man-made structures. Soon, all he saw was greenery.

The young man who sat across from Coll spun the cylinder of his revolver repeatedly like it was an amusing toy. He stared at Coll as he played with the pistol, trying to project his dominance over his captive. Coll stared back and never blinked. After a while, the young man tired of the inane activity and jammed the gun into the back of his waist band.

"What happened to the tall guy and his midget friend?" Coll asked.

"I heard they died," the younger man said.

"Car accident?"

"Swimming accident. Both drowned."

"You should always wear a life preserver."

"They don't make ones that'll float half a yard of cement."

"You saw them take that dip?"

"I was fresh outa school, but I was on the boat where they's took. Reason I know is, it was my daddy's boat."

"That your daddy driving?"

"Yup."

"Family is everything."

Coll could easily imagine how Bartel Vandermeer rewarded failure. Even from jail, he was executing his unsatisfactory help.

The van turned onto a very bumpy road that almost jostled Coll to the floor. During the rough ride,

Coll managed to use the violent movement of the vehicle to his advantage. He rubbed the ligatures on his wrists against the raw metal edges of the exposed back supports of the steel bench. Five minutes later, the van slowed and stopped.

When the rear doors of the van opened, the black-haired woman stood outside and beckoned for the young man to bring Coll out. The young man pulled Coll to his feet and shoved him hard toward the open door of the van. The woman trained her gun on Coll as he stumble-jumped to the ground. In the same motion, Coll tripped headfirst toward the woman, only three feet away, and butted her backward hard. The move caught her completely by surprise and she threw her hands low behind her to lessen her impact with the rapidly rising dirt road, Coll following on top of her. Her gun hand collapsed on impact with the ground, painfully twisting her index finger trapped in the trigger guard. Coll's free hands made a lightning move for her gun and ripped it from her damaged hand. The young man fumbled for his pistol under the back of his pants and took several seconds yanking it free of the shirt material snarled around its hammer. Two shots boomed into the peaceful pastoral setting. The younger man fell out of the van and hit the rutted road head-first in a heap.

Coll fired another shot at the back of the driver's seat, but the older man had bailed out of the vehicle in time to miss the bullet that blistered through the vinyl seat and perforated the windshield.

Coll had two choices: stay behind the cover of the van, or run for the thick woods next to the road. The woods won out, but as he scurried for cover he ran over the downed woman attempting to sit up and kicked her hard, squarely in the face. Her body flew backward like she'd been tackled by a pro football linebacker, her head smashing on the washboard road with an audible thunk.

Coll took a quick glance back as the older man cautiously peeked around the back of the van. Seconds later, four shots ripped through the trees, but Coll was already in the protective forest and, for the moment, he was safe.

* * *

The large trees offered more than enough cover for Coll to stay concealed, and offered options as to the direction he could take. But he knew what his first choice had to be: The nearby assassination crew needed to be eliminated. No more coming back for seconds on him. Bartel could send them, and Coll would bag 'em, if that's the way he wanted to play it.

Running away wasn't on the menu. Coll wasn't about to plod home for more than ten miles. Coll was going back in that van. But first, he had to survive an armed father with a dead son.

Coll was close enough to the van to hear things like an engine being started, but he was sure the older man was administering to the injured woman, if she was still alive. She appeared to be in charge and it would not bode well for the surviving man to abandon her in her time of need, unless he wanted to see how long he could tread water with cement scuffies. Coll heard no engine sounds, but he knew older guy was still around.

The tree branches before him slowly parted and the van came into Coll's full view. He approached from the front of the vehicle. There was activity near where he'd punted the woman's head. A closer look and the older man came into focus bent over the woman. Coll could hear him speaking to her, but he couldn't make out all the words. He managed to pick up a few.

"Billy's dead," the older man said to the woman. "My boy's dead."

Coll moved in closer and took cover behind a thick maple parallel to the side of the truck. The older man was holding the woman up with one arm, but her eyes were closed and her mouth was open. Blood was on the ground where she'd lain, a lot of it. As the man eased the woman's body back to the ground, Coll could see her head bobbing with an unnatural motion. He had seen that condition before and knew what it meant. The woman's neck was broken and she was dead.

The older man rose and turned back toward the van on unsteady legs. He stopped by his son's body for a moment and leaned down and touched the boy's face. He straightened up and began to trudge toward the driver's side.

Coll circled to the rear of the vehicle and called to the man.

"Drop your gun and get on the ground," Coll said.

The man swung around and faced Coll only thirty feet away.

"Die, you motherfucker," the older man said and raised his gun toward Coll and fired.

At almost that same instant, two bullets exited Coll's commandeered Colt .357 snubnose.

* * *

Coll left the bodies of the three kidnappers for the sheriff's department to sort out. On the upside, he'd saved Bartel Vandermeer the cost of about a yard and a half of Portland's best cement.

Chapter 27

The sheriff in Bozeman investigated the kidnapping and subsequent shooting incident and ruled it a model case of self-defense. Coll was never charged with any wrongdoing, but his popularity in Gallatin County skyrocketed. A reporter for the Daily Chronicle wanted to do a series of interviews with Coll, and a retired librarian wanted to write a book based on the incident and the events surrounding it. High profile publicity was the last thing Coll wanted or needed. He refused any invitations for notoriety, and pulled back his activities to taking care of the Community Center's chores and an occasional fishing trip, nothing more. Trouble was, the damage was done. Coll Nolan wanted invisibility, yet managed to become Bozeman's most famous celebrity.

Months later, after the hubbub died down about the kidnapping and triple killing, the chatter at Judson's almost returned to its normal topics, like where the best fishing holes were, and the influence that upcoming cable television would have on children. Bozeman parents weren't keen on having life in the fast lane paraded in living color in their homes where impressionable minds could be swayed into leaving Montana to take up the surfing life in

California. The uproar from the shooting had died down, but was far from forgotten. The outside world was creeping into the sanctity of northwestern life, and most Montanans didn't want New York, Miami, or Los Angeles coming any closer. A stranger had come to their town, and crime and killing had followed. Coll could feel the distance in the eyes of the people he greeted every day. The smiling warmth and friendly welcomes were all but gone. Coll knew his days in Bozeman were numbered, but he would first need a little more time and a Santa Claus sack full of money.

Coll kept abreast of what was going on in major league baseball and continued to make mock bets with himself throughout the summer seasons. He was doing okay, but he was going to have to keep polishing his craft if he was ever going to put a serious dent in any of the Las Vegas casinos' bank accounts. Betting ten dollars to win twelve back wasn't going to cut it. Okay was not going to do. He had to do much better than okay.

Past seasons of mock betting had resulted in less than stellar outcomes. His 1983 season, which included a winning World Series for his beloved Baltimore Orioles, turned out to be about break even. Break even results weren't going to make him the Vegas betting champ of all time. Break even was for chumps who gambled their winnings off just to walk away the way they started, if they were lucky. A delirious waste of time. He knew he had to figure out something soon or join the ranks of other notorious failures, like that guy who invented nasal floss, or that idiot who came up with solar flashlights. Failure: a word that made every U.S. Marine cringe, a concept unacceptable in any strategic plan. Pro baseball betting was his objective. He would have to figure out how to conquer it– and soon.

* * *

Coll knew that pitchers, particularly relievers, had to be studied extra closely, and hitters, even the mediocre ones, would have to be more carefully factored into every game. He looked into home game statistics for each team, and checked the historical patterns of wins versus losses when compared to away games. Ballparks and their orientations to the sun and their varied outfield depths and fence heights were worked into his formulas. A good, left hand batting, pull-hitting slugger would have a definite long ball advantage in a park with a short right field wall, wouldn't he? Which stadia were prone to high winds, and from which predictable direction? Which teams generated the most runs per game, and how many bases were attained by each club in an average game and during an entire 162-

game season? Thousands of variables entered Coll's computations and were tried out for consistent results. He studied books on test validity and reliability to find out if his experiments were testing what they were supposed to test, and if they were giving him the same results time and again. When the day came to go to Sin City, he'd be able to tell you which umpires used the letters-to-the-knees strike zone and which ones favored a much tighter area over the plate; which ones favored hitters and which ones favored pitchers. When Coll came to town to play he would be the Master of Memorial Stadium and the Ace of Anaheim.

In the 1985 season, Coll began to see a dramatic turnaround in his win-loss average. The reason was simple. Instincts were brought into his formulaic mix. Not very scientific, but simple. Coll discovered that, at some point in the complicated conjuring with the myriad factors that baseball betting involved, one had to plug in some gut feelings. When a game, according to all the facts, could go either way, play your best hunch. Gut-guessing could raise some goose bumps, but the simple truth was, it was working.

Alfred Hitchcock had popularized a concept he called a "MacGuffin" in his movie plots. It simply was a cryptic unknown that the audience had to unravel to solve the story's mystery. A man on a train who carried a briefcase handcuffed to his wrist literally carried a MacGuffin. What was in that briefcase was a secret something that had to be discovered or revealed to understand the intrigue and resolve the crime, murder, or unanswered question the suspenseful story posed. MacGuffin later evolved into meaning a special talent devoid of a factual basis for existence. A gambler who could consistently win eight out of nine horse races definitely was blessed with an equine MacGuffin.

This was that gray unknown where the "MacGuffin Factor" came into play for Coll. If he could win a large percentage of games in cases where opponents' plus and minus factors were virtually a toss-up, he could be consistently victorious. He could win where others would fail. It was an edge that all of Las Vegas casinos banked on having, but not by fortunate guessing.

Slot machines paid out 96% of what was paid in, giving the casino or hotel a consistent 4% profit. It appeared as if the casinos were crazy to allow such payouts, but they racked up that seemingly small profit twenty-four hours a day, every day, times the huge number of slot machines they had in operation. It added up to astronomical dollars in the coffers of the gambling establishments and players loved the frequent jackpots. Casinos offering blackjack might only garner as little as a 1.5% winning edge against an competent player who made all the correct bets and employed the soundest playing decisions. But that was only when dealing to *experts*, who were, by far, in the minority of people who played the game. Most players were hapless tourists visiting Vegas for a good time and some comped drinks. The point being, that Las Vegas made a winning percentage off every game they ran, regardless of how enticingly low it appeared in the eyes of the public. But when that tiny edge was multiplied over ever hour of every day, it amounted to income in the billions.

One last question lingered in Coll's mind: What would Las Vegas do if someone came to town with an edge they couldn't figure out, counter, nor defeat?

Chapter 28

The Minnesota Twins finished in last place in the American League West Division in 1990 with a record of 74 wins and 88 losses. The following year the Las Vegas statisticians were laying odds of anywhere between 200 to 1 and, in some extremely rare instances, as high as 500 to 1 against Minnesota making it to the World Series. The odds against the Twins actually *winning* the series fell between 250 to 1 and 300 to 1. Coll knew these odds would be available in Las Vegas casinos before the 1991 season started. And he had a feeling about that as a possible side wager as well.

The Atlanta Braves finished last in the National League West with a record of 65 wins and 97 loses in 1990. The Las Vegas odds against the Braves winning the World Series in 1991 were around the same as the Twins, if not a little higher. Coll had a feeling about this heavily disfavored team too. There was more than one way for him to bet on baseball in Las Vegas and he was going to open that door all the way. Coll knew that long-shot horses paid huge money when they crossed the wire first, but, when it came to baseball, he sure wished he had a peek through Amachee's "long eyes" on bets like that.

The 1990 season had the statistics leaning toward a handful of teams that could stay atop of that magic .600 game-winning average: Boston and Toronto in the American League East, Oakland and Chicago in the AL West, Pittsburgh and the New York Mets in the National League East and the Reds and Dodgers in the NL West. Coll set a well-charted course toward the league championship games and subsequent World Series and ended up correctly backing the right guys. The secret to making money on the right guys in baseball was to bet a lot on the underdogs, which Coll did to great advantage. The Cincinnati Reds beat the Oakland Athletics four games to none in the World Series and Coll, had he been wagering real dollars, would have come out on top that season to the tune of $2.4 million.

At last, Coll's 1990 season, on paper, proved that he could take Vegas on and win big. The problem was that $2.4 million wouldn't even come close to the biggest money winner in Las Vegas history. He was going to have to up the ante considerably to be the Vegas chip champ. He was going to need to risk a big part of his bankroll at the beginning of the betting season, even though that was when betting on baseball was most precarious because of unpredictable spring weather and the introduction of unproven new players. It was tantamount to betting on maiden horse races. Always an iffy proposition.

He would have to escalate the amounts he wagered early on. Coll was ready for the challenge, but he knew Vegas casinos, at worst, looked to break even on straight baseball bets and made their profit on the vigorish, or "vig," as it was known. That vig could be high when the casinos raked off favored team bets when the favorites lost, and it could work against him. One more reason, Coll figured, to play the underdogs whenever they looked due and probable to upset the favorites. Bottom line: he was going to have to make heavy bets.

The only concern remaining was would the casinos play big time ball with him?

Chapter 29

Coll realized that the government people were trying to protect him, shoddy as their efficiency was. But after almost thirteen years he wanted out of his bucolic and laughable invisibility, even if it meant that he'd possibly have to confront those who would want his hide if they ever ran into him. He felt like his current existence was a harsher sentence than what was meted out to his former Dutch employer and his band of yardbirds years ago. They only had to do a finite number of years; in Bozeman he was doing life without parole.

His yen to go to Las Vegas to bet on baseball included an added gamble. It was, as fate would have it, the one place outside of New York City that Bartel Vandermeer's organization regularly visited. But Coll actually began to expect and welcome confrontation with the bastards. He began to savor the idea that he might be the one to make Vandermeer and his murdering mutts actually endure their proper punishment. Why act like a scared cat and work in the shadows of dark alleys when he could be an attack dog and strike first? A strong offense would be a sight better than a cowering defense. He smiled at the thought and a silent, U.S. Marine "Oorah" welled up in his body.

Robert "Bob" Smith, AKA Coll Nolan, had pretty much made up his mind. He was now thirty-six and determined not to let any more time go by prohibiting him from the one thing that made life worthwhile. The government folks that contacted him in secret over the years had hoped their Mr. Smith would find a love interest in Bozeman, maybe settle down, have a family and live the whole Cinderfella story. Bob Smith couldn't imagine providing for a wife and family on the money one made mowing grass at the Bozeman Community Center, but he knew that was just a lame excuse. He'd had his romantic flings, and even liked one of the women he'd met to the point of joining her theatre group at the town center just to see her more often. But he knew well that he'd put up with the long rehearsals, and acted in a couple of plays with her, only for the friendship-with-benefits aspect. The moment she talked of making their relationship more permanent, Coll withdrew his attention, and eventually cut out the thespian stuff altogether. Some efforts weren't worth the few moments of ecstasy they provided. Besides, he didn't mind being her leading man on stage, but he hated leading her on offstage. Someday, he hoped the perfect woman would come into his life, but who was he kidding? Perfection was something that could be attributed to a superbly cut diamond or a perfectly-pitched baseball game, but a lifelong mate? Dream on.

Coll's simple life in a town where a nickel still could buy something had allowed him to save up a substantial chunk of money, and he decided to gather up what he had and slip out of town after the winter. The thought of going to Las Vegas lifted his recent hangdog spirits. He took a deep Montana Big Sky breath and felt like someone who'd just won the Irish Sweepstakes.

He started planning his escape from his pabulum life. When the time was right, he'd take a bus to Billings and fly out of there to confuse those government suits, who later might be looking for him, trying to protect him. He smiled at the ironic thought that now everyone, good guys and bad guys, would be searching for him. It wouldn't matter. He was going from the least likely gambling place on earth to the world's most likely place in one shot. But Las Vegas was a place that could kill you financially quicker than six golddigging ex-wives. He would have to be very careful with his money, and if physical trouble stalked him, he'd be calling on all that the United States Marine Corps had taught him: adapt, improvise, adjust, invent — *prevail*.

Chapter 30

On a cool March day in 1991, Coll got off the bus at the terminal in Billings, flagged a cab and headed for the airport. The excitement that billowed up inside him was at a level close to lethal. He took only a single suitcase and a carry-on bag, but surrounding his waist was over fifteen years of savings in a money belt capable of holding a small fortune in hundred dollar bills. There was a broad smile on his face as he watched the countryside flying by the taxi's window and thought of the million things he planned to do once he got to Las Vegas. He was at last beginning his dream and it wasn't merely a fantasy with mock bets anymore, it was actually happening.

Coll paid the cab driver, got his bags, and went into the airport ticketing area. He'd checked ahead to determine which airlines flew to Las Vegas and knew he was in time to buy a ticket. A man at an information kiosk directed Coll to the airline's reservation desk. A pretty lady at the counter told him that there was a non-stop flight going to Vegas in about a half hour and it wasn't fully booked. Coll paid cash for his ticket, checked his suitcase, and headed for the boarding area.

As he marched down the corridor leading to his plane's boarding pier a most unexpected thing happened. Standing before him in the distance was Amachee.

Coll couldn't believe his eyes. He hadn't seen him since the incident with the hit men, but he was elated to see the chief and embraced him warmly when he reached him.

"How the hell did you find me?" Coll asked.

"I'm FBI. We know everything."

"One day I'm going to be walking on the Great Wall of China and you'll be coming the other way," Coll said.

"My people say I'm like manure on a cattle ranch; I'm everywhere," Amachee said. "And, of course you know, I have that ability to see everything."

"Want to go to Las Vegas with me? I'll buy."

"Thank you, no. I gamble like I make baskets, and I've never made a basket in my life."

"You have to tell the FBI I left town?" Coll asked.

"They will know soon enough, but not from me."

"You could come along and watch me play," Coll said.

"I came here to see you off, not to go with you." Amachee said. "I have something I want you to have."

Amachee took a silver necklace from a leather pouch on his belt and spread it open. It had a silver cross at its lower part with a feather attached to it.

"Talk to your spirits to help you on your journey. They will listen," Amachee said.

"It's been a long time since I spoke to my spirits. I doubt they'd want to listen to me."

"I have a son that I haven't seen for more than ten years, but he's still my son, and always will be my son," Amachee said, placing the necklace around Coll's neck.

"You have chosen to walk a dangerous path," Amachee said. "Keep this with you. It will comfort you when the difficult times come."

"What's this feather from?" Coll asked.

"A hawk…who can see far into the distance."

The Crow chief turned and walked away. Coll watched him until he disappeared among the bustling people far away.

Coll stroked the hawk feather and wondered just how dangerous his path would be.

A decade had passed since Bartel Vandermeer had made an attempt on his life, and Coll wondered why. The answer came to him in seconds.

The diamond magnate would be getting out of prison soon. And Bartel Vandermeer would want to do the job himself.

Chapter 31

When Caesar crossed the Rubicon, Coll mused, he must've felt a lot like he did at this moment. And, like Caesar, he knew there would be no going back. Coll's mind took him to places like this where his courage had been tested before.

He remembered getting in line to go on a roller coaster when he was ten at Gwynn Oak Amusement Park in Woodlawn, Maryland five miles west of Baltimore. He bought his ticket and shuffled, guts a-twitter, with the line of people toward the awaiting cars of that incredibly scary ride. It was, to Coll, like the Bataan Death March that his father had told him stories about. At one point, a sign over a stairway exit said: "This is your last chance to exit before taking this ride." Coll had felt his stomach turn over, and cold perspiration had beaded on his face and dampened his palms, but he wasn't going to cop out and take that exit to where he was sure was a place of sanity and safety. He somehow knew that if he took those stairs down and out of the ride platform he might always take those stairs in life, and opt for the easy way out. Instead he went on the ride, almost soiled himself during the terrifying run, and left that ride like he was St. George and had killed the Chimera, wrestled King

Kong to the ground, and kicked Godzilla squarely in the his frank and beans.

Caesar too had hesitated at that little stream he had faced, and thought over the decision that lay before him. But on that fateful January day in 49 B.C., Gaius Julius Caesar crossed that tiny bridge over the water and stepped into history crying, "Let us go where the omens of the Gods and the crimes of our enemies summon us! The die is now cast!"

This day Coll was going across his own Rubicon to lead his talents against his fears and any obstacles fate could throw at him.

Coll wondered if Caesar ever had sweaty palms.

* * *

It was near dark on the first day of spring when Coll got out of the airport minibus at the middle of the famous Las Vegas Strip. He put down his suitcase, panned his eyes across the brilliantly lighted attractions and took it all in. The place looked like it had exploded since Coll had visited there with Bartel Vandermeer years ago. It was all he'd remembered and so much more. The new casinos, hotels, and buildings were magnificent. The glare, flicker, and dazzle of what truly must be the biggest electric light extravaganza in the world was mesmerizing; the glitz blinding and hypnotic, even at twilight. Whoever named Paris the City of Light had never been to Las Vegas, Coll thought.

He felt like a stagestruck young actor on his first trip to Hollywood.

Chapter 32

The world outside Las Vegas carried daily headlines about President George Herbert Walker Bush and the Persian Gulf War, newly elected president of Poland, Lech Wałesa, being the first Polish president to ever visit the U.S., Mike Tyson's barometric boxing career, and the Academy Award for Best Motion Picture of 1990 won by Kevin Costner's *Dances With Wolves*. But within the carefree town the outside news paled in the lights of the marquees and flashing signs on the famous Las Vegas Strip, which boldly proclaimed unbelievable hotel deals, $2.99 steak dinners, dynamite shows, and celebrity headliners. Stars like The Grateful Dead and Santana at the Sam Boyd Silver Bowl, and Frank Sinatra coming to the Riviera, were emblazoned in colorful, sequentially moving lights, confusing and tempting the ambivalent tourist as to where to eat, drink, and be entertained. There was even an upcoming outdoor National Hockey League game between the New York Rangers and the Los Angeles Kings being hyped by Caesar's Palace.

Coll strolled off the strip and beyond the major attractions. He stopped to look at a marquee down a side street that promoted:

Rooms - $9.00

Coll looked up higher at the hotel's main sign that proclaimed it as the Bon Chance, then angled over to the lobby door.

It seemed to be a very nice place that contradicted the expectation that nine-dollar rooms could only be hovels with a community toilet down the hall.. Coll went over to a line that had formed in the back of the lobby and started to queue up with the others. A woman, middle-aged and dressed like a slot machine regular, was at the end of the long line and turned to face him.

"Would you believe, we've been here since five o'clock?" she said.

A man next to the woman, who Coll assumed to be her husband, appeared to be in his late fifties, and nodded in agreement as the ash from his cheap cigar cascaded down his yellow plaid, double-knit, polyester suit jacket. He took a small bottle, wrapped in a brown paper bag from the Pleistocene Epoch, from his back pants pocket and took a long swig of its contents.

"The line's that slow?" Coll said.

"Oh, no, it's moving fast enough. Me and my husband started out down the street and around the block. I sure as hell hope there are some of them room specials left," the woman said.

"Is spring their peak season?"

"I don't think this town has a peak season. You think drunks and gamblers got a peak season?" She said with a gravelly laugh. "Look at him," she said, indicating her husband, "Been drunk since the moon landing."

The woman's husband laughed, revealing a toothless smile.

"They got rooms," she said. "This joint's huge. It's them nine-buck jobs I'm worried about. They sell outa them, see, then they try to stick you with one of them big, three room suits. Know what I mean?"

"Aw, that stinks. That's not right. People like us don't need them big, three-room suits," Coll said, enjoying her idiomatic usage.

The woman took out a pack of cigarettes, plucked one out with her inch-long nails, and dangled it on her moist lip. She fumbled through an oversize beach bag that presently served as her purse.

"George, you got any matches?" she asked her husband.

George frisked himself and dug into every pocket he owned, and his Spike Jones, signature plaid suit had plenty, but he came up with nothing. Coll reached into his jacket and pulled out his Zippo lighter.

"Got a light right here, ma'am," Coll said.

"Oh, thanks. Shit, where's my manners? Would you like one?" the woman said as she held out her cigarette pack to Coll.

"Oh, no. But thanks very much. Gave 'em up years ago," he said.

"Gave 'em up, but still carry a lighter?" the woman said.

"Keep it as a memento to surviving life's battles," Coll said.

"Yeah, quittin' these damn weeds is tough business."

Coll struck the flint on his lighter and extended it to the woman who leaned forward and took the light.

"If I was smart, I'd give the damn things up too. Shit, if I was smart, would I be with him?" she said, pointing a thumb toward George.

George brightened, baring his liquor-soaked, gummy smile as the woman rubbed his head with affection and rasped out laughs between bronchial coughs.

"Hell, I don't know why I love him sometimes. He's shitfaced as a drugged lab monkey and stiff everywhere 'ceptin' where he should be."

"He looks like a nice man and I'm sure he loves you," Coll said and thought how remarkable love can be on almost any level. Someday, he thought, he'd like to find some semblance of what this colorful pair had, but for now, the casinos beckoned.

Chapter 33

Coll entered his nine-dollar hotel room, put down his suitcase, and took a cursory look around at the décor. He was pleasantly surprised that it was a real room and not the college dormitory he had expected for that absurd price. *They must be desperate for gamblers in Vegas*, he surmised, as he flopped on his back on one of the two double beds in the room and stared at the ceiling. Well, he thought, he'd finally done it. After more than thirteen long years he'd made the move he'd always dreamed about. He'd come to the most ideal place in the world where he could bet on pro baseball games. For that matter it was the ideal place where anyone could bet on just about anything.

 Coll had heard the stories about guys coming to Las Vegas and betting huge amounts of money on a mere coin flip, but his bets would be far more complicated. Over the years he had done his homework and kept up with whom was doing what in pro baseball, and now it was time to bet. It was time to trust his research and his gut. It was time to put his life savings on the line. He was in fabulous Las Vegas, and this was greatest city in the world to do all that. He was almost giddy with joy that he was, at last, lying in his own room in that very special tiny dot on the world map.

Coll got up and pulled up his shirt revealing the fat money belt around his waist. He removed it, opened a zipper on the belt's back side, and removed a considerable amount of cash and laid it on the dresser. He lifted up one end of the dresser and slid the money belt under it in the cavity between a drawer bottom and the carpet. Coll crossed to the open curtains on the balcony door and started to draw them closed, but hesitated. He opened the balcony's sliding door, stepped outside, and took in the view. A smart soldier always checked out his environs, surveyed possible escape routes, and assessed the security of his position. A large parking lot half-filled with cars, part of a street with moderate traffic activity, and a large swimming pool were directly below him more than a hundred feet down. There was no moat with crocodiles down there, but he felt he was in a reasonably secure place. He leaned out over the railing and checked what was above him. There were more balconies, several of them, rising to a roof another five stories up.

He stepped back inside, closed the sliding door, drew the curtains, and went into the bathroom. He looked at himself in the vanity mirror. He looked pretty good, he judged. Pretty good for sneaking up on forty. All that sun and fresh air while mowing grass in Montana had left at least one positive result: a sweet beach bum tan. He conceded that he wasn't Cary

Grant in his prime, but he still looked damn good; at least present-day Robert Redford good.

Coll ran water for a shower and began to remove his clothes. Coins and a wallet from his pockets were placed on the vanity top. He took out his lighter and set it upright with the other items, and started to take off the necklace that Amachee had given him, but decided to leave it on. A shower wasn't going to harm the gift. After all, in the wild, water wouldn't damage a hawk's feathers, and Amachee and Coll found magic in falling water.

Coll finished undressing and got into his shower. The warm streams ran over his body like the baptism of a born again person and seemed to wash his past troubles down with the draining water. This was going to be a new life for him, a fresh beginning. He smiled at the thought.

When Coll stepped out of the shower, he started to towel himself off, then looked at himself again in the mirror. Coll knew he was about to go into the devil's playground and longed for some vestige of the fighting man he used to be. He stroked his chin and stared deep into the glass. An old gleam still shone brightly in his eyes, and he smiled knowing that Gunnery Sergeant Collin Valerio Nolan was back on duty. He recalled an old Celtic melody and spoke its simple refrain. "Oh, my Johnny, I hardly knew ya," he said, in his best Irish brogue.

Knocking came from the hall door to his room.

Chapter 34

Being naked and still wet from a shower was not the best way to greet a visitor, but Coll wrapped a towel around his waist and crossed to the door.

"Yes?" Coll said.

"The front desk forgot to give you your complimentary information book and coupon pack for your stay in Las Vegas," a man's voice said from the hall.

Coll reasoned that the caller was legit, but erring on the side of caution, he didn't open the door.

"Just got out of the shower. Can you leave it in the hall?"

"You bet, sir. Have a great stay at the Bon Chance."

"Thank you."

Coll was surprised how early his suspicions had arisen, but he knew a careless man was like a dog that chased cars: not long for this world. Every stranger he met was going to be a reason to exercise suspicion. It irked him to have to live that way, but to live was the whole point of the exercise.

* * *

The next morning, Coll walked down a street on the outskirts of Las Vegas. When he'd come here with Bartel years ago, there hadn't been time to make any bets, but he never forgot the magical spell the town had cast upon him. Now he wanted to look around the place to see what was new since he'd been here, and to inspect some of the outskirts of his new environment. He also wanted to determine what major casinos would be involved in his betting plans, but he had absent-mindedly passed those places minutes ago, and now was in the less-traveled part of the renowned gaming capital. He paused at the front of a tiny wedding chapel with its semi-inviting sign:

WEDDINGS PERFORMED 24 HOURS
Elvis wasn't married here,
but he thought about it.

Coll smiled and ambled on down the street. He soon arrived in front of a nondenominational Christian church, stopped, and stared at its red front doors for a long moment. Something drew him up its six steps and compelled him to go inside.

It was a beautiful little sanctuary, illuminated by the bright sunlight passing through its stained-glass windows. A life-size Corpus Christi dominated the room and drew the eye above the altar. The church was empty of people, but since it was early morning and this was, after all, Sin City, an empty church was probably not a rarity.

Coll slowly walked to the front of the church and, for reasons he couldn't fathom, knelt before the depiction of the crucified Christ. He had been to mass with his family as a young boy, and he had attended religious studies in parochial school, but religion wasn't something he ever took to seriously. Young boys had better things to do than chant church flummery every Sunday. If religion was such a hot ticket, why were his parents taken from him while they were barely into their middle years? If being religious gave assurance of spiritual protection, why were they dead, and why did it turn out that he'd never see his whole family together again after he got tucked away in that wonderful Southeast Asian wildlife resort where the government had sent him?

Coll also thought that maybe if he'd been a more Christian person than he had been in the past, perhaps prayed for things once and a while, maybe life would've turned out better for him. He had rebelled against formal religion when he couldn't get his mind around why God would want some folks to wear little hats and others full beards. Then there were those God-fearing people who played with rattlesnakes, and Baptists, Methodists, Catholics, Presbyterians,

Pentecostals, and on and on, but which religion had it right. Which one truly taught what God intended? Did God preordain what happened to us, or did He actually give us free will to keep our own appointments and create our own destinies? It couldn't exist both ways.

So Coll decided to make the Bible one of his great storybooks to read and found that God didn't really give a whit about all that denominational foolishness. All He wanted, it appeared to Coll, was for people to love one another. If not, why did His book say that so often? *Maybe I can start now.* Maybe God would forgive him, he thought, and allow him another shot even though his life was fraught with war, killing, and seemingly no good purpose that God would ever find to be a sweet sound in His ear. It was a gamble, but gambling was something Coll religiously believed in.

Coll stared at Jesus.

"I know you probably don't think much of me," Coll began, as he found himself talking to the Corpus Christi, "but I just needed to talk to you. My life's not exactly turning out like I planned. In fact, it's not turning out much at all. There are people who come here who'll want me dead, and I may need to settle that score once and for all. I'm through looking over my shoulder. I know you helped guys like David, Joshua, and Gideon in the past to fight battles, so I guess it's okay in your eyes to fight a righteous fight. I've been away in a wilderness for a long time now. Well, you know what that's like. I need to do the only thing I'm any good at: betting on baseball. Now I know betting's not on your top ten list of great things to do with a life, but it's all I know how to do. So what I'm asking here is this: Can we cut a deal? You and me? A win-win kind of deal. You give me a little help so I can have it out with these guys who're after me, and help me get the money to steer my life in a better direction, and I'll do something good with the money. Your kind of good. What do you say?"

Coll held his bowed head in his hands for a long moment, then looked back up at Christ.

"Please help me," Coll said as he rose to his feet. He started back down the aisle toward the front doors, then stopped halfway and turned back toward the altar.

"By the way," he said, "I don't know if you know this or not . . . uh, . . . of course you know this. You know everything. Anyway, I want you to know I never cop out on a bet. But you already knew that too, didn't you? Well, thanks for listening... I know ... I know you're busy."

Coll turned and walked out of the church sanctuary. As he did so, his jacket brushed past a rack of religious pamphlets in the vestibule. A single pamphlet fell to the green marble floor. Coll picked it up and looked at it. The cover page read:

"And all things, whatsoever ye shall ask in prayer, believing, ye shall receive."
— **Matthew 21:22**

He put the pamphlet in his pocket and exited the church.

Outside, the sun shone warm on his face and he felt he'd just made the best bet of his life.

Chapter 35

Coll sat in the sports amphitheatre of The Palacio Hotel & Casino with its wall-to-wall TV monitors showing games in progress, betting results, and previews of every conceivable sporting event. A large screen at the center of the banks of monitors gave the odds and results of every significant sports contest going on in the world.

The large screen graphically announced:

**MAJOR LEAGUE BASEBALL
BEGINS TOMORROW**

The message was followed by the following day's team match-ups which Coll studied intently as he scribbled notes on a legal pad. He made a notation of the first day of the season and wrote *"Monday, April 8, 1991"* at the top of the page. He looked at that date like a new father seeing his child for the first time, then underlined it several times to emphasize the fact that he was at last about to embark on his career betting campaign. He added a final phrase:

It begins.

A tall, rugged-looking man dressed in western apparel sat one seat over from Coll. He looked to be maybe fifty, but had that trim, cowboy build characteristic of rodeo riders. After several minutes the man looked over at Coll and waited for an appropriate opportunity to speak.

"How're you hitting 'em, partner?" he asked.

Coll turned his head and looked suspiciously toward the voice.

"The name's Creeger. Jim Creeger. Some folks call me Jimbo, but you can call me anything but late for dinner," Jim said with a gentle smile as he extended his large right hand to Coll.

Coll looked at Jim for a long moment, unsure how to regard this talkative stranger. He was alone on precarious turf in a very public place and felt he'd better hold any conversations with unknown people to a minimum.

"Bob Smith," Coll replied and shook Jim's hand.

"Like that fella that used to be on Howdy Doody." Jim said.

"Beg your pardon?"

"Buffalo Bob. The guy with the buckskins and fringe on the old Howdy Doody television show back in the early days. His name was Bob Smith. I bet you get a lot of that."

"All the time," Coll said.

"You don't favor him much, though."

"Well, I wouldn't want to copy the man's act."

"I guess not. Been done. And back in the '50s, at that. I come here 'bout every day for the horses. What's your affliction?" Jim said.

"Uh . . . baseball."

"Baseball? No stuff. Not many people here in Vegas make a living bettin' on baseball."

"I'll let you know if it ever becomes a living." Coll said and went back to writing on his pad.

"Bettin' on baseball's hard, partner. Like puttin' pantyhose on an ostrich." Jim said as he studied the TV monitors.

Coll stared at Jim for a moment, shook his head, and smiled at Jim's home-spun comparison, then consulted a newspaper under the pad in his lap. After a few moments, he got up and took a few steps toward the archway that led to the casino's main floor, paused, and turned to Jim.

"The secret is to be prepared," Coll said.

"My old Aunt Tal from Texas used to say something like that. She'd always say, 'Son, don't trim your fingernails if you're fixin' to pick your nose.' I think she had something there, don't you?" Jim said.

Coll grinned at Jim's likeable manner and colorful speech. He gave Jim a so-long wave and left the room.

Minutes later, Coll stood at a betting window and consulted his newspaper. The cashier waited patiently for Coll to look up and acknowledge him. Several moments passed before Coll broke from his newspaper trance.

"I'm sorry. I'd like to bet on baseball," Coll said.

"No problem. What game did you want to bet on?" the cashier asked.

"All of them."

"All of them?" the cashier said.

"Yes. That's all right, isn't it?"

"Yeah, sure. We seldom get a bet quite that expansive."

"Or did you mean, quite that expensive?" Coll said.

"Don't know about how expensive yet, but you give me the team match-ups, and how much you want to bet, and I'll give you the starting pitchers and the odds on each game," the cashier said, consulting a pile of typewritten pages and a computer screen.

"Excellent. Opening day. Let's start with Houston at Cincinnati. To keep it simple, my bets each day will always be for the same amount for each game. Today it's five dollars." Coll said.

"Five dollars on every game. That'll amount to a tidy little sum," the cashier said with a ration of sarcasm.

"Will you need to get approval from your supervisor?" Coll asked.

"I think I'll just go ahead out on a limb on this one and okay this deal myself."

"You're a good lad."

"Houston is plus 140 with Scott on the mound," the cashier said, reading from his information. "The home team Reds are minus 110 with Browning starting.

"Give me the Reds with Browning," Coll shot back.

Coll continued with the cashier until they went through every game being played that day, and bet on every one.

Later, Coll walked into a different casino and headed for the cashiers' windows. Coll talked to a smiling cashier for a few moments, then rattled off his picks for the day. He handed his money to the cashier and was handed back his betting tickets.

Coll went down the famous strip and entered every noteworthy casino and betting establishment, making the same bets that he'd made at the first casino. At the end of his rounds, he hiked back to his hotel room to monitor a few of the day's baseball games in progress, and study some of the upcoming west coast games on his busy schedule.

The happiness he felt was long in coming, but no less well received. He was betting on every major league baseball game being played every day.

Coll Nolan was in paradise.

Chapter 36

Coll knew that betting on baseball in Las Vegas was different than betting on other sports. In football, one chose a team and either took the favorite and let the underdog have a certain ration of points designed to even the bet. If the favorite exceeded the given game points, the favorite would win the bet. Conversely, the underdog could lose the game, but stay within the "point spread" they were given and still win the bet. If the final score had the favorite winning by exactly the "point spread," the bet would be a "push," or a tie, with neither side winning the bet. Often the odds makers stuck half a point into the spread to eliminate any chance of ties. The amount wagered was always a single set amount that both sides agreed to, say $10. It was a fairly simple kind of wager that almost anyone could follow.

While Coll studied baseball he also looked into the Las Vegas wagering systems that applied to other sports, such as professional football. He learned that the casinos or bookmakers handling sports bets liked to see the point spread be such that wagers were nearly even on both teams in play, regardless of the sport. The "house" made its money, or "vig," on the losers, usually ten percent. But, unlike a typical barroom bet, football wagering in Las Vegas got a bit more complicated. The simple point spread was used, but the system required bettors to pony up more money to back a favored team to win back less than a person betting on the underdog, which took less money to win more, if your team could overcome the expected performance of the favorite. Of course, there were other bets available, such as on the total score, a figure estimated by the odds makers on the combined points of both teams. One could bet that the total score would be higher than the estimate and win by selecting "over" as the bet. Conversely, an "under" bettor would hope that the total points scored in the game would fall short of the predicted estimate.

Betting on baseball presented a different set of lines, rules, and odds, although the mathematics were almost identical. Coll had studied baseball betting and knew that it could be based on different systems. To be sure, Coll checked the rules for the current method being used in Las Vegas and was given the following overview:

To wager on baseball, the bettor was asked tell the ticket writer the "bet number," if he had it, of the team he wished to bet on, and the amount he wished to wager. If he didn't have the bet number, he could specify the team by name. If his team won the game, he'd win to bet. The payout varied according to the odds posted. Baseball odds were shown using a

"Money Line." The Money Line was the odds for a particular game based on 100. A "minus" (-) preceding the number indicated which team is the favorite. A "plus" (+) preceding the number indicated the team was an underdog.

Coll read the example provided by the casinos. The pitchers listed were the starting pitchers.

BET #	TEAM	PITCHER	ODDS
301	Dodgers	Brown	+110
302	Braves	Maddux	-120

He noted that the bottom team, as on all baseball scoreboards, displayed the home team, unless otherwise specified. The Braves' odds shown were -120, meaning a $12 bet would win $10, for a return of $22. The Dodgers' odds were +110, meaning a $10 bet would win $11, for a return of $21.

Coll knew the baseball betting formula was complicated. He also knew that betting odds could change right up to game time, and a bet could be refunded if a purported starting pitcher for that game had changed. A game had to go at least nine innings, or eight and a half innings if the home team was ahead after the top of the ninth. Some casinos had their own house rules regarding baseball bets and Coll had to learn those nuances too. It was tricky business and made Jim Creegers' statement understandable about how very few people in Vegas bet on baseball because it was so difficult to figure out. But as Coll had told Eddie, "If it was easy anybody could do it."

Coll didn't take the exit stairs at the roller coaster ride. He went on the ride. He hadn't turned and run away from difficulty, or from his fears that sprang up in his past life, and he wasn't going to change direction now.

He was going on the scary ride all the way to the end.

Chapter 37

The Royale was one of the places that upper crust clientele sought out whenever they could finagle accommodations there. It was always in demand and typically packed with high rollers, millionaires, celebrities, and successful gangsters. It was small wonder that it was also the favorite hotel of Bartel Vandermeer and his gaggle of merry murdering geese.

A uniformed doorman opened a huge glass door, framed in polished brass, with fancy gold lettering that proclaimed The Royale Hotel & Casino. Big Al Marko, now in his early fifties, walked into the hotel carrying two large suitcases and an airline carry-on bag. He paused a moment to take in the grand scope of the place in its spacious and elegant lobby. It had been a long time since he had reveled there with "the boys" and tarried a moment to survey the many changes. He then plodded to the registration desk and deposited his heavy baggage on the Italian marble floor. The desk clerk, a precise man in a sport coat bearing the hotel name and logo, warmly greeted him.

"Good afternoon, sir," he said, smiling.

"Right," Al said.

"Will the gentleman be staying with us this evening?"

"Is the Florentine Suite available?" Al said while staring at the man through his gnarl of eyebrows.

"The Florentine Suite, sir?"

"Yeah. You know, the one you always reserved for Bartel Vandermeer."

"Bartel Vandermeer… Bartel Vandermeer…" the desk clerk mumbled, at sea with the name.

Big Al looked around for relief and spied the concierge at a nearby desk.

"Excuse me. Could you get me someone here who knows current events past last week," he said to the small man at the desk.

"How may I help you, sir?" the concierge said jumping to his feet and moving onto the scene.

"I want to stay in the Florentine Suite. May be here for a while," Al said.

"Ah, a man of fine taste, I see," the concierge said as he consulted a computer screen. "But of course, sir. Here we are. It is unoccupied. And how will we be paying today?"

"How will *we* be paying? My half will come out of this," Al said as he tossed a credit card on the counter. "But I can't speak for your half, can I?"

The concierge forced a weak smile at the jape and examined the credit card. "Hmm, a diamond credit card. We don't see one of these every day, do we, Charles?" he said.

"No, sir, we certainly don't," the clerk said.

"Get Mr. Marko's things taken to suite 1711," the concierge ordered as he looked at Big Al. "If you'll be so kind as to sign right here, sir."

The concierge pushed a pen and the credit card transmittal slip across to Al. Big Al signed the slip and was handed back his card and a receipt.

"The Florentine is a fabulous suite," the concierge said, "Very elegant and spacious. Eight king-size bedrooms. Will the gentleman be staying alone?"

"I may ask a friend over," Al said and winked at the concierge.

"Oh, yes, I see, indeed," the concierge said, his face in full blush. "Thank you, sir. You have a wonderful stay."

Big Al stuffed his card and receipt into his pocket and trekked to the elevators, led by a young bellman who toted his luggage.

At the six-elevator platform, the bellman put the weighty luggage down as they awaited the next elevator going up. The bellman checked the number on the room key.

"Boy, Suite 1711. That's a lucky room number," he said.

"I'm hopin' your right, kid," Big Al said.

Albert Marko was practically born into the mob by several generations of fathers and uncles who were enforcers and underbosses for the Vandermeer family going way back to the 1920s. Al had made his bones by accident when three goons from one of the rival families had decided to send the Vandermeers a message by working over the twenty-year-old nephew of Pavel Marko, a ruthless man who had more than once roughed up some of their relatives.

The three would-be assailants had tragically misjudged who their intended victim was, and when they thought they had him cornered in a church courtyard they paid a dear price for their lack of foresight.

Al hit one of them so hard in the solar plexus that his heart stopped, killing him instantly. The other two tackled Al and tried to get him down on the ground, but Al put a headlock on one that crushed the man's neck. By the time the last one realized that he was now woefully under-manned and tried to flee, Al tripped him up and beat him so severely that he lost the vision in his right eye and had to have three surgeries to re-align his jaw and cheekbone. Al let him live to tell the tale. No one ever tried to do anything untoward to Al "The Bear" Marko, after that, except to cross to the other side of the city when they saw him coming. When he got older and wider, the "bear" moniker was replaced with simply Big Al.

The bellman parked Al's luggage on the baggage bench in one of the exquisite bedrooms, opened the draperies, and checked to make sure the bathrooms were in perfect order. He came back to the hall door where Big Al stood and wished him a pleasant day. Al countered with a hundred-dollar bill to the young man, who thanked him four times before Al could get him out the door. Once again Al knew the value of having someone to tell the tale and knew also that he'd be getting the best room service and hotel attention a guest could get during his stay in Las Vegas.

At his age, handing over C-notes had proved to be a hell of a sight easier and smarter than busting a guy's head into tapioca pudding.

Chapter 38

Coll sat in the same seat he had the day before in the Palacio's media room. He scanned the wall of TV monitors for the baseball scores from the previous day and jotted notes on his legal pad. Since clocks in Las Vegas casinos were scarcer than blizzards in the Sahara, Coll wisely wore a watch. It was 8:47 AM local time.

Jim Creeger entered the room and Coll saw that he'd spotted him. The lanky man walked over and took a seat near his new friend, Bob Smith.

"Well, how's Bob the baseball expert doin' today?" Jim asked.

"So far, I'm up at least eight dollars," Coll said.

"Whoa, where do we want to eat in Paris tonight?"

"Now, I've only had time to check one of my bets."

"Didn't mean to interrupt."

"No interruption. So, you like eating in Paris?"

"Yeah, right. Truth is, I've only been out of Las Vegas during my military service. Born and bred right here in fabulous LV," Jim said.

"What kept you here?"

"You grow up, draw a couple of tours overseas, start a business, get married. Before you know it, you're stuck like a moth in a spider web, waitin' for life to roll up what's left of you and suck you dry."

"What do you do?" Coll asked.

"I was a cop for over twenty years, then I started a private security business," Jim said. "Did pretty damn well, if I do say so, but when you get past fifty, you need to do things you've always wanted to do. For yourself, you know? So, I sold the business to some younger fellas, made a couple of bucks, and now I'm a loose cannon. Miss the action, though. Maybe I sold out too soon."

"I had a business all laid out for me once too."

"You sell it?" Jim said.

"Yeah," Coll said, paused for a moment, then added, "I sold out too."

"Still miss it sometimes, I bet."

"Sometimes."

"Ever in the service?" Jim asked.

"Nope. Managed to get deferred. Bad feet and asthma. You?" Coll said, looking down at the floor.

"Marine retread. In country mid '70s," Jim said. "Probably would've gone for more, but took the discharge in '75. War was over. They gave me a Bronze Star, a Purple Heart, two aspirins, and a swift kick in the ass."

The baseball games for the day appeared on the monitors and media boards. Coll turned his attention to the screens.

"I've got to get over to the betting windows to get something down on today's games. I bet every day so I won't lose the rhythm," Coll said, getting up from his seat.

"And Bob, don't you forget to collect that eight bucks from yesterday," Jim said.

"Count on it, cowboy. I can taste that '61 Lafite Rothschild and the escargot at Maxim's already."

Coll strode into the casino's main hall and made his way to one of the cashiers he placed bets with the day before. Today his bets would be different.

* * *

"Well, looks like you did pretty well for yourself, mister," the cashier said as he counted out several ten dollar bills on the counter. Coll left most of his winnings where they lay but pushed a couple of the bills toward the cashier.

"This is for you. Today I want to bet on all the baseball games again, but I'm upping the bets to ten dollars a game."

"Thank you, sir," the cashier said and displayed the two bills at a video camera before pocketing the tip. "Okey-dokey. Start with the American League again?"

"I'll give you the teams and you pull the numbers, okey-dokey? Give me the Cubs over the Phils, Oakland over the Twins, the Giants over San Diego . . ." Coll continued to rattle off the game match-ups until every game being played that day was covered.

Coll placed his bets at the various casinos as he had the day before, and went on making his bets and doubling the stakes as the days and weeks went by. At every casino where he placed bets he collected large amounts of money from their cashiers. So large, Coll figured, he had to get himself a sizable safe deposit box at a local bank. He leased one at a small savings and loan on Fremont, plugging itself in their front window as: "The Commonwealth Bank, the safest bet in Clark County." He started by placing most of his money belt savings there, and later his daily winnings.

The down side of his wagering windfall was that many eyes were starting to cast their attention his way. Jim Creeger was becoming more than a casual casino acquaintance, and seemed to ask all the right questions needed to piece together a person and his past. Jim was, after all, a cop. Maybe it was just in his nature to be inquisitive, but Coll sensed there was much more to his congenial banter than idle curiosity. Maybe he was like that Lieutenant Columbo on TV who politely "niced" you to the gas chamber. Maybe.

By late July, the casino owners and management nabobs were starting to feel the hit they were taking from Coll's daily baseball bets, which continued to escalate with every playing of the National Anthem. The eyes of Las Vegas were looking at him attentively. Generous contributions were being made to the Internal Revenue Service, which added another group carefully monitoring his successes.

Coll also knew there were other eyes coming that hadn't surfaced yet. Eyes that would be inordinately pleased to see him.

Chapter 39

A few weeks later, Coll and six other men were playing poker at a large game table in the Las Palmas Casino. Coll, wearing a New York Yankee baseball cap and a pair of dark sunglasses, had a tall column of chips and a stack of paper money in front of him. One of the other players shoved a pile of chips into the pot and looked at Coll. Coll said nothing, but studied his cards for a moment, thumbed and riffed the stack of bills in front of him, then shuffled his chips. He glanced at the mound of money in the center of the table, took another peek at his cards and then, one-by-one, snapped his middle finger against each of the five cards in his hand.

"I guess I'll have to keep you boys honest. I'll see the bet," Coll said as he pushed matching chips into the pot. As he did so, he looked up, beyond the dim light falling off behind the players, and saw a curious face that caused him to stare. The face was hard to make out through his dark sunglasses, so he tilted his head gently forward to see over the rims. He clearly made out the emotionless face and cold eyes of Kyler Rotermund, now in his forties, staring back at him.

Coll suppressed his anxiety and put on a fair act of nonchalance by attending to his game. He won the hand and gathered in all the chips in the pot. He figured if something was going to erupt with Kyler right then and there, he'd make himself ready. Coll stood up and put his chips and folding money in his pockets.

He set his jaw and looked back at where he had seen Kyler, but the man had vanished.

Chapter 40

The Las Vegas Strip at night was an electric luminary show of the highest order. Even more so when the street traffic and pedestrian movement became sparse like they were in this particular early morning darkness. The blitz of radiance bounced from one sign to another without the interruption of cars and masses of people dressed like racetrack hacks. It was four o'clock in the morning, but Vegas was still in her primetime array, calling out into the night for her players, like Circe wailing her irresistible enticements to Odysseus and his men on the seas of ancient Greece.

Siegfried & Roy signs beckoned with promises of 500-pound tigers live onstage, and The El Rancho Hotel offered a prime rib dinner for under five bucks. The Tropicana advertised *The Follies Bergere* with an entourage of leggy beauties in breathtaking costumes. Las Vegas promised unforgettable entertainment for every taste and every age.

Barging through all this dazzle, a classic convertible weaved down the street with its top down. Two men inside the beautifully preserved, black, 1956 Lincoln Continental held cocktails in their hands and brandished them outside the open car as if toasting the passing casinos. The young, good-looking one was Augie Palermo, a man perhaps in his early thirties. The driver was a forty-something Vince Bartolo, the owner of both the car and a veteran face of frequent frontal assaults.

"You know why blind people don't bungee jump?" Vince said with slurred speech.

"Nope," Augie said after thinking a moment, as if preparing a sensible answer.

"It scares the shit out of the dog," Vince said and roared at his insensitive joke.

Both men laughed like howler monkeys, toasted each other's madness, and polished off their drinks. The glasses were carelessly tossed onto the street, scattering broken glass shards over the asphalt.

"Hey, we're outa drinks," Augie observed with rapier wit.

"Oh, no," Vince said as they approached the classic front of Caesar's Palace.

"Look, Vince. It's Caesar's. Bet we can get a drink in there," Augie said.

"Ten-four, good buddy. We're headin' in."

Vince steered the car onto the sidewalk outside Caesar's, bounced violently upward from the curb, and crashed into Caesar's landmark fountain. The car knocked over the seven-foot statue of Winged Victory of Samothrace and ended up in the pool's center. Water from the large fountain surrounded the vehicle's body and streamed into the open convertible's interior and down the windshield.

"Well, piss," Augie said rubbing his head from the bang it got slamming into the sun visor.

Vince put up the power windows and turned on the windshield wipers, but failed to put up the top. The deluge continued to pour in on them and fill the car with water.

"There, that's better with the windows up," Vince said.

A police car pulled up to the curb, its lights flashing. Two uniformed officers got out and slogged over to the stranded convertible. One of them tapped on the driver's window with his nightstick, water surrounding his legs to his knees. Vince looked up at him, then put down the window as the water continued to rain down.

"Hey, no hot wax, okay?" Vince said.

The two drunks convulsed in laughter.

Vince noted that the cops were not nearly so amused.

* * *

Later that day, Joseph Penuto, a well-dressed man of about forty-five, was led into the lock-up cells by a police officer. They arrived at a cell containing a dozen unsavory-looking characters who looked like cast members from *Les Miserables*. In the back of the cell, passed out, were Vince and Augie. Drool ran down Vince's fat lower lip and onto his lemon yellow, Italian knit shirt.

The officer motioned to Otis, one of the lock-up's regular detainees, a man of advanced but indeterminate age. The cops often referred to him as the western counterpart of the famous Mayberry drunk, Otis Campbell, on the 1960s *Andy Griffith Show*. The local jail was his home when he wanted a change of scenery from his street digs, which was a refrigerator box behind a nearby appliance store. Otis added a colorful personality to the otherwise stodgy hoosegow's drunk tank, which was always open for business, no reservations required. The officer knew that Otis stood as a reminder of how cruel a town with so much money per capita could be with an individual who gambled everything and lost.

"Come here please, Otis," the officer beckoned.

The old man reluctantly trudged over to the officer.

"Go wake up Peter Pan and Tinkerbell over there for me, will you?"

"What's in it for me?" Otis said with a scowl.

"You get to spend the night without having to worry about getting killed in your sleep," the officer said.

"Say what?"

"Those two are the famous Mendez brothers," the officer said.

"No shit? The ones who killed all four of their parents?" Otis whispered.

"Then went out and buried them right where they had conceived their own stepchildren," the officer said.

Otis cautiously went over to the two sleeping men.

"Hey! Get up. I think you dudes been sprung," Otis boomed.

Vince and Augie came around grumbling and, through squinted eyes, saw the suited man with the officer outside the cell. Vince stood, wiped his mouth on his collar, and followed Augie over to Penuto.

"Hey, paisan. How long we been in here? A week? What? You get laid in Hollywood?" Augie carried on. "What the fuck kept you, Joe? Me and Vinnie got Social Security checks coming in, for shitsakes."

The officer opened the cell door, let out Vince and Augie and relocked the cell.

"I'm a lawyer, not the governor," Penuto said. "You're lucky they're letting you assholes out at all."

"What? One little pissant, cheap, imitation, cement statue, for cryin' out loud," Augie said. "It didn't even have a head. You'da thought it was the damn statue of the Mona Lisa."

Penuto looked at the officer and shook his head as they exited the lock-up.

Chapter 41

Kyler Rotermund held a cordless phone to his ear at the elegant bar in the Florentine Suite. He poured himself a Chivas Regal scotch and sipped it as he listened. Big Al Marko and Two Ton Teddy De Groot were seated in the sunken living room, watching pro wrestling on television. Tony, now in his mid-fifties, had not jeopardized his two-ton standing by dieting, and Big Al had managed to maintain his tonnage and continued to look like a barn with legs.

"Yeah, I understand, Bartel," Kyler said. "I didn't see him close up, but some things you never forget about somebody. He was a little older-looking and wearing a Yankee cap and sunglasses, but underneath it was him. He had that tell when he played his cards, like back when. Yeah, sure, I'll be careful. I got Joey Peanuts to bail out Vince and Augie. The two idiots got themselves locked up for boozing it up. I set it up for Cammy Delano to pick you up from the joint if the parole board signs the release. You want air tickets here? Right. Goodnight, sir."

Kyler pressed a button on the phone and placed it on the bar. He sipped more of his drink and ambled over to the two big men.

"The boss wants us to make sure what I saw is what I saw last night," Kyler said. "He's coming here if all goes well with that dumb ass parole board. What-the-fuck. Thirteen years is enough time for an old man to serve."

"It was plenty of time for me," Teddy said.

"Right." Al said. "What's the boss gonna do at his age? Knock over a nursing home? Makes no sense."

"What about this poker player? Teddy said. "You think it's our boy?"

"Check with the dealer at Las Palmas," Kyler said. "Find him."

Big Al and Teddy got up and tromped to the door.

"And guys . . ." The two big men stopped and looked back at Kyler. "Bring him to me able to talk, okay?"

The two big men nodded and held up at the door.

Kyler looked out the glass balcony door at the magnificent view of nighttime Las Vegas. He took a last slug of his drink and put the empty glass on the bar.

"I've had a lot of time to think about Mr. Nolan," Kyler said, staring out at the lights of Las Vegas. "A hundred and fifty-six months, two weeks, and four days, not that anyone's counting. You two bring him to me."

Teddy and Al looked at each other, and exited the suite.

Kyler imagined his reunion with Coll Nolan, what he was going to say to him and how it was going to feel to crush him under his power.

And how he was going to kill him.

Chapter 42

It was mid-summer and Coll sat in the Palacio's media room reading a newspaper. His eyes regularly peered above the pages of the paper to scope out the room's numerous people. A hand clamped on his shoulder from behind. He reacted instantly with a backward flail of his fist and a lightning turn to see behind him. He found himself staring into the face of Jim Creeger.

"Hey, partner, didn't mean to spook your deer," Jim said.

"Sorry, Jim, my mind was somewhere else," Coll said.

"Gonna bet on baseball today?"

"Done that. Collected some winnings too. We'll be able to afford a villa on the French Riviera," Coll said.

Jim sat down next to him and stared straight ahead without his usual engaging smile. Several moments passed in silence.

"First day I met you I sensed some kind of trouble in you," Jim said. "I was a cop, remember? After twenty years, you can't just stop being one. You learn things. You seem like a nice enough fella, and I've enjoyed our little chats, but I think it might be time to talk a bit, if you care to."

Coll stared long and hard at Jim, then looked around to see who was within earshot.

"Know somewhere private?" Coll asked.

Jim studied Coll carefully. "If this is about anything shady, let me warn you, son, you're dealing with a straight shooter here," Jim said and opened his jacket enough to reveal a large handgun in a shoulder holster, which Coll duly acknowledged with a nod. "And I do mean *straight* shooter."

"I have something I want to show you," Coll said, pointing to his jacket pocket and waited for permission to go there.

Jim nodded and Coll reached into his pocket, took out his distinctive lighter and a laminated card from his wallet and handed the two items to Jim. Jim looked at the engraved Zippo lighter carefully, then at the card. The card was the certification of Coll's Congressional Medal of Honor.

Jim handed the items back.

"My car's right outside, gyrene."

* * *

Jim and Coll drove up in Jim's Jeep Cherokee to the front of Jim's modest, but homey rancher on a tract of isolated land in the desert. Jim's wife, Dina, a woman of about forty-five, was on a ladder leaning against the front of the house painting a window frame. She was a tall blonde woman with classic Vegas showgirl looks. She turned toward the car as they drove up. Coll's eyes went right to her and stayed there as he and Jim got out of the vehicle.

"That's Dina, the one I told you about. She's only woman in the world who could've put up with me for almost twenty-five years," Jim said as the men approached. "Hiya, cupcake. This here's Coll Nolan, my replacement. You've done wore me out, honey. I had to call for backup."

"He looks okay. Long as he can go four or five times a night," Dina said from high on the ladder.

"And you thought I was in trouble before?" Coll said.

"He says he'll slow down to five times, if that's the way you want it."

"Nice to meet you, Coll. Where'd you get that cute smile?" Dina said as she came down off the ladder and approached the men.

"A really good dentist in Baltimore."

"Let's get out of this hot sun and get us some cool drinks," Jim said as he gave Dina a quick peck on her mouth and pointed Coll to the front door.

Shortly afterward, Jim and Coll sat in the living room as Dina brought in cold beer.

"I'm going down to the store to get us some steaks for supper. You make Coll stay," Dina said and left the room.

"You don't want to miss her country-fried steak," Jim said.

"You see me moving?" Coll said.

"Now, take a pull on that brew and fill me in on these past years since '75," Jim said.

Coll took a chug of his beer and leaned forward on his chair toward Jim, his forearms resting on his thighs.

"I'd just turned twenty-one, Coll said. "In one of the remaining marine units. Most of the regular combat troops had been gone for months, but we were assigned to stay and protect our installations and help in the evacuation of Saigon. It was in the last weeks for the city, and the NVA was making its final push into the south. My men were scattered well outside the city where this big firefight was going on. We were spraying and praying along with some SVA troops, and they were hitting us from everywhere and throwing everything in their bag at us. The men who were already in the middle of it were trapped without a good way to safely withdraw. We found a corridor that the NVA hadn't bottled up and pulled those trapped marines out to a safe position farther to the south."

Jim raised his hand almost as a reflex to what he'd just heard.

"My god, I was one of those marines. Now I remember you," Jim said.

"You remember *me*?"

"Yeah. You're that fella everyone was talking about. Sergeant Collin Nolan, a regular John Wayne in action. You pretty much saved our outfit single-handed."

"Hardly a John Wayne. I just did my duty. Marines don't leave marines in trouble on the field," Coll said. "You know that."

"Well, I consider this my lucky day. I get to pay back the favor to another marine in trouble. Semper Fi," Jim toasted and extended his beer toward Coll, who clinked it with his bottle.

Having a friend in Las Vegas was unexpected, and Coll never figured much on finding good luck outside of the betting arena, but this was special, very special. Crossing paths with a friend and former marine who actually knew of him overseas? Even for Vegas the odds were astronomical.

Coll's thoughts trailed back to the little church he'd visited.

He wondered …

Chapter 43

Coll filled in Jim on his past with the Vandermeer family and his stay in Montana as they lounged on the patio in the back of the Jim's house.

"I think I saw Kyler Rotermund at Las Palmas last night. The jig may be up for me," Coll said as he stood and crossed to the back edge of the patio. He looked out into the desert night and at the glow of lights coming from the distant center of Las Vegas.

"What's out there?" Coll asked.

"Rattlesnakes, Gila monsters, scorpions, and tarantulas."

"Ah, my kind of people."

"So, what's the next move?" Jim asked.

"I came to Las Vegas because I couldn't lay a two dollar bet where they put me in Montana," Coll said. "I came here to bet on baseball; every game, every day. I love the game. I study it, and I can make money betting on it. Decent money. I'm not letting some jackasses from my past run me out of the one place where I can plop a grand on the Yankees at minus 160."

"That's not a move, that's a whole philosophy," Jim said.

"I'm going to need help for the next step. I had to leave what little battle gear I owned back in Montana. You still miss the action?"

"Come with me. I want to show you something," Jim said as he rose from his chair. "It's inside."

Coll followed Jim into the house and through a door that went down a flight of narrow stairs. The basement below had been converted into a cozy club cellar with fashionable furniture, a pool table, and warm, indirect lighting. Jim told Coll that basements were rare in the sandy desert soil of that part of Nevada, but some home owners had contractors dig them in anyway. He related how when he and Dina had moved into their home the basement shell was there, but nothing had been done to make it into an practical living space.

"I built this clubroom back when Dina and I used to entertain a lot," Jim said.

"It's a lot nicer than my room at the Bon Chance," Coll said.

"What did you expect for nine pesos a night?"

Jim led Coll to an art arrangement on the wall and moved aside one of the paintings. The move revealed a brass escutcheon and keyhole. Jim turned to Coll.

"I've built my reputation on being able to know when to trust people and when to put the steel to their chin. No one that I don't trust sees what's behind this wall." Coll looked at Jim straight and steady in his eyes.

"I don't feel any steel," Coll said.

"I was sure I could trust you the moment you didn't deny that you were in trouble. A lesser man would've picked up and walked away," Jim said and placed a key into the lock and turned it until it clicked.

A push by Jim on the key, and the entire wall section began to move. Two wall panels, whose center seam had been concealed by a vertical molding, separated and parted inward to reveal a narrow opening. The passageway it revealed had been virtually undetectable.

Jim led Coll through the passage into a dark room. Jim flicked a switch and the hidden space became bathed in light. Coll gazed at the most complete arsenal this side of Fort Knox. Guns and ordnance of all varieties hung from the walls. Boxes of ammo and explosives covered the floor. Camouflage apparel and military gear hung in an open closet, as well as black SWAT uniforms and helmets.

"Good Lord," Coll said.

"You said you needed some help. Well, here's some help. The First Marine Division was tied up, so I guess this'll have to do," Jim said as he picked a Beretta 9-millimeter handgun off the wall and handed it to Coll along with a box of ammo. "I know you can't buy a gun here legally without tipping your hand to the wrong people, so here's a little personal help in case that Kyler character pays you a visit and I'm not around."

"What can I ever do to repay you?" Coll said.

"Baseball's giving you back your life. Nailing bad people will give me back mine. You're giving me something I thought I'd never see again. Who could ask for better payment than that?" Jim said placing a firm hand on Coll's shoulder.

* * *

When Dina returned, they sat down to a sumptuous steak dinner, and later had drinks in the den. Jim excused himself and left the room while Coll and Dina chatted. Their conversation touched on Coll's current love life, which Coll explained was nigh on to nonexistent. Dina suggested a possible remedy for him in the form of a close friend she claimed was very single and quite attractive. The friend worked at the same bank where Dina was a teller and, Dina added, they had been friends since their earlier showgirls days.

Coll thanked her for the tempting offer, but politely begged off since he was involved with matters that didn't leave much time for dating and romance. Besides, he had heard that "close friend who was very single and quite attractive" recommendation before, and found that it usually was skewed from the matchmaker's perspective and often over-hyped.

Jim returned in time for Dina to say her goodnights and go off to bed. Jim directed Coll out to the garage where a beautiful, candy apple red 1966 Mustang occupied one side of the multi-car garage. He hefted a large black duffel bag from the floor to the top of a workbench.

"I put you together some things that'll remind you of your active duty days. I included a complete burglary kit in the event you have to get in, or out of, a tight spot. If you need anything that's not in that bag, let me know," Jim said.

Coll stared at the bag and shook his head. He wandered over to the Mustang and peeked inside at its dashboard.

"That's my baby," Jim said. "She's four hundred cubes, blown and balanced."

"Jumps when you hit it?"

"If you had a pointy butt, it'd drive you into the trunk," Jim said.

"Jim, I really couldn't take this. I'd be—."

"Not to worry, Bunky. You're not getting my 'Stang. You're taking the Jeep outside."

Jim handed Coll a set of keys and stepped out to the driveway and opened the Jeep's rear hatch. Coll plodded behind with the heavy duffel bag and swung it into the back of the vehicle.

"This Cherokee looks brand new. You sure you want me to take this?" Coll asked.

"Yeah, shit. Otherwise I gotta drive your jarhead ass back to the hotel. I offered you to stay here. Sofa pulls out downstairs, never been used; not a pecker track on it."

"I've got to see some cashiers in the morning. I made that vow to myself that I'd bet on every game, every day as long as I have the money to play. It's part of the deal I made."

"Deal?" Jim said.

"Yeah. I made a little deal with Him," Coll said pointing skyward. "It's my edge. My MacGuffin."

"Your McWhat?"

"MacGuffin. It's a special ability, an advantage. I've got kind of an inside track with baseball, that and a deal I made with a man at a church; a MacGuffin. It's what keeps me hummin'."

Jim strolled back to the garage, stopped, and turned back to Coll.

"Now here's my McMuffin: I'm going to bed. And if I can get up tomorrow, I'm taking a shot at the old lady. That's my edge, partner," Jim said, smiling, then saluted Coll and disappeared into the garage.

The garage door closed, leaving Coll alone in the driveway. Coll slid into the Jeep and started the engine. He looked toward Las Vegas and thought of the day he had ahead of him. Was running into Jim Creeger an extraordinary stroke of his own Irish luck, or was it all part of the deal he'd made? And was the fact that he was now armed to protect himself a thing that would keep him from harm, or thrust him headlong into deeper trouble? He factored in his betting rounds and realized that his high visibility in his daily routine could be easily monitored by those who wished him harm. If trouble wanted to find him, it would have little difficulty doing so.

Coll put the Jeep in gear and drove out onto the road leading back to town. He felt the tightening in his jaw. It was the same feeling he had experienced in Vietnam when the battle was on. He welcomed the sensation the way an ancient soldier was comforted by his armor and weapons before the clash of armies.

Coll knew he was a warrior. And he knew it was time to prepare for war.

Chapter 44

Coll tramped from the hotel elevator to his room with the duffel bag that Jim had given him tugging on his shoulder. He took a key from his pocket and opened his hotel room door. He reached inside from the hallway and flicked the light switch, but the room lights didn't come on. He quickly withdrew his arm, closed the door, and backed into the hallway. He bolted down the deserted corridor lugging the black bag and disappeared around a corner.

* * *

"Damn it," Teddy De Groot said, moving into the lone stream of light slicing into Coll's otherwise black hotel room from the balcony door. A large hand fully parted the door's draperies, allowing in a wide ray of light from the outside city glow. Big Al Marko emerged from the shadows on the balcony and tiptoed into the room.

"I think he's on to us." Big Al said. "I shouldn't've unscrewed the light bulbs. They work by the wall switch. Time to retire. I swear, I'm starting to slip."

"I'll check the parking lot," Teddy said as he opened the door to the hall revealing the lighted corridor. He looked in both directions, then slipped into the hallway and eased the door closed behind him.

Minutes later, Teddy waddled out onto the hotel parking lot, studied it carefully, then lit a cigarette. He rescanned the area and caught a glimpse a head bobbing far across the parking lot at the rear of a parked car. Teddy hiked over to investigate.

Teddy drew a handgun from a shoulder holster, held it low against his rump, and took a closer look. A man stood at an open car trunk with his back to him. Teddy quietly approached the man and aimed the gun at the man's upper body from a few feet away. The man at the trunk turned to the side enough for Teddy to see that his profile didn't belong to Coll Nolan. Teddy holstered his gun and trudged back to the hotel.

More than twenty minutes had passed, and Teddy didn't want to leave Big Al by himself any longer than he had to. He was sure that Coll Nolan was not a man you'd be eager to tackle alone in the daylight, much less in the dark, but feeling a bit peckish, he detoured into the hotel bar where he'd seen complimentary hors d'oeuvres.

* * *

Upstairs a pair of eyes watched Al Marko slide open the balcony door and step outside. The big man bent over the railing and searched the parking lot. The watchful eyes silently descended on a rope from above the balcony. Big Al turned to go back inside the room just as a shadowed figure swung his feet in Al's direction and kicked him hard in the chest. The huge top-heavy man staggered to the railing and barely kept himself from going over. The shadowed figure dropped down onto the balcony deck and landed on his feet as Big Al regained his balance and hastened away from the rail.

"That you, Coll?" Al said as he fumbled in his jacket and withdrew a gun.

"Put it down, Al," Coll said. "I've got a bead on your head and you know I won't miss."

Big Al hesitated for a half-second, then bent over as far as he could and dropped his pistol on the deck.

"Jesus, man, I just came to talk," Big Al said.

Coll came out from the shadows. He wore black clothes and a knit cap that made him look like a Ninja. He had the Beretta automatic pointed at Al.

"Yeah, talk," Coll said. "That would explain hiding in the dark and pulling your gun on me."

"You scared the shit outa me," Al said. "I didn't know who it was. What do you expect?"

"I expect you to step into the room," Coll said. "Now."

Al did as he was ordered, with Coll close behind. As Coll stepped across the sliding door threshold, Al spun around with his enormous elbow flying backward and struck Coll hard on his gun arm. Coll's weapon flipped onto the carpet and skipped across the room. Al followed up the move with a glancing right cross to Coll's head that sent him reeling against the wall near the bed's nightstand. Al tromped in for the kill as Coll grabbed the lamp on the nightstand to use as a weapon, but it was secured to the table and wouldn't budge. Abandoning the lamp, Coll dove across the bed a split-second before Al closed within striking distance. The big man's forward momentum slammed his sumo-size body into the wall like a runaway freight train.

Coll rolled to the edge of the bed and jumped to his feet as a dazed Al Marko composed himself for his next assault. The big man was panting hard as he glared across the bed at Coll, who grabbed a pillow and sidled into the open center of the room.

"Cheap-ass, nine buck rooms. Don't even trust you to not steal the lamps," Coll said.

"So now you're gonna smother me with a pillow?" Al said.

"I have to do something to shield me from those pork butts you call hands."

"Let's see how that works out for you," Al said, heaving breaths as he stalked Coll with clenched fists.

Coll braced himself for a volley of blows from Big Al and held the pillow at the ready at his chest, but Al turned for the nearby balcony instead. He plodded for the gun he'd left on the deck. Coll charged after him as Al scooped up the gun and pivoted toward the onrushing black and white blur. As Al clumsily tried to get the gun oriented in his hand, Coll hit him hard in his face and upper body with the extended pillow. Al's gun fell from his hand as the top-heavy man was propelled over the railing and plummeted toward the swimming pool far below. His body violently crashed onto the roof of a cabana below and caromed off onto the diving board of the adjacent pool, breaking it off clean. Al's battered body sank to the bottom of the illuminated, crystal water, blood streaming from his head like red snakes.

Coll checked to see if anyone below witnessed Al's fall, but saw no one. He picked up Al's gun on the deck, stuck it in his waistband and went back inside his room. He retrieved the Beretta from the floor and kept it in his hand at the ready. He left the sliding door open, but moved to a dark position on the far side of the room and waited.

Coll didn't have to wait long before the door to his room swung open.

Two Ton Teddy slipped into Coll's dark room from the hall and closed the door. He saw the balcony curtains wafting inward in the soft light at the open sliding door and headed for it.

"I didn't see nobody outside, Al," Teddy said to the balcony. There was no response. Teddy cautiously stepped toward the narrow doorway of the balcony and drew his gun from his shoulder rig.

"Hey, Al, what's going on?" Teddy leaned through the balcony doorway and peered outside.

"Drop the piece, Teddy," Coll ordered from the darkness. Teddy wheeled around toward the voice. Coll stood directly behind him with the Beretta leveled at his head.

"Coll Nolan. Been a while, pal," Teddy said.

"If you don't want to die, Teddy, lose the piece."

Teddy complied and dropped his gun on the floor.

"Now have a seat on the foot of the bed. Put both hands down at your side. You make one move for the knife or the second piece you carry, I send you to hell early."

Teddy did as he was instructed.

"So how've you been, amigo?" Teddy asked.

"Well. You?"

"Besides the little stretch in Sing-Sing, or just in general?"

"I think I saw Kyler the other night. This is starting to look like a family reunion. Is big boss still with us?"

"Pulling twenty to life in Attica for the feds and the state of New York. You seen Big Al?"

"He was here a minute ago. Oh, yeah, let's see, he was out on the balcony trying to kill me, but apparently he decided to take a dip in the pool instead," Coll said.

"You're an amazing man, Coll," Teddy said and shook his head. "Am I going off the high dive next?"

Coll sat across from Teddy on the other bed.

"I'm going to make a deal with you. It's a one-time, get-outa-jail-free deal. You go back to Kyler. I assume he's pulling the family puppet strings these days," Coll said.

Teddy gave a noncommittal shrug. "The boss gave him some juice 'til he gets out. Kyler said you was playing poker in one of our old joints. We got your picture from one of their security cameras and asked around. And here we are, one big happy Boy Scout troop again."

"Kyler's like fire, Teddy. He's a scary servant and a dangerous master. I want you to go back to him and tell him to call off the hit on me. He'll laugh in your face. When he does, I want you to shoot him. You'll be doing all of us a favor."

"You having an agent orange attack, Coll? What're you talking? Do Kyler? He just wants to talk. Make sure you're not after him," Teddy said.

"That's the deal. Or, if you come after me, I'll kill every one of you murdering assholes," Coll said as Teddy clenched the bedspread in both fists. Coll stood up and placed the muzzle of his pistol against Teddy's forehead.

"There's only one reason I don't cap you right now, you big tub o' guts. I don't need the publicity. So you dump out your metalwork on the bed, ever so easy, and then beat your number twelve Florsheims back to Kyler and tell him . . . tell him the game's still afoot." Coll said and moved away from Teddy. He gestured for Teddy to get to his feet. Teddy did as he was directed, then emptied his pockets of a switchblade knife and a small revolver and tossed them on the bed behind him.

"What about the one you keep on your ankle?" Coll said.

"Don't do that one no more."

"Too fat to get to it?"

"Yeah. I like my tacos and pasta," Teddy said with a nervous chuckle.

"Indulge me. Pull up your pantlegs," Coll said.

"Geez, man, you don't trust me?"

"Not as far as I can throw the pyramids," Coll said. "Now get the pants up past your socks or I shoot you in both knees and do it myself."

Teddy grimaced and hiked up his pant legs revealing a small Derringer pistol in an ankle holster.

"Take it out, with two fingers only, and toss it on the bed with the other ones."

"This ain't like the old days, Coll. We never had to do stuff like this back then," Teddy said as he strained to reach his ankle holster, extracted the small pistol, and slung it on the bed.

"Time to go," Coll said. "Remember, to see any of you ever again is to put me into a self-defense mode. I recommend you guys try Reno from now on for your gambling rake-offs. The price of poker here has gotten way too high."

Coll followed Teddy as he headed out the door and lumbered down the hallway. He watched him as he reached the elevators and pounded one of the down buttons with his knuckles, then bashed his fist into the gypsum wall, leaving a hole the size of a volleyball.

Coll backed into his room, secured the hall door, and went toward the balcony. Since he was certain that there would be a crowd by now around Big Al's body, he avoided going out onto the balcony. Instead, he stooped down and picked up Teddy's gun and tossed it with the others on the bed.. He reached outside and pulled in the dangling rope he had used to hover above Big Al. It was still tied in a continuous loop through the railing of the balcony above. He pulled the rope into the room and tugged on one side until he had drawn in the knot that made the loop complete. Once the knot was untied, he pulled on one side of the rope until the remainder fell to the deck and wriggled into the room. He slowly slid the glass door shut, drew the draperies, and pushed the rope under the bed. Coll gathered up all of Teddy's weapons, Al's gun, and dumped them in the nightstand next to the bed. He paused for a moment to consider the irony of putting instruments of killing on top of the Gideon Bible that lay in the drawer.

Coll took off his knit cap, doffed the black outfit, and changed into street clothes. He left the room, walked down the hall and took the elevator up one flight. On the ride up, he put on a pair of surgical gloves he had in his pants pocket. He made sure that no one was in the hall on that floor, then went to the room that was directly above his. The door was closed but unlocked. A piece of folded paper had been placed in the door frame over the latch so it couldn't lock when it was pulled to. He removed the paper, ducked inside the room without turning on any lights and made sure the balcony door was closed, latched it, and drew the draperies. Coll went to a closet and retrieved the black duffel bag he had left there, and placed it on the small dining table in the room's kitchenette. He took a set of lock picks from his jacket pocket, returned them to a leather case in the duffel and zipped it up. He checked to see if there was anything he'd left behind. Satisfied that there was nothing, he left the room, pulling the door to until it locked. He ambled down the deserted hall to the stairway with the duffel bag slung over his shoulder and disappeared.

After all these years, Sergeant Collin Nolan was back in action, and he had to admit he liked the feeling.

Chapter 45

Coll got up early the next morning and took the elevator down to the hotel lobby. The scene there buzzed with uniformed policemen and several plainclothes cops as they questioned the hotel management and staff about the death of the large man discovered in the swimming pool. Coll marched past them, exited the building, and blended into the people out on the street.

He had picked up voices and footsteps coming from the balcony above his room earlier that morning and heard them leave after a brief stay. He knew there would be questions asked of everyone who could have been involved or had seen anything on his side of the building. He hoped that they had entertained the possibility that Al Marko could have accidentally fallen or been pushed from any number of balconies in the building, or even the roof. It was too difficult to tell where he'd fallen from with any precision. In addition, Coll knew a background check would no doubt reveal that Mr. Marko was a career criminal and ex-con. That might help to divert any investigation pursuing a foul play angle that might point back to "Bob Smith" in the room below. Truth be known, any number of people might have had it in for a wise guy like Al Marko, especially in Las Vegas where plenty of rival gangsters spent time.

Rather than take the Jeep, Coll decided to walk down to the casinos where he placed his daily bets, and later go to the Palacio's sports media room. Vehicles got stopped by the police a lot more often than pedestrians. The more invisible he could be, and the less time he tarried around the hotel, the better, he judged. The last thing he needed was a bunch of cops turning his life history inside out while he was on his baseball quest. Cops and gambling didn't go together with what he was doing. Not in a good way.

After placing his bets at all but one of his casinos, Coll made his way to the Palacio. He spotted Jim Creeger as soon as he entered into the media room and signaled to him that he'd be in the cashier area. Jim nodded and followed him, but kept his distance as Coll approached one of the betting windows. The cashier and Coll exchanged a few words after which the cashier doled out a large amount of money. Coll noticed that the ever vigilant Jim stood off to the side of the window and scoped out everyone who came by.

"There you go, pal," the cashier said. "Your winnings from yesterday's games, minus a cut for Uncle Sam. I think we'll be looking forward to the football season."

"What do you mean?" Coll asked without looking up as he counted his money and placed the bills into separate piles. "You tired of me betting with you? Tired of my tips? There're other casinos in this town. I've seen them. They welcome my money," he said as he looked up from his pile of cash and glared at the cashier. "You telling me to take my business elsewhere?"

"No, no, sir, not at all. I was only making a comment. A joke. No offense intended," the cashier said, his brash demeanor shaken.

"I wonder how your boss would feel about your little comments? Think he'd like the way you talk to customers?"

"C'mon, sir. I meant nothing derogatory by it. I apologize . . . completely."

"Suppose I want to up my daily bets to a grand a game, huh? What about that? You going to tell me to go bet elsewhere?" Coll said, glaring at the man. "Tell you what. Let me speak to your sports book manager."

"Sir, for God's sake. The casino wants your bets. You can bet any amount you want. I'll get it okayed."

"Good thing," Coll said. "I don't want to have to go to the news media with this. I closed a joint in Atlantic City for less. So you mind what you say to customers. You better watch your damn step."

"Yes, sir. You *were* kidding about betting a thousand dollars a game, weren't you?"

"Kidding? Does this look like I'm kidding?" Coll said with a piercing look as he indicated the mound of money on the counter in front of him. "See this? This little stack here is enough to bet a grand right now, here in this establishment, on every game that's being played today. Now you start putting down the games and the odds like always, or we go have a chat with one of those people on *60 Minutes*. What do you say to that, Mr. Jokes?"

"I say, the Giants with Wilson are favored at minus 130 over the Cubs and Maddux," the cashier said.

"Good. Now you're talking. Give me Frisco on that one for one large."

"Uh ... one thousand it is," the ashen-faced cashier said, and wiped his brow. "The Braves and Smoltz are even up with the Mets going with Gooden."

"Put me down for Hotlanta," Coll said and looked over at Jim, who grinned and shook his head in amazement at what he'd witnessed.

Coll and Jim walked out to the parking lot and sat in Jim's Mustang in an area away from the concentration of cars near the casino.

"Remind me never to be your cashier. Hell, that boy's gonna need therapy," Jim said.

"You have to cut off the protests to the high bets before they happen. I've watched gamblers in casinos in Atlantic City. When the house loses bad against a player over a few days, they sometimes get timid about raising the ante," Coll said as he looked around the parking lot like his head was on a swivel. "I need the house to stick with me when the bets get heavy."

"At how many joints are you placing those bets?" Jim asked.

"All of them."

"What's that amount to?"

"Let's just say I can afford any kind of ride I want."

"Something in the neighborhood of a 700 series Beamer?"

"More in the neighborhood of a 700 series Boeing."

"Shit fire and save the matches," Jim said.

"Thing is, I have to blow a couple of betting days and let the casinos win," Coll said.

"You're takin' a dive?"

"For a day or two. The casino bigwigs have to think they have a chance to get even. If I win every day, they may get gun shy and cut me off."

"And I thought betting on horses was complicated," Jim said.

Coll and Jim sat for several minutes staring at the growing activity around them and on the streets beyond. Another day in Vegas was coming to life. Cars began to fill the back lot where they were parked and people streamed past them, turning a quiet place into a public thoroughfare. Coll looked over at Jim and broke the silence.

"I think I'd better stay clear of my hotel," Coll said. "They frown on people falling from the upper floors into their pool."

"Who fell?"

"One of my old mob buddies. Paid me a visit, and not to tell me how much he missed me while he was in jail where I put him. By the way, you didn't tell me about all the goodies that were in that duffel bag."

"They can carry more than firearms."

"That bag was a second story man's dream gift. Had everything but hi-tech explosives."

"Didn't you look in the side pockets?" Jim asked.

Coll looked at Jim askance.

"Anyway, I'm gone from that hotel," Coll said.

"The offer still holds at my place."

"You're on. I packed up my things this morning before sun-up and put everything in the Jeep. I'm paid through the end of the week, so they won't have any issue with me stiffing them. The cops were starting to ask a lot of questions before I left. It's the right move."

"Think they'll trace anything to your room?"

"I busted into the room above mine and rappelled down to my room." Coll said. "They taught us rappelling in basic, but I never found much use for it in country. Came in mighty handy last night, though. They won't find out much in that room. I cleaned it up after I used it. No prints, nada. Besides, the hotel thinks I'm Bob Smith from Baltimore. That'll be a mother for the cops to check out. Couldn't be more than two million Bob Smiths in this country.

"Think they'll check?" Jim asked.

"My sister lives in Baltimore. I got a message through to her last night. She'll cover me if it comes to that."

Coll stared out the windshield for a moment.

"I think I'm going to need a passport," Coll said.

"Gonna run for it?"

"No, no rush. I'm here for the duration, but afterward I may be heading to one of those far-away places with strange-sounding names. I don't have the back-up I used to."

"If need be, I have some friends in the back-up business who can lend us a hand," Jim said.

"My life seems to hang on the generosity of strangers. I hate putting people out because of the jams I get myself into."

"It's what friends do. When the time comes, they'll be there."

"I think the time's here," Coll said with undisguised gravity in his voice.

Jim started the car and drove out of the lot and onto the street. He headed to Coll's hotel and pulled up alongside the Jeep Cherokee. Coll climbed out of the Mustang, took out the keyless entry remote, and opened the doors of the Jeep.

"Dinner's at six," Jim said. "Dina's having her best girlfriend over tonight, so lose the Droopy Dog face and set yourself up for some fun."

"You trying to fix me up?"

"Hell, why not. You haven't been laid since they discovered fire."

"Got any sex vitamins?" Coll said as he got behind the wheel of the Cherokee.

"Not to worry. Word has it that Dina's friend's good looks actually *caused* the Petrified Forest," Jim said and drove off.

Coll started the Jeep's engine and followed Jim's car out onto the street. He couldn't help thinking that earlier that day he had handed over more than a quarter of a million dollars to complete strangers, and yet he was on the run like some ragamuffin fugitive. Life had its unpredictable bounces, but like a professional golfer playing at the Masters, he knew that how one dealt with unfavorable situations made all the difference between losing and being a champion, and getting to try on one of those fabulous green jackets. To win, a pro had to stay alive through all four rounds to the final hole. No matter what fate threw at him, Coll was going to stay to the finish. He was a 44-regular and had set his mind to winning that shamrock-colored coat, Vegas style.

Chapter 46

Dinners at the Creegers' were not only some of the best meals Coll had ever eaten, they were enjoyed without the constant over-the-shoulder checks to see who might be approaching with bad intentions. Add to that the fact that the Creegers had gained his complete trust and had provided a warm, growing friendship as well, which shifted an incalculable safety quotient into Coll's confidence and sense of well being. Coll discovered that, more than anything else that might happen as a result of his winnings, he wanted to be safe. Right now, the Creeger home was the only place on Earth that Coll felt completely secure. The value of that was immeasurable.

Connie Hannigan, the girlfriend that Dina had alluded to the night before, was everything Dina had said she would be. She was a stunning woman in her mid-thirties with fire-red hair and skin like an airbrushed Playboy centerfold. Coll had never been a believer of that love-at-first-sight phenomenon, although immediate lovemaking interest had often influenced his past affairs. He couldn't take his eyes off Connie through the entire dinner, and it took every "guy" ploy Jim knew to get him to join him on the patio for some man-time.

Jim tugged Coll outside to have drinks and watch the last rays of a brilliant sunset. The enjoyment and the beauty of the day's end suffered from the interruption of Coll's thoughts, thoughts of that lower world outside the Creegers' comfortable hospitality. He hated allowing them to intrude on the few moments of peace he could depend on, but he hadn't come to this corner of the world to frolic and loll about like the tourists; he had come here on business. And now that business had become a life-and-death enterprise.

"It's only a matter of time," Coll said. "Rotermund's not going to go away. He's killed many people for far less than what I've done to him."

"How big's his crew?" Jim asked.

"Hard to say. He's got money to buy all the help he needs, but I doubt if he'll bring in a lot of soldiers."

"Why's that?"

"He's going to want to take care of me personally."

"Is that smart?" Jim asked.

"It's not about smart," Coll said. "It's about ego. It's about revenge and pride. The prisons and graveyards are filled with men who let these things dictate their actions. Kyler hasn't learned that pride is the most deadly sin a person can commit."

The two men stared at the final glow of daylight in silence for several minutes. Their near-hypnotic state was pleasantly brought to a close as Dina came out onto the patio, followed by Connie. Both men stood and welcomed the two women with broad smiles.

"Enough of this male bonding crap. We're here, we're dear, and we're in your face. And now we want some attention," Dina said.

"Aw, no," Jim said. "Coll and I were having a lovely chat about toning up our unsightly thigh bulges."

"I know an exercise that firms that right up," Dina said.

"Will it mess up my golf swing?" Jim asked.

Coll locked eyes with Connie.

"Hiya," Coll said.

"Hiya back," Connie said.

"Coll, do you remember what we had for dinner?" Dina asked.

"Nope. Sure was good, though," Coll said, never taking his eyes off Connie.

"Uh-huh. Connie, I'm going to get myself a glass of wine. You want one?" Dina said as she turned for the house.

"Nope. Sure was good, though," Connie said, with her eyes steady on Coll's.

"Oh, yeah, they're not going to get along. I just knew it," Dina said.

Dina went into the house while Jim watched and enjoyed the obvious affection between Coll and Connie. Dina re-entered the patio, grabbed Jim by the wrist and towed him into the house.

"See that desert out there?" Coll said.

"Yeah," Connie said.

"I did that."

"You did it good," she said as they began to move slowly toward each other.

"Jim says I haven't been with a woman since they discovered fire. He exaggerates. Maybe it was not since the Tet offensive."

"The what offensive?" Connie said.

"Tet, Tet."

"Yeah. Got two of them," Connie said as their bodies almost touched.

"It's an Asian holiday, a celebration," Coll said, their faces an inch apart.

"You do whatever you want with them," Connie said as they softly kissed. Coll felt weightless in the moment. After what seemed like an eternity, their mouths slowly parted.

"It's an Asian holiday," Coll said, oblivious of the redundancy.

Dina returned to the patio from the house.

"Do you two want ... Who am I kidding? The only thing you want is me out of here," Dina said and then shot back inside. "Brace yourself, big boy. We've got the house all to ourselves."

Chapter 47

Later that night Coll and Connie lay, fully clothed, on the pulled-out sleep sofa in the Creeger clubroom.

"Connie Hannigan. That's a lovely Irish name," Coll said looking at Connie, propped on his elbow.

"Irish as Paddy's pig." Connie said.

"There's an image."

"I was born in Cong, Ireland."

Coll cocked his head and thought a moment.

"Isn't that where they filmed *The Quiet Man* with John Wayne and Maureen O'Hara?"

"Before my time, but yes."

"Mine too, but what a great movie," Coll said. "Barry Fitzgerald, Victor McLaglen, Ward Bond. Wow. They don't make 'em like that anymore. Is Cong as pretty as it was in the movie?"

"Still beautiful, the last time I saw it," Connie said with a note of sadness in her voice. "Dina says you're some kind of super baseball fan."

"The boys of summer and I do okay. You're a professional dancer?"

"Dina and I used to be in lots of shows around town. That was years ago. Now we work at a bank."

"Married? Kids?" Coll asked.

"No and no. Showgirls have a habit of intimidating men. I went home alone almost every night after the shows. I always thought there'd be a line of men waiting at the stage door with flowers and invitations to late night, romantic dinners. All I ever got was Dina and a diner."

"Hard to believe," Coll said.

"It's a common scenario in Vegas," Connie said. "I came out here to find an adventurous man and romance. Ends up, I'm an over-the-hill showgirl without even a pet goldfish. You have family?"

"Everybody's gone but my sister in Maryland. No wife, no kids. Funny thing is, I always loved kids. I'd've been a good baseball coach to some young Cal Ripkens," Coll said.

"I would've taught little girls to dance," Connie said as she waved a shapely leg in the air.

"Breakfast's at seven, you meatheads," Jim hollered down into the basement.

"What a charming place. You here next to me, and Archie Bunker in the kitchen upstairs," Coll said as he sat up and looked intently at Connie. "I want you to know that nothing's expected tonight. We can… you know, just sleep here tonight without anything… happening."

"Coll, I'm tired to the bone of waiting at the stage door for someone special to meet me. And I'm too old to hold off until the traditional third date to get to second base, even for a baseball expert."

"And so... ?" Coll said.

"And so," Connie said as she pulled Coll close to her, "ditch those duds and get your gorgeous butt over here and make me scream out religious names."

Chapter 48

Jerry Cohen, a sharply-dressed businessman in his fifties, sat at the center of a large banquet-style table having coffee with several other men. The remains of what had been breakfast lay on some of the plates in front of them, but they hadn't been assembled there for the eggs Benedict. These men were the owners and upper management people of the most prominent hotels and casinos in Las Vegas. The group gathered regularly for a little breakfast and coffee, but, more importantly, they convened to compare notes and discuss the goings-on in their businesses. Lately, they had been getting together almost daily to deal with what was becoming a growing concern.

Jerry held the floor at the moment as the other men looked attentively in his direction. He was the owner of the Palacio and Hermosa casinos where they often held these meetings, two of the top-ranked establishments on the Vegas Strip.

"This cashier of mine says this guy's bets have gone from five dollars a game to several thousand a game since spring training," Jerry said. "Normally I wouldn't mind, but this guy seems to be beating my brains out, and he's doing it betting on *baseball*, of all things."

"He's into us too, but what're you going to do? Cut him off?" Charlie Mazio said.

Charlie was an old school casino owner who went back to the heyday of the Sands and the Stardust when celebs like Sinatra, Tony Bennett, and the Rat Pack headlined there. "Some big raghead from Saudi hits my joint every year with big bets. Sometimes I take a couple of mil on the chin, but over the years, the house is up on the guy."

"Policy says we should cut him off," a bald man said.

"I know the goddamn policy," Jerry said. "I thought of limiting the bets on this baseball maven, but my guys here tell me he threatened to take it public."

"So what?" a fat man with three chins chimed in. "The Nevada Gaming Commission allows us to refuse bets from anyone, with no reason given at all."

"I don't know about you, but I don't need CBS doing a special on my joint," a man with thick glasses said.

"So we either ban him or hope his streak goes sour," Jerry said as waitresses and bus boys began clearing the breakfast plates and topping off coffees.

Jerry waved a hand and the others withheld further comments until the wait staff left and had closed the double doors of the room.

The room immediately became a press conference with questions and comments coming rapid-fire from many of the men.

"Who is this guy? We know him?"

"No one's ever seen him before. Some mamaluke named Bob Smith, if you can believe that one. Says he's from Baltimore. Yeah, I can believe that. With all of Brooks Robinson's golden gloves in his suitcase."

"And Secretariat's horseshoes up his ass."

"If he was a card counter or working with a dealer I could shut him down without any problems from the outside, but baseball? How the hell do you fix baseball? He'd have to be Shoeless Joe Jackson."

"Maybe he *is* Shoeless Joe Jackson. He sure as shit knows the game."

"You been watching too many Kevin Costner movies."

"In 1919 Shoeless Joe got caught. And so will his guy if he's not on the level."

"Nobody thumps us every day in baseball," Jerry said. "No way. I think this guy is headed for a big fall. I want him in my casinos betting big when he goes down."

"Maybe we should start keeping closer tabs on his betting. See if there's a pattern."

"Oh, there's a pattern, all right," Jerry said. "He bets every friggin' game, every day, and kicks the crap out of us. That's his goddamn pattern,"

"Jerry, is there anything we can do with the odds?"

"Like what? You gotta know who he's going to bet on ahead of time to make that work. Plus, you've gotta know who's going to win. Okay, try this: The Giants are playing the Dodgers tonight. So who's going to win?"

There was silence at the table.

"See what I mean?" Jerry said. "There's no way to know. You can't fix baseball bets."

"Maybe we should stay out of doing sports books altogether."

"Are you nuts?"

"Hey, fungu this choo-choo from Cooperstown," Charlie Mazio said. "I make a ton of jack on sports books. All of you do. So get off the whining about one guy who's making a small living on us. And who sets the odds so we get action on both sides of the bets? We do."

"He's right," Jerry said. "We can't burn down the house just to get rid of one roach."

"Wanna off him?"

"What the fuck's wrong with you? Jerry said. "Off him? You ice this schmuck and I'll watch them strap your ass in the goodbye gurney. We don't kill people anymore for winning. Off him? Shit, we usually up their credit line."

"It was just a thought."

"And it stinks," a big-nosed man next to Jerry said.

"All right, gentlemen, let's do this: get the numbers boys to figure what he's into us for," Jerry said.

"What good'll that do?"

"It'll give me an idea of how much I gotta raise the prices in my restaurants and nightclubs," Jerry said. "Maybe cut the slot payouts from 94 percent to 90."

"The way I see it," a short man at the far end of the table said, "we have to let this guy keep betting and hope we go in the win column when he's got the volume way up on the bets. That way, we can get even with Mr. Baseball in a few big swings… No pun intended."

"There's a man talking sense. He's absolutely right," Jerry said. "We have to let this guy double-down and hope the lady turns our way."

Jerry studied the faces at the table as they looked at each other and nodded in agreement, coupled with tacit resignation. Jerry knew it had been many years since these powerful men had shown concern over a single player, who got deep into their pockets and seemed to have no intention of going away anytime soon. He watched them as they left the room, hoping he was right about lady luck turning their way, but he knew gamblers could sometimes have incredible winning streaks. Maybe there was no such thing as luck, but there surely were streaks.

No matter how much he wanted to be encouraged, he felt every person there still had a nagging worry biting at their bank accounts.

Chapter 49

Coll knew there were only two days in the summer schedule of big time professional sports when no games were played: the day before, and the day after, major league baseball's all-star game. Coll had already placed his bets on the all-star game and had three off days in a row to himself. It was a perfect time to get away and take in a change of scenery. It would be even more enhanced if he could share that time with Connie Hannigan, who was rapidly becoming a most important aspect of his life.

He knew she was looking forward to the break from baseball, but studying his betting had to be priority one, now more than ever. Things could abruptly change as the season progressed. Coll would have to make astute adjustments to stay on top. He decided to take Connie out to dinner and explain his need to stay in Las Vegas and continue to pore over his twenty-six unpredictable schedules and rosters.

Coll had another project to strategize. A project as unpredictable as baseball. One that didn't abide by any rules. A project named Kyler Rotermund.

* * *

Coll stared at Connie across the table at Chez Beleau.

"I knew what I needed to know in the service to be a good soldier, to survive. And in baseball? Well, who's more on top of things than I am? But this? You and me? I'm at my first day at school," Coll said and swirled the wine in his glass.

"I'm not much of an expert on this either. Look at me. Going into middle age with little to justify my existence. You're not dealing with Dear Abby here."

"One step at a time then?" Coll said.

"One step at a time," Connie said and reached over and touched Coll's hand.

Chapter 50

It was late in August, not so one would notice in a place like Las Vegas where the seasons seldom showed dramatic change. But one man took particular notice. He knew that in the world of professional baseball, this was when time was running out, and the World Series loomed ahead, ready to accept the sport's two most victorious teams.

Kyler Rotermund was keenly aware of that baseball clock ticking away the days. He felt the urgency. Time was drawing short for his chance to capture his nemesis Coll Nolan and dole out the comeuppance he richly deserved. He knew Coll was in Las Vegas to bet on baseball, and baseball was in the final days of its season. To get to Coll he'd have to catch him somewhere he knew his prey couldn't avoid; someplace like the one depicted in that oft-shown nature scene at the edge of an African river where crocodiles lie in ambush for the wildebeests to come to cross or slake their thirst. That watering hole in Las Vegas was where Coll came to place his bets, a place where Kyler's crocs would be lurking just beneath the surface.

Kyler paced up and down in the elegant living room of the Florentine Suite talking on a cordless phone. Two Ton Teddy sat in front of the TV in a big leather recliner with the footrest up under his thick legs. Kyler's conversation was an angry one, but he was an angry person by nature. Kyler liked his anger, embraced it like a valued friend. Anger made people fear him, empowered him. Anger was his drug of choice.

"Well, you get them up and on their feet right now," Kyler said. "My guys won't be here 'til tonight and I need some extra eyes on the street. One hour. You have them at Charlie Mazio's place in one hour." Kyler turned off the phone and slammed it on the bar counter.

"Teddy, did Joey fix you up with new hardware?" Kyler asked.

"Yeah. No problem."

"I still can't believe that sonofabitch got to Big Al. Al must've been slipping."

"Yeah. When he killed all the lights in the hotel room it tipped Coll off. He'd've never done that in the old days," Teddy said.

"And those stupid local dicks think he fell from the roof," Kyler said as he picked up a handgun from the bar counter. "What a bunch of a-hole Sherlocks they've got in this burg."

Kyler took out the magazine from the automatic pistol and checked it for ammo. Satisfied, he replaced the mag and slid the gun into his shoulder holster.

"I want you to go over to the Bon Chance again and see if you can find out where he is," Kyler said to Teddy. "Call me soon as you know something. I've been putting off getting him because Bartel wanted to be here when we grab him, but Bartel's delayed. Time's running out. I'm taking charge now."

Teddy grumbled and slammed the footrest down on the recliner, got to his feet with some grunts, and tramped to the door. Kyler paced in front of the glass door to the balcony and looked out at the Las Vegas panorama as Teddy banged the hotel door shut.

The rage in Kyler kept forming the same promises: *I'll find you, Coll Nolan. No matter where you are, I'll find you. And when I do, I'm going to kill you slow.*

Chapter 51

Coll went into the Commonwealth Bank and straight to the manager's desk with two weighty briefcases. The bank manager looked up from his work and greeted Coll cordially.

"Ah, Mr. Smith, good morning."

"I need to go to my safe deposit box," Coll said.

"Of course," the manager said and crossed to a room in the back of the bank with Coll close behind. He took out a set of keys from a security box on the wall and handed Coll a pen. Coll put down his cases and signed a large register. He picked up the cases and the manager led him into a vault containing stacks and rows of safe deposit boxes of all sizes. They arrived at one of the largest boxes where the manager put in his key and turned one of its two locks. Coll set down his cases, took out his key, and opened the second lock. The manager pulled the steel container from the wall and placed it on a narrow table in the center of the room. Satisfied that his client had his box, the manager turned to leave.

"Can I get cash reduced to a single bank draft and sent somewhere?" Coll asked.

"Certainly, sir. Whenever you like," the manager said. "We can wire funds to anywhere in the world you specify."

"Good to know."

The manager left and Coll took everything into a curtained cubicle in back of the vault. He opened his cases on a shelf provided in the small space, transferred numerous packs of bills into the large safe deposit box, and arranged them into neat rows. He then made a cursory count of the contents and put one pack in his pocket. He closed the box, replaced it in the vault opening, and relocked his side. He pressed a button on the wall near the doorway. Shortly, the manager re-entered the vault with his keys and relocked the bank's side of the large box. Coll smiled at him approvingly and exited the vault with the empty briefcases.

Coll left the Commonwealth Bank, and drove the Cherokee down the street and parked a few yards from another bank. He donned a pair of aviator sunglasses he took from the glove compartment, and watched the front door of the Prospect Bank like Willy Sutton casing the place for a future heist. Momentarily, Connie Hannigan, the true object of his surveillance, emerged from the bank and walked toward the Jeep. Coll opened the passenger door from inside and Connie climbed in.

"I told them I was only going to be a minute," she said.

"I need you and Dina to take care of an account for me. It's at another bank right now, but I want to put it where someone I trust can handle it."

"Come into the bank later today and we'll get you set up."

"Good enough," he said as she leaned over and kissed him.

"You have a passport?" Coll said.

"Yeah. Got one when Dina and I went to Aruba two years ago. Why?"

"No reason. Just curious. Want to get in the back and mess around?"

"Much as I hate to pass that up, I've got to run, love," she said, and checked her face in the visor mirror, hopped out of the car, and hurried toward the bank.

Coll started the Jeep and moved along parallel to Connie striding on the sidewalk.

"There're laws in this state to protect older men from beautiful young women, you know," Coll said, growling like an old man as he bent low in the car to see Connie's face. "How do I know you're not one of them trick rollers out to steal my money?"

"Going to arrest and handcuff me, big boy?"

She winked at him and entered the bank.

Coll drove off down the street until he was stopped by a red light at a busy intersection. On the far corner he saw Two Ton Teddy De Groot talking to a pair of rough-looking men he didn't recognize. Coll took a good look at the two strangers talking with Teddy as the traffic light changed to green, then drove through the intersection, unnoticed by the trio on the corner.

Maybe Kyler is recruiting soldiers after all, he thought.

Chapter 52

Kyler Rotermund sat in the finely-appointed lounge in the Las Palmas casino. Charlie Mazio stood nearby, leaning on the bar as Kyler studied the gambling activity in the adjoining room though a wide archway.

"Looks like your joint's jumping, Chaz," Kyler said.

"We do okay."

"So what's new?"

"A lot since I last saw Bartel. Mostly good," Charlie said.

"A few nights back there was a high-roller in here playing poker. Guy wearing a Yankee hat. You remember him?"

"Yeah, I watched him for a while. Had a bad tell. Flicked his cards before the laydown. I put some of the boys from the pit on him, but they couldn't spot anything irregular about him, except he was kicking everybody's ass, even with that give-away with his cards. Nothing hinky about his poker playing, anyway."

"What do you mean?" Kyler said as he leaned toward Charlie.

"Back in spring, this guy starts betting on baseball. He bets on every game every day. Starts out slow. Five bucks a game, then ten. All of a sudden we turn around and this chooch is into us for heavy metal."

"Same guy?" Kyler said.

"Same guy. Now we gotta hang in there and hope his streak goes sour."

"What happens if he up and quits? Like tomorrow," Kyler said.

"Then me and a bunch of other casino owners flirt with goin' in the red for the baseball season. Your boss included. Bartel's got big bucks invested in this joint too."

"Bartel don't like losing money. This guy's got you that good?"

"If he was the flu, we'd all be in intensive care."

"And if he hangs out 'til baseball's over?"

"We may get back something, but I think the harm is done," Charlie said. "We're in damage control right now. If we can't stop the bleeding, we'll do what we can to up our interests elsewhere."

"Like what?"

"We don't ever allow one facet of our business to be able to sink us. We diversify our capital, invest in other projects. Hell, right now I'm losing my ass to this guy on baseball, but I've made a killing this year on slots and the craps tables. Made some bucks on a few outside ventures. I'm okay. We're all going to be okay. I'd be the last to tell you that I'm ecstatic when someone lightens me up of a coupla hundred grand, but shit, that's Vegas, baby. You gotta love the action, even from where I sit."

"He bets here every day?" Kyler asked.

"Every friggin' day," Charlie said, "like it's a religion. He has the luck of the Irish, as they say."

Kyler scowled at hearing the phrase and got up from his stool.

"Maybe I'll see you later," Kyler said as he started to leave, then stopped at the end of the bar. "By the way, I'm in the Florentine Suite at the Royale. Give me a buzz if you see this guy again. I think I know him." Kyler headed out of the room.

"Will do," Charlie said.

* * *

Charlie Mazio knew Kyler's request wasn't because he was trying to hook up with an old friend. He knew damn well that all of Kyler's friends were either dead or employed by him. And those who worked for him weren't exactly friends to him like Damon was to Pythias, or even like Laurel was to Hardy. Charlie knew that Kyler was interested in this "guy wearing a Yankee hat" the same way a cheetah was interested in a Thompson's gazelle.

Chapter 53

The days went by in frenetic blurs for Coll as he went about his baseball bets. Darting from one betting parlor to the next and keeping a careful watch over his shoulder made for high tension as he precariously walked open streets and public places where an enemy could lie in wait for him. Then there were the daily bank deposits to add to his vulnerability. His only respites came at night at the Creeger home where he could feel safe among trusted friends, calm his nerves, and see Connie Hannigan.

His affection for Connie had grown immensely in the past weeks, and while he hadn't figured on romance during his intense betting quest, he now welcomed it with her. A meaningful love relationship had eluded him all his life. Perhaps because he never allowed time for it, or maybe because he distrusted the notion that anyone could possibly love him to the same degree that he would dedicate himself to the partnership. He had been with numerous women, but no one ever made him feel that the commitment he demanded of himself was reciprocal.

Coll had dismissed love as being something no longer important on his bucket list. But then he met Connie. She was all he had ever thought love should be and, as a bonus, she was Irish. Someone once said that not everyone "grieves on universal bones," but he and Connie had numerous features in their backgrounds that made for a wonderful fit.

One evening in late summer, Jim, Dina, Connie, and Coll sat at the Creeger dinner table finishing up the evening meal. Dina had put in extra time making the food for her guests and saw their appreciation for her efforts in thumbs-up gestures from Coll, and smiles and nods from Connie. Dina also beamed with personal satisfaction at seeing Connie with this accidental Montana visitor who had dropped into their lives, and who seemed to be a perfect match for her best friend.

Dina had been saddened that Connie had never, in all the time she'd known her, found the love and home life she desperately wanted. She also knew that Connie Hannigan was very discriminating about what she liked, and distrusted most men. Las Vegas was a place where the boyfriend pool was often what one scraped off the bottom of the septic tank: gamblers, drunks, philanderers, lowdown pigs, oafs with money, and con men who'd do almost anything for a tumble with a looker like Connie, only to go back to whatever sewer had produced them and never look back.

Dina knew that her friend was not going gently into that broken-hearted good night. She would rather be alone the rest of her life than settle for less than her ideal of a man. Dina knew Connie had her dreams that guided and fortified her every day of her life. And like Scarlett O'Hara, if they didn't pan out today, there was always tomorrow. For the first time in Dina's experience, Connie seemed truly at home with a man; albeit a man who was mysterious, had an uncanny passion for baseball, and was in trouble.

"I was hoping to get out of town before they make a try for me, but, for some reason, Kyler and his crew seemed to be laying off. But that may be changing. Looks like they're recruiting some heavies now," Coll said, looking across the table at Jim.

"Leave now. You've got plenty," Jim said.

"I came here to bet on baseball for the whole season, all the way through the World Series. I'm not letting ghosts from my past run my life."

"Is this that pride thing again?" Jim asked.

"Whose side are you on?"

"Come on, Coll. You know where I stand. I just don't want to see you become like them."

Dina looked over at Connie's saddened face and shook her head. Coll stood up from the table.

"Maybe I need to stop looking over my shoulder every time I go out to get an ice cream," Coll said as he crossed to the bar and poured himself a stiff drink.

Connie rose from her chair

"The sweetest man came to visit me at the bank today. He was funny and charming. Everything I've ever wanted in a man. Each day, I wonder if I'll ever see him again."

She walked outside onto the patio.

"She's quite a gal, Coll," Dina said. "And she's been madly in love with you since the night she met you. And so have we."

Dina went to Coll at the bar.

"In your pursuit of the World Series try not to destroy any more people than you have to," Dina said.

She kissed him on the cheek, turned, and strode down the hallway toward the bedrooms.

"Boy, can I clear a room or what?" Coll said.

"Yeah, you're a regular Baby Ruth bar in the swimming pool," Jim said.

Coll downed his drink and went out onto the patio to join Connie. She was sitting on a wooden bench looking out into a beautiful, starlit desert night as he ambled over and sat beside her.

"See that desert out there," Connie said.

"Yeah."

"I did that."

"You did it good," Coll said and pulled her to him and kissed her for a timeless moment. They gently broke from the kiss and Coll held her hand. "A Crow warrior took me to a very special place in Montana. He had been a great warrior and hunter, and later he became a chief. People from all around came to see him for his wisdom and good counsel. He took me up this winding river to a mountain lake that had the most beautiful waterfall at its end. We sat there by the falls just looking at it for the longest time without saying a word. It was a magical place, like something out of a fairy tale. He told me it was his heart place. I understood what he meant as he and I became rapt in the beauty of that special spot. When he wanted to think of something to lift his spirits, he would recall an image of that river and the waterfall."

"And where's your heart place, Coll?" Connie asked.

"Never found one," Coll said, staring out at the desert. "I searched all over Montana. And trust me, I saw some pretty places. Then, like a bolt out of the blue, it appeared right in front of me."

"The desert out there?"

"It's wherever you are," he said softly.

Connie put her head on his shoulder.

"We're going to be okay," Coll said.

"I want us to get married in my little village in Ireland. In Cong, north of Galway, between Lough Corrib and Lough Mask," she said, "and to the west where the Maumturks Mountains look down to the sea."

Coll looked into her eyes and smiled.

"If that's a proposal, it's a date," he said.

"I know you must think it's stupid to love some old forgotten town in the Irish countryside, but I guess it's *my* heart place. I never wanted a movie star lover, or some famous lawyer, or a rich businessman for a mate. God knows I met plenty of them here. I just wanted to meet someone on the run from life like me. On the run from time that flies by so fast a mind can't catch it. Someone kind, who'd go to Ireland with me, and see a place in the world where time stands still. I'm getting old here. In Cong, I think I could find once more the girl who used to be me."

He held her face in his hands and kissed her tenderly as Dina charged out from the house.

"Guess what movie's on TV tonight?" Dina said with elation. She saw their embrace and spun on her heels. "Crap, every time I come out here . . ."

Dina barged back into the house.

* * *

Dina stepped into the kitchen where Jim was putting dishes in the dishwasher.

"Well, honey, I guess it's just you and me for watching *Casablanca* tonight," Dina said to Jim's behind as he bent over the open dishwasher.

"You know, Dina, this could be the start of a beautiful friendship," Jim said.

Coll and Connie entered from the patio and came into the kitchen.

"Okay, okay, we'll watch the damn movie with you guys," Connie said.

"It's *Casablanca*," Dina said like it included a personal visit from Bogart and Bergman.

"Why of all the gin joints in all the world did you have to end up in mine?" Coll said in something resembling a Humphrey Bogart impersonation.

"You guys have seen this movie, right?" Dina said.

"Everybody on earth has seen the movie,... everybody but you," Connie said.

"What the hell, play it again, Bogie," Jim said.

* * *

As the foursome filed to the den, bullets sprayed through the large living room window, disintegrating it and puncturing the walls overhead and around the two couples. Coll grabbed Connie and tackled her to the floor. Jim yanked Dina down the hall out of sight.

"Kill the lights!" Coll yelled.

"I'll hit the breaker. Dina, call the cops," Jim said as he flew into the basement.

"Crawl back into the bedroom and stay down on the floor," Coll said to Connie.

Connie heeded the instruction and wriggled her way toward the back of the house. Coll followed her part of the way, but then opened the basement door and slipped downstairs. Jim was already there at the circuit breaker box throwing switches. The house lights went dark and Jim turned on a large flashlight he held in his hand.

"That ought to do it. You got your gun?" Jim said.

"It's in the Jeep," Coll said. "Didn't think I'd need one at dinner."

Jim opened and ducked into his secret ordnance room and came out with two M-16 rifles.

"Take this. Remember how to use it?" Jim said while shining his flashlight on the weapon. Coll darted a stern glance at Jim and snatched a rifle from him.

"Had to ask. You know, old age, Alzheimer's and all," Jim said.

"I got your old age. Let's do some recon."

Coll and Jim went back upstairs and surveyed the outside of the house from concealment behind the draperies of several windows. Nothing moved outside.

"Must've been a drive-by," Jim said.

"Not a very efficient method for assassination," Coll said.

"I'll go out first. I know the grounds," Jim said and sidled to the front door and cautiously opened it.

"I'll cover you," Coll said as he moved stealthily into the front room. Jim slipped outside and dashed for the left end of the house. Coll kept him in sight until he disappeared around the corner.

Minutes passed. Coll panned the outside through the broken glass of the living room window, but saw nothing of the shooters. He maintained his position until he heard measured footsteps coming from the darkness behind him. Coll spun around with his rifle leveled at the shadow's body mass and squeezed a millimeter off the trigger play.

"Easy, partner. It's me, Jimbo."

Coll exhaled through puffed cheeks and lowered his weapon.

"You were a four pounds of pull away from being Jimbo the Swiss cheese."

"Sorry. Came through the patio. Looked all clear. They must've rode on."

"Why would anyone spray a few of rounds and run like hell?" Coll said. "If they're after me, they're going about it in a strange way."

"Maybe they're not really after *you*." Jim said.

Coll looked at Jim, puzzled.

"Shit, son, you think you're the only one in the world with enemies? I've put plenty of bad people in the calaboose, you know. Sometimes they get out and harbor downright unsavory attitudes."

"This has happened to you before?" Coll asked.

"Not like this here at my home, but I've ducked a few pot shots," Jim said as Dina and Connie emerged from the shadows in the darkened hall. They each carried pistols in their hands.

"You guys all right?" Dina asked.

"We're okay, honey," Jim said.

The women tiptoed into the room and joined the men.

"Pretty nice ordnance you got there, baby," Coll said to Connie.

"I know, but how do you like my gun?" she said.

"What are we going to do, Jim? I don't like cooking dinner in Kevlar," Dina said as sirens wailed in the distance.

"I'll put some of my boys here for the rest of the week," Jim said.

"Now they know where you are," Connie said to Coll, as the sirens became louder and the lights of approaching vehicles danced on the walls inside the house.

"And now I find out where they are," Coll said and snapped on the safety of the M-16.

"Come on, Connie," Dina said. "Let's go downstairs and get the lights back on."

The women left and Jim moved over to Coll.

"Before you have any dealings with the Prospect Bank you ought to know Dina's boss, Gibbs, has ties with mob people," Jim said.

"Kyler and company?" Coll said.

"The mafia, I'm betting, but bad guys for certain. I got folks lookin' into him."

"Is he paying off cops?"

"Doubt it," Jim said. "I got a crapload of domestic stuff on him. Good for Dina's job security, but I got more comin' in."

"Keep me posted," Coll said.

Chapter 54

Jonathan Gibbs, a short, portly man in his fifties, sat behind his large desk in a tastefully decorated, private office talking on the phone. An engraved sign on his desk displayed his name and his title of Bank Manager. Through his open office door, he watched the uniformed guards on duty around the doorway of the Prospect Bank and the people who moved in and out of the building transacting business with tellers at the main counter and with customer service personnel at desks on both sides of the lobby.

"He's moved his funds here to our bank," Gibbs said into the phone. "Quite a tidy sum, I might add." He paused for a moment, then resumed talking. "Well, he makes his deposits here daily, it seems, though not in person. One of my employees makes them for him." Another pause. "Hannigan, Connie Hannigan. A pretty girl. Friend of Dina Creeger that you met here. Another pause. "Yes, my assistant manager. You're certainly welcome, sir. Anytime, Mr. Rotermund."

Gibbs hung up the phone, got up and crossed to a large credenza. He opened a drawer, removed some papers and looked through them. A framed photograph on the credenza showed a smiling Gibbs with his arms around two other men. A sign behind the three in the picture said "Banking Association of Las Vegas Golf Tournament."

The two other men in the photo were younger versions of Kyler Rotermund and Bartel Vandermeer.

Chapter 55

Coll's winning bets were starting to fall off as the season waned. He found himself losing day after day and it confounded him. The bets he made now were huge and the losses were heavy. He reviewed his meticulous notes, but could find no tangible reason for the negative turn. There had to be a reason, and he had to find it and correct for it — and do it fast.

Looking over the season thus far he noted one very peculiar fact that didn't quite fit other seasons he'd used as tests for his 1991 Vegas debut. The two championship teams that led the American League and the National League in 1990, and ultimately played in that year's World Series, were currently faltering. At the same time, the two 1990 teams that ended up on the very bottom of their respective leagues were leading all other teams and making a bid for the pennant. This phenomenon had happened with a single team in the past, but rarely. However, this was an instance where *both* of the former season's cellar dwellers were currently in first place in their respective leagues. If the season ended with the two of them on top, it would constitute an unparalleled situation in modern, major league baseball history. Maybe this, Coll thought, was skewing the odds and giving the

Vegas casinos a shot at winning the betting game in this season's bottom of the ninth.

The World Series loomed on the horizon and Coll's former net winnings were looking more and more like they might have to be put at risk. He had hoped he could finish up the season by only having to tap into his current winnings, but with his recent losses he doubted that he could end up being the biggest money winner in Las Vegas history without drawing on every penny he owned. It was a thought that ate at him like the locusts that plagued the Pharaoh in ancient Egypt. What was next for him, he pondered?

Is Lake Mead going to part like the Red Sea and drown me too?

Chapter 56

Jim Creeger and Coll Nolan stood in front of a rustic cabin that looked like it hadn't been inhabited since the Lewis and Clark expedition.

Jim's had parked the Cherokee, covered with a thick layer of tan dust, near the two men on what would have to be upgraded to be considered a dirt road. The surrounding desert stretched as far as the eye could see in every direction. Distant mountains and a few boulders were the only things that broke up the far, otherwise flat, horizon.

"I dug out and dragged stones from around here, and brought out a couple of loads of lumber and modified this place fifteen years ago, even before I built my house in town. I was told it was originally an old miner's cabin. I used it to get away from it all when I was younger. Do a little desert hiking. Bring out the boys from the force for poker weekends," Jim said. "But I haven't tended to it for a long time. It's kinda gone to seed."

"This certainly is away from it all," Coll said as his eyes panned the desolate wasteland.

A distant dust plume swirled on the western horizon. A vehicle approached, moving fast down the twisting dirt road.

"Looks like we got company," Coll said.

Jim followed Coll's gaze to the vehicle and nodded in that direction.

"I asked some buddies to meet us out here. You're going to need some help and I've got to be with Dina 'til this drive-by shooting stuff settles down. You'll like these boys. They're like me. They'd rather bang a bad guy than a thousand-dollar hooker."

"These boys pretty dependable?"

"Steady as a bronze sniper."

"I think Kyler's onto my routine at the betting windows. I think that's how he traced me to your place. But I don't think he was trying to do me in with that pathetic drive-by. He wants to have a face-to-face, *then* do me. He likes it when people squirm and beg for their lives. He gets off seeing fear."

Coll paused for a moment and felt reluctant to go on about Kyler, but changed his mind and continued.

"He bought a cute little rabbit from a pet store in New York when we were both working for Bartel Vandermeer," Coll said as he squatted and began piling up a some desert rocks around his feet. "I was told that when he got tired of feeding it and teasing it, he decided to torture it. Rabbits don't make vocal sounds very often, and he wanted to hear it scream. He started by clipping off his ears. Then he blinded it with an ice pick. He finished up by dousing the poor thing with lighter fluid and setting it on fire. The guy who told me about this said Kyler laughed while the animal screamed for mercy. He'll want me to die like that. He's the cruelest person I've ever known. Before it's over, one of us will kill the other. I just hope it's before he blinds me and lights me up."

Coll rose and kicked over the rock pile he'd made.

Minutes later, a large, Dodge utility vehicle pulled up next to the Cherokee. What could be seen of the dust-covered truck body was metallic green paint with dark tinted windows. Three men, all with holstered side arms, got out and sauntered toward Jim and Coll. The driver was a trim, buff-looking man of about thirty-five, followed by a younger, slight-built, tan man, and a huge fellow who looked older than the other two.

"Coll, this here's Bill Ashton, about the best man with a pistol and rifle as you'll find this side of Carlos Hathcock," Jim said with his hand on the shoulder of the athletic man. He then turned to the younger and smaller of the three men. "Next to him here is Remo Morales, our Spanish-speaking, martial arts brother who can track a fly across a glacier. And lastly, this big old dude is Don Braxley, a guy whose horse you *do not* want to steal." Jim then turned toward Coll. "Boys, this is Coll Nolan. He's my friend and a former marine war vet who needs a little help watching his back. Things that come up in front of him he can pretty much handle."

"Appreciate your help," Coll said shaking the hands of the three men.

"Coll, did Jim tell you that the air conditioner in this joint is a little short on air and conditioning?" Bill said, indicating the cabin.

"What air conditioner?" Don said.

"See, they love it here," Jim said with a Cheshire cat grin.

Jim led the way to the cabin, unlocked the padlocked door, and they all filed inside. The interior of the unmercifully hot, stale-aired cabin was something out of Abe Lincoln's early years. It contained, in a single large room with a stone fireplace: a cast iron stove, four bunk beds, a farm table with rustic chairs, and a filthy porcelain sink under a long-handled water pump. Fully exposed in one corner, was the pearl in the oyster: a galvanized steel camping toilet. It was to living accommodations what a week-old road kill was to fine French cuisine. A rusty lever-action rifle rested against the wall in a corner of the room, and a box of large caliber shells lay open on a nearby window sill. The men stood and stared in silence at the desperate room.

"There's absolutely no place like home," Jim said, breaking the silence. "And it's a hell of a sight cheaper than those big-name motels."

"Is this what a Motel One looks like?" Don said.

"And, if you're lucky, they'll leave the light *off* for you," Bill said.

"Where would you plug one in?" Remo asked.

"Jeremiah Johnson wants his house back," Coll said, piling on.

"Make the best of it, boys," Jim said. "It's going to be our secret hide-out for a little while. Coll's got the World Series to get through yet. And he has to go in and out of town every day 'til it's over. A couple of days here will sharpen your competitive edges."

Remo stepped around the perimeter of the room searching under the bunks and peering behind the stove.

"World Series? Next couple of weeks, right? So where's the TV?" Remo said as the others focused on Jim.

"I'll think of something," Jim said.

"Try Radio Shack," Don said. "Way out here we're going to need a tall antenna, too."

"And lots and lots of them batteries that keep going and going," Bill said, tweaking his full moustache and smiling like a happy walrus.

"You sound like my wife," Don said. "Never understood why she needs so many damn batteries all the time."

"Maybe she has a cordless hand mixer," Remo said with a snort.

Coll moved to the window, his hand on his mouth.

"Maybe she has a cordless friend," Bill said, stifling a laugh.

"You mean like one of them kitchen robots?" Don asked.

"More like one of those *boudoir* robots," Jim said as everyone there but Don howled so loud they could be heard in Reno.

Chapter 57

Dina Creeger and Connie Hannigan stood outside Jonathan Gibbs' office at the Prospect Bank as Dina tapped a cup of water from the company's cooler. The manager's door was open and Gibbs was working at his desktop computer. It was during the bank's late afternoon slow time, so there were only a few people in the lobby as Coll Nolan calmly sashayed in wearing an orange and black Baltimore Oriole tee shirt and baseball cap, dark sunglasses, and sporting a thick, full lip mustache *a la* Pancho Villa. He walked straight over to Dina and Connie and stood in front of them for a long moment.

"Coll?" Connie whispered to the man as Dina stared wide-eyed.

"Don't you love the get-up," Coll said.

"What are you doing here?" Dina said.

"I'm going to be making my betting rounds in this from now on," Coll said. "It feels lucky."

"You'd better get your lucky get-up the hell out of here," Dina said as she thumbed behind her to Gibbs' open office door.

"Well, gee, I'm glad to see you guys too," Coll said, then turned and strode out of the bank. The two women shook their heads in disbelief and returned to the tellers' area.

*   *   *

That night, after bank hours, Jonathan Gibbs sat alone in his office and carefully watched a color monitor playing back the scene at the water cooler when Coll Nolan had dropped by.

Gibbs picked up his phone and punched in some numbers.

"Mr. Rotermund? Jonathan Gibbs over at Prospect Bank. I've been looking at some security camera footage here at the bank I think may be of interest to you."

Chapter 58

Kyler picked up the ringing phone on the bar in the Florentine Suite and pushed the receiver's incoming call button.

"Tell me something good," he said and listened for several seconds. "Excellent," Kyler said as an uncharacteristic smile appeared on his sullen face. He ended the call and laid the phone on the bar.

"Good news?" Teddy asked from his entrenched position in the recliner in front of the television.

"The boys got Coll while he was collecting his bets at Charlie's. They're coming up on the service elevator," Kyler said and poured himself a drink. "Put that in your Oriole hat, Mr. Nolan. Ah, Teddy, life can sometimes be so sweet."

* * *

In the service elevator of the Royale, Augie Palermo and Vince Bartolo stood on either side of their bound captive, while two other accomplices, dressed in Dallas Cowboy football jerseys, positioned themselves near the elevator doors. Augie pulled a pistol from his belt and stuck it roughly in the back of the man's Oriole cap.

"You make a sound, any sound, Nolan, and the last thing you'll hear will be this cannon taking off your fuckin' head. Got it?" Augie said.

To punctuate his threat, Augie jerked the brim of the baseball cap downward over his prisoner's eyes, forcing the sunglasses to slide under his nose.

At the 17th floor the five men got out of the elevator and plodded down a long corridor to the suite marked 1711, practically dragging their blind captive. Vince knocked three times, paused and knocked once more on the door. Teddy De Groot answered and let them inside.

Kyler Rotermund sat in a large, throne-like chair in the middle of the suite's great room as his henchmen guided their captured prize before him.

"Play time's over, Coll," Kyler said with a smile as he took a sip of his drink and nodded to his men.

Augie snatched off the Oriole cap covering the man's eyes. Vince removed the displaced sunglasses, grabbed a fistful of hair, and jerked his captive's bowed head upward, revealing the mustachioed face of Bill Ashton.

Kyler's smile vanished. He stood up and bellowed. "Who the fuck is this?"

Auggie shrugged.

"That's not your guy?" Vince asked.

"Assholes," Kyler said and hurled his drink across the room toward Teddy, causing the big man to jump out of its trajectory.

"We don't know what the guy's supposed to look like except you said he'd be wearing a Baltimore Oriole outfil with sunglasses and a 'stache," Augie said. "We told the cashier to tip us off when the baseball guy came to collect. Whaddaya want from us?"

Augie shoved Ashton hard enough to trip him over a large ottoman near Kyler's chair. Ashton'r duct-taped hands, bound behind him, provided no help in keeping his face and upper body from planting into the ottoman's upholstery.

"I want you to get me Coll Nolan," Kyler said, staring at Ashton, face-down on the ottoman. "And kill this imposter. *Now.*"

"On the fucking furniture?" Augie said.

"Now!" Kyler yelled.

Vince and Augie drew their pistols and marched over to Bill Ashton and aimed at his head.

The safety glass in the balcony doors in the bar disintegrated from rapid gunfire from outside. Bullets danced across the marble floor and ricocheted into the walls. Coll and Remo Morales crashed into the room brandishing automatic weapons. Two rappelling ropes dangled outside on the balcony from above.

Vince and Augie ducked behind Kyler's chair. Bill Ashton rolled off the ottoman onto the floor.

Coll and Remo stormed into the larger room with weapons shouldered and aimed at Kyler and his men.

The suite's hall door exploded inward at almost the same moment, and into the suite charged Don Braxley, armed with an Uzi machine pistol. One of the jersied kidnappers drew a pistol and fired toward Braxley. Coll and Don pumped several automatic rounds into the kidnapper's chest and head, reeling him backward against a nearby wall. His riddled body slid to the floor, trailing blood on the wainscoting and lower white marble panel.

The other Dallas Cowboy accomplice attempted to draw his gun, but Remo chopped him in the neck, kung-fu style, then kicked him hard in the chest. The blow sent him staggering into an open fireplace, crashing backward into the andirons in an unconscious heap.

Kyler raised his hands to his men to keep them from further harm.

"Do what they want," Kyler shouted.

The room fell silent. Coll stepped over to Kyler and stood directly before him.

"So, how've you been, Kylie?" he said.

"You look a lot older than the last time I saw you, you mick prick," Kyler said.

"I never thought you could possibly get any uglier, but I was so wrong."

"Twelve Christmases in Dannemora will do that to a guy," Kyler said.

"I told you Santa would know if you'd been naughty or nice," Coll said.

Coll slung his M-16 onto his shoulder, drew his Beretta 9-millimeter, and held it on Kyler as he patted him down. He ripped the Glock automatic from Kyler's shoulder holster and stuffed it into his own waistband.

"Check the rest of them for ordnance," Coll said, "and I'll cut Bill loose."

Coll took out a snap-blade knife and cut off Bill's duct tape restraints. Bill removed the tape from his mouth, while Don and Remo patted down Vince, Augie, and Teddy De Groot. They tossed the found weapons onto a Queen Anne wing chair, except for one pistol that they handed to Bill.

"Get a pillowcase from the bedroom and put all the guns in it. We don't leave anything here that's useful," Coll said. Bill Ashton nodded and dashed for the bedrooms.

"Guess what happens next, Teddy?" Coll said to the big man.

"Beats me, Coll."

"What did I tell you in my hotel room?"

"You said if you saw us murdering assholes again, you was gonna do every one of us," Teddy said.

"Now correct me if I'm wrong, but it looks like I'm seeing you lollipops again. What's a mother to do?"

Coll pulled a fistful of nylon cable ties from the back of his belt and handed them to Don.

"Cuff these guys good and snug," Coll said to his men. "After we finish here, gather up that van driver downstairs and meet us in the alley behind the hotel. Cable-tie him too, and blindfold the whole bunch with some towels when you get them in the truck. Steal some from this joint. That'll be original."

Don disappeared down the hall, as Bill returned with the pillowcase and collected the weapons on the wing chair. Remo herded Kyler and his remaining three henchmen to the hall door.

"What about the casualties, Coll?" Bill asked.

"Leave the down and dead," Coll said.

Coll crossed to the three men in custody.

"Let's get them cuffed and out of here," Coll said and handed more cable ties to Remo. "We've got to roll, men. Use extra ties on the big boy," he said, pointing to Teddy. "I don't have to tell you bozos what happens if you yell or act up, do I?"

The four captives remained silent.

"Good. 'Cause I really don't like shooting people in a nice place like this. I mean," Coll said, sweeping a hand from the ravaged bar to the two downed men, "look at the mess it causes."

Coll faced Kyler, inches from his hateful eyes.

"Just like old times, eh, Chuckles?" Coll said to Kyler, who spat on the floor near Coll's feet.

Coll went to Kyler's back and cinched his hands tightly behind him with the nylon cable ties.

"Remember that little rabbit you killed?" Coll said directly behind Kyler's ear as he took out a keychain with a rabbit's foot on it and dangled it in front of Kyler's face. "Funny how one man's cruelty can be another man's good fortune."

Don came out from the hall with the towels and handed one to Coll to put on Kyler. Coll took Kyler's upper arm and led him toward the front door, paused, and turned Kyler toward him so their faces were only an inch apart.

"You wouldn't happen to keep any lighter fluid around here, would you?"

Chapter 59

The last multi-colored glow of daylight persisted behind the distant mountains west of the cabin. The dry desert air that was baking hot earlier, now began to cool. Coll had learned about the desert and knew by late evening the temperature could fall to under fifty degrees and would be a chilling contrast to the midday heat. Darkness would come on fast, almost as if someone switched out the light in the western sky, and only a bright moon could stave off the blackness of the coming night.

Kyler, Teddy, Augie, Vince, and the van driver remained bound and were seated on the wooden floor of the cabin. Their towel blindfolds were removed. Don Braxley stood near the door, Remo Morales kept watch at the cabin's only window, and Bill Ashton sat at what served as the cabin's dining table and adjusted the flame on a Coleman gas lantern, which provided the only light in the room. Coll faced the five prisoners, burning his eyes into each face.

"If the series goes the limit, you could be here for a couple of weeks. Food's not exactly like the Four Seasons', but, you have to admit, the desert air alone is worth the trip. If my Twins win in four, things could go better for you."

"You make more money if it goes seven games?" Teddy asked.

"Yeah, but not as much as CBS and Budweiser," Coll said and nodded at Don who stepped outside, followed by Remo.

"We're going to go into town and get some nice chow, have a cold beer or two, see some ladies, catch some TV, and later have a goodnight's sleep in a nice soft rack," Coll said. "You guys have a cozy time here and we'll be back to slop and water you in the morning."

"Hey, paisan, you can't leave us here like this. I mean alone and all with no TV and nothing to eat. C'mon, man," Teddy said.

"You're right. What was I thinking?" Coll said. "My friend Don came up with an idea that will help sustain you during your stay."

Don and Remo re-entered carrying a large trunk.

"In this trunk are things you can eat. Many people think it's a delicacy. The tricky part is that you have to either catch them with your teeth or try like hell to avoid them."

The two men turned the trunk so the men on the floor could see its contents through a Plexiglass window on one side. Dozens of rattlesnakes of various sizes squirmed and rattled inside.

"Oh, Jesus," Augie muttered.

"For the love of God, Coll," Teddy said.

"What the fuck's wrong with you, you goddamn psycho," Augie Palermo said. "You think this is funny? Those bastards can kill people. There's something seriously wrong with you, baseball man. And you two grinnin' yo-yos too. Seriously."

Bill maintained his broad smile, welcoming his inclusion in Augie's invective.

"You yokels need a serious check-up," Augie continued. "By a real good shrink. If I get outa this I'm gonna remember you jokers. I'll be lookin' for you, you sonsabitches. You better hope I fuckin' die."

"Stop, with the complaining. At Trader Jack's Wildlife Farm the skunks were all taken," Coll said as the rattlers wriggled around each other and up the trunk window looking for escape. "So here's the deal. I know as soon as we leave, you're going to try to get free of those cable ties. That's only natural. Even dummies like you can figure that out. Now we're going to dump these little nippers all around outside. But, if you stay here, safe in this cabin, my little vipers over there won't get nervous and bite you, which will probably kill you, being that you're way out here on this moonless night with no help to get you to a hospital, get antivenin, yadda, yadda. However, should you take a notion to get your cuffs off and wander outside in the dark, well, let's just say I'm taking eight to one on the snakes, and ten to one on the desert doing you in."

"You miserable fink mutherfucker," Kyler said.

"This from a man who blinds rabbits with an ice pick and sets them on fire," Coll said as he, Remo, and Don filed out of the cabin and closed the door.

Several moments went by. The front door reopened and Coll stuck his head in the doorway.

"Oh, did you think we were leaving the lantern? Sorry. Fire hazard," Coll said as he stepped inside with a canvas water bag and placed it near the door. He grabbed the lantern and held it up. "Besides, I'd rather you didn't see where you were stepping, in case you stumble into one of my venomous friends outside."

Coll took a large padlock from his pocket.

"I'll lock the door so nobody can come in and molest you. Some water is here by the door," Coll said. "Don't forget to ration it out. By the way, you'll stay warmer if you guys kinda cuddle. I promise not to tell the *National Enquirer*. By the way, snakes like people because they're warm and they can follow the vibrations made by human voices to find them. Read that in National Geographic."

Coll left, closed and padlocked the cabin door. He joined Don, Remo, and Bill at the Dodge SUV.

"Think we need to leave some guards out here to make sure they stay put?" Bill said as they clambered into their truck.

"If they can survive the snakes, the desert, and each other out here, they can go with my blessing," Coll said. "Can't say I'm not sporting. Hell, we even left them a gun."

"I don't know..." Remo said.

"Look, all I need is a few days to wrap up the season and then get through the World Series. Those guys are going to have to think about survival. That gun and those snakes can be their salvation out here."

"How's that?" Bill said.

"They're going to need water and food and we left them both. Now I'll be the first to tell you that eating a rattlesnake is not my idea of a choice entrée, but you do what you have to do in a situation like this, or you die. Let's figure that a couple of them get lucky, or are smart enough to make the right choices to stay alive. By the time they get free and find their way back to humanity I'll be somewhere out of reach, maybe long gone."

"It's your show, Coll," Don said. "We'll play it any way you want."

Bill Ashton cranked up the Dodge and roared down the road toward Las Vegas, more than thirty miles away.

Coll didn't like lowering himself to the level of Kyler and men like him, but the time clock was counting down the hours he had left to win his final bets. He had to do what was expedient and at his disposal. And he certainly didn't need killers coming after him wherever he had to do business. He'd improvised, invented, adapted, and now he had to adjust. There were still a few playoff games left to bet on, but the Series would restrict him to wagering on only two teams a day, not many. He would need to increase his bets to several million dollars per series game if he hoped to achieve his ambitious goal.

One possible scenario gnawed at his insides.
What if the casinos refuse to take my bets?

* * *

"We gotta get these handcuffs off," Kyler said. "Anybody got anything sharp?"

"Maybe I'll cut the cheese," Augie said. "Maybe it'll be sharp cheese."

Inside the cabin, the morale level plummeted to its lowest point as Kyler and his men heard their only connection with civilization roar down the road and fade away.

"They took everything when they frisked us," Teddy said. "We ain't got shit."

"What the fuck," Augie said. "Who'd a thought ten years ago that I'd be tied up, sittin' on my ass on the floor in some goddamn dump where Lawrence of Aruba's camel wouldn't even take a shit. With rattlesnakes, no less."

"Did I mention that Augie is available for Bible readings?" Vince said.

"Kiss my Sicilian ass, you fat guinea faggot," Augie said.

"You really need to go to mass more often, August," Vince said with an exaggerated lisp.

"I'd sure as hell rather be at mass right now than here," the van driver said. "And I'm not even Catholic."

"No one told me what a bad-ass this Nolan guy is," Vince said.

"I think I know now why them Vietnamese called him Nightmare," Teddy said. "Uh-oh. I think I feel them snakes coming closer. They might crawl up my pant leg. It's warm in there."

"There aren't any snakes in here ... Are there?" the van driver said.

"Shut up, Teddy," Kyler said. "I don't want nothing crawling up my leg but a dick."

Kyler, even in the blackness, felt Vince's eyes looking over at him with dancing eyebrows.

"*My* dick," Kyler said.

Chapter 60

The next morning, Coll and Connie were seated in a booth having coffee at the Horseshoe Diner on a side street in North Las Vegas. Connie's face looked uncharacteristically solemn as she leaned over the table toward Coll.

"Gibbs has been asking a lot of questions," Connie said with fear in her voice. "He wants to know why I'm making deposits for you. Wants to know what you do to make so much money and why you leave it in such a low interest bank account."

"Jim got me some serious intel on your bank manager, so don't worry about him," Coll said. "Seems he's got a thing for the showgirls in town. Several of them are Dina's friends. Funny thing is, Gibbs' wife doesn't seem to know about his little penchant. If she finds out he'll have to go to another bank to get a loan to pay her off after the divorce. I've got enough to bury the bastard. Also, I'll be able to move more freely from now on. Those guys who took the pot shots at us are out of the picture for a while."

"What do you mean? What does *any* of that mean regarding what I just said?"

"Your boss is not like the nice bank manager act he puts on. But I used him to get to Kyler and his goons."

"How?" Connie said.

"With the Oriole outfit. You have to trust me, Connie. If I tell you everything about my business, it could come to no good."

"God, I feel like I'm with Michael Corleone. What kind of 'no good?'"

"The kind that several million dollars will buy," Coll said.

"I don't care about money. I handle money all day, tons of it. A little bit is enough for me. I want us, not money."

"Yeah, but I know what money can do. And what it does to people who want it, good and bad."

"What happens now?" Connie asked.

"Soon I'll need you to send my money to an account in Zurich and destroy the transaction. Can you do that?"

"Dina can."

"That'll work. I got some business to take care of out of town. I'll contact you and then we'll go find an Irish priest in your old home town," Coll said, taking Connie's hands in his.

"Are you sure?" Connie said.

"It's the only thing I'm surer of than the Twins beating the Braves, but if I'm wrong, you may have to apply for unemployment."

"Remember, Coll, money can't buy what we have."

"Remember, honey, happiness can't buy money."

* * *

That afternoon, Coll called on every casino where he'd made bets all season and requested that they accept substantially larger wagers on the World Series. He had taken a beating during the last weeks of the baseball season and wanted to go for broke. The casinos held a meeting about the issue and passed on their verdict to their cashiers. Coll was pleasantly surprised that all the casino nabobs unanimously agreed to the huge bets, but he was sure their recent winning streak against him, plus the fact that they were still far from breaking even on this strange baseball betting phenomenon, was at the heart of their decision.

He would bet on each series game, one at a time, to the end. He either would leave Las Vegas as its greatest money winner ever, or as the biggest loser in the history of the gambling.

Maybe Connie was right. Money shouldn't define them or affect their love for each other. He had come to Vegas and done what he'd yearned to do all his life, no regrets. Jesus probably despised gamblers, he mused. After all, there were those biblical moneychangers. And MacGuffins are just hopeful feelings you get about your abilities, not actual, surefire things. Hope was a concept that someone had described as only a delay of the inevitable. He'd been living life on hunches, and hunches can be, as often as not, dead wrong.

* * *

Later that day, Connie and Dina were working at the copying machine in the Prospect Bank as Coll entered the front door. He barreled past the two security officers without so much as a howdy. The women watched him as he marched past them and winked on his way to the manager's office at the rear of the lobby.

A woman of perhaps fifty, whose severe appearance and tight-bunned hair made her seem schoolmarmish, intercepted Coll at the office door.

"May I help you?" she asked, with deadpan expression.

"Yes, you may. By getting out of my way." Coll nudged her aside, strode into Gibbs' office, and closed the door. Gibbs was on the phone and looked up, annoyed by the intrusion. Coll went over to him, took the phone from his hand, and hung it up. Gibbs snaked a hand to the underside of his desk.

"Before you press that alarm button, Jonathan, I've got tapes and pictures enough to put you in prison for a long time and, at minimum, severely damage your married life," Coll said.

Gibbs withdrew the hand.

"What is it you want?" Gibbs asked.

"I'm the man who bets on baseball and makes those large deposits in your little bank. I understand you've been pumping one of your employees for information about me."

"Well, I merely wondered why an account with so much money wasn't being put to better financial advantage," Gibbs said as the schoolmarm stepped into the office.

"Do you need anything, Mr. Gibbs?" she said, staring coldly at Coll.

"No, I'm quite all right, Miss Chalmers. That'll be all, thank you," Gibbs said.

The stodgy secretary reluctantly retreated to the lobby, but left the office door ajar.

"Your interest in your clientele is admirable, John," Coll said as he sidled to the door and firmly closed it. "But from now on, you will make no further inquiries regarding my accounts. No more discussions of my money with the trusted friends of mine who work here and are empowered to conduct my business for me. Is that quite clear?"

"Why, of course. As I said, I meant no harm."

"Then I wonder why you shared information about me with that man," Coll said pointing to the golf picture on the credenza of Kyler standing with Bartel and Gibbs.

"I shared no information with anyone," Gibbs said with indignation.

"Make that your last lie. If I ever hear about any further inside information coming from this bank you'll get a chance to hear the tapes ... in court, along with your wife," Coll said.

Gibbs looked checkmated and unable to reply.

"I think this meeting is over, Mr. Gibbs." Coll said and stepped to the door, opening it wide. He raised his voice loud enough to be heard well outside the office. "Not to worry, Mr. Gibbs. Those tapes and pictures will never reach your wife. You have my word on it," Coll said as he exited Gibbs' office.

He smiled at a pale Miss Chalmers as he strolled to the front door. A parting wink at Connie and Dina on his way out of the bank concluded Coll's visit.

Gibbs would go on lying and cowtowing to the Vandermeer family. Of that, Coll was certain. As certain as he was of publicizing the tapes as soon as he and Connie departed town. But Gibbs would steer clear of Connie and Dina regarding Coll's personal business. That was the purpose of his visit. The ultimate destination of Coll's money had to be kept secret.

Chapter 61

A day had passed and Coll thought he should go out to the desert cabin to see how Kyler and his men were holding up. He knew their survival skills would be put to the test and he wanted to buy himself some time by sticking them there, but the outright murder of those men was not in his makeup. Doing that would make him no better than Kyler Rotermund and the rest of thugdom. He put together water and food, some medical supplies, and gathered up the troops for a trip back into the desert.

That afternoon, the green utility vehicle pulled up to Jim's desert cabin. Coll and Jim's crew stepped out and looked over the cabin cautiously before approaching. There was no discernible activity in or around the place, but the door was wide open. The padlock, hasp, and a portion of the door frame lay strewn on the ground.

"Awfully quiet," Coll said.

"Maybe too quiet. You gag those boys?" Jim said.

Coll shook his head.

"Keep aim on that window," Jim said, shifting a black pouch hanging from his shoulder, clearing access to his holster.

The five men moved closer to the door of the cabin, side arms pulled and at the ready.

Don light-footed up to the open doorway, and peeked in. He disappeared inside. A moment later, he came back out.

"They're gone. Plenty of snakes, though," Don said.

Remo Morales checked the ground around the cabin door. "They headed that way," he said and pointed in a direction away from town.

"Shit, that's into the deepest part of the desert. That's the wrong way. Town's this way," Bill said and pointed toward Las Vegas.

Remo continued to study the ground leading away from the cabin.

"They'd better be related to lizards if they're going that way," Jim said as he scanned the barren landscape.

"Kyler Rotermund and reptiles may very well be related," Coll said.

"Wonder why those snakes didn't bite them?" Bill asked, removing his wide-brimmed hat and wiping the dust sticking to his sweaty brow.

"Professional courtesy?" Coll said.

"Three of them went this way," Remo said as he moved around the corner of the small building and moved slowly toward the back of the cabin.

"There were five of them. Where'd the other two go?" Coll said.

"We're going to need a chopper," Jim said.

"Why? How far could they get?" Coll asked.

"You'd be surprised," Jim said. "Besides we're not going out there no better off than they are. I want ... What do you call it, Coll? A McMuffin?"

"What the hell's a McMuffin? You mean a sandwich?" Bill asked Jim with a look of befuddlement.

"A *MacGuffin*," Coll said.

"Well that clears things up," Don said.

"It's something Coll has. Gives him an edge," Jim said.

"Damn, I gotta get me one of them," Don said.

Coll shook his head at Jim. Remo came back to the area in front of the cabin and made a closer study of the ground.

"Somebody, at least two or three of them, went this way toward the back," Remo said as he retraced his steps. They all followed Remo's lead toward the back of the cabin. Remo led them to a large wooden box with a hinged lid.

"That's our old toolbox," Jim said.

"Looks like there was a scuffle," Remo said pointing to the crusty sand near their feet. "The footprints are blotted and flattened out in front of the box. Someone fell here, then rolled around on the ground. That's why the prints are gone over here. Three sets lead to the box, then one set goes back the other way, around front. The other set joins up with two others over here and they head out there into the desert."

"What does that mean, Remo?" Bill asked.

"It means three people came here to this box, but only two left," Remo said.

They all stared at the wooden box. Jim went over to it and lifted the heavy lid until it was fully open. Inside was the wide-eyed van driver with literally a death grip on a huge rattlesnake that had imbedded its fangs into his throat. Both were very dead and starting to smell foul.

"Mother of God," Jim said.

They all felt a powerful force that obligated them to peer inside at the macabre scene. They quickly withdrew in disgust.

"Two of them must've put him in there after he struggled and died here on the ground," Remo added.

"Right neighborly of 'em," Bill said.

"One down, four to go," Don said.

"Well, according to Remo, looks like three of them went that way," Coll said as he pointed away from town. "But bachelor number four is MIA."

"Maybe he had the good sense to head toward civilization," Jim said.

"I never saw anyone on the road driving in," Bill said.

* * *

As the distant voices of Coll and the other men carried from the toolbox, the earth rose on the sandy ground near the green Dodge truck. The soft, dusty soil parted and quietly erupted as the dirt-covered face of Kyler Rotermund emerged from his shallow grave-like hiding place near the vehicle. Loose earth cascaded from the subtle disturbance and pushed a ball of tumbleweed gently into an adjacent gully. Kyler slowly rolled onto his side to face the cabin and determine where Coll and the others were. Satisfied that they were out of sight, he scrambled to the truck and slid inside where he saw the most welcome thing his eyes could behold: keys dangling from the ignition. Had he been a religious man he would've hallelujahed, amenned, and rejoiced in the spirit, but since he was Kyler Rotermund, a man of no spiritual bent, he just squeezed out a tight-lipped "Hot damn."

* * *

The men conferred at the back of the cabin and mapped out their strategy by drawing with sticks on the ground. Their planning was interrupted by the sound of a throaty V-8 engine being cranked to life.

They scurried to the front of the cabin in time to see the dust trail of their departing vehicle as it raced down the road toward town.

"You've got to be kidding," Coll said to the sky.

"Son of a flippin' bitch!" Jim said and kicked at the ground with one of his Tony Lama boots, just as a patch of dry soil near the men exploded, followed by the sound of a distant rifle report.

"Incoming!" Jim yelled as a second bullet ricocheted off a small boulder near the cabin, followed by another resounding boom. The men dashed for the far side of the cabin and drew their pistols.

"One of them must've grabbed that old Henry Big Boy of mine. Damn thing'll shoot a mile," Jim said.

"That's great. And all we got are these fifty-yard pistols," Coll said.

"Look, we need a lift out of here, anyway, so let's get a chopper in here to do a little double duty," Jim said.

"And how might you be thinking of doing that? Write 'Help' in the sand?" Coll said.

Jim extracted a wireless phone from his shoulder pouch and wiggled it in front of Coll's face.

"Let's forget I said that, okay?" Coll said as Jim extended the phone's antenna and pressed some buttons.

"George, it's Jim Creeger, I'm out at my cabin in the desert." A short pause. "Yeah, yeah, right. The one with no TV or air conditioning. Listen, we're under fire here by some loonies. Got us pinned down with nothing to throw back but small arms fire. Can you get us a chopper out here and something big on the ground with four-wheel drive? And bring us a long piece that shoots more than a hundred damn feet." Jim paused a moment to listen. "Good man. Fast as you can, okay? I owe you, George." Jim pressed a button on the phone and returned it to his pouch. "The cavalry's on the way."

Coll and the others hunkered down to wait on the shady side of the cabin, which offered protection from the direct sun and incoming gunfire. An hour passed; a 108-degree, hot, dry hour that made even conversation a chore. Finally, the roar of a helicopter was heard coming at them from across the far horizon at high speed. Down at ground level, a large white vehicle raced over the dusty road toward the cabin.

The men got up from where they were huddled and watched the helicopter as it moved earthward and prepared to touch down. Dust, sand, and small pebbles blew everywhere from the mechanical tornado that hovered a few meters above the cabin grounds.

A rip appeared at the center of the copter body, spewing metal shards out its opposite side. The familiar, distant rifle report followed, muted a bit by the helicopter's roar. The chopper struggled to maintain stability. The blades slowed their rotation and smoke poured from the engine compartment as it wobbled to the ground with a less than graceful, bouncing landing.

"The bastards got the chopper," Jim hollered.

The approaching GMC Suburban stopped well short of the cabin.

The pilot and his rider bailed out of the crippled helicopter and ran for Coll's group. The rider carried a high power, hunting rifle with a large scope mounted on the receiver.

"Anybody here know how to use this?" the rider asked holding up the rifle.

"Give me that bad boy, son," Bill Ashton said.

The man handed him the rifle and Bill checked out the action on the piece, popped off the scope's protective caps, and made some adjustments on the telescopic sight. "I need higher ground. Help me get on the roof."

Remo and Don boosted Bill up onto the roof. He crawled to a position behind the stone chimney and scanned the far horizon through the scope for the fugitives.

"He's trying to get a fix on them," Coll said, "We need to draw some fire from the shooter."

"Let's see if this'll do it," Remo said and darted across fifty yards of open desert to the side of the cabin, then u-turned back. A huge blast of dirt kicked up six feet behind him followed by the far-off rifle boom. He made it back to the cover of the cabin breathing hard, but unhit.

"Yep, I think that oughta do it," Jim said.

"Got him in the hairs," Bill reported from the roof. "Well, go figure. It's the gay one."

"Vince?" Coll asked as a loud shot cracked through the air.

"Make that ex-Vince," Bill said from up top.

"We won't have to worry about him helping his buddy get us 'sonsabitches' now," Don said.

"What about the other two?" Coll said.

"Can't get a good bead on 'em. They're running around all over the place, but they're avoiding picking up that Henry," Bill said. "Can't imagine why. Looks like the mouthy one and the fat guy."

"That'd be Augie and Two Ton Teddy," Coll said to Jim. "Guess who stole our ride?"

The stopped GMC Suburban came to life again and raced up to near the men at the cabin and slid to a halt. Coll's group helped Bill off the roof and everyone piled into the getaway truck. The vehicle turned around and sped away, trailing a yards of thick dust.

"What about the two left out there?" Coll said.

"I give them about two days," Jim said. "Three at the outside, unless someone comes for them."

"Get on the radio," Coll told the driver, "and send a rescue unit to pick up Vince's body and those other two nitwits out there. Tell them to come armed."

The driver nodded and picked up the radio's microphone.

"And give the coroner's office directions to the cabin to pick up the body of that van driver," Coll added.

* * *

Out in the desert, Teddy sat in the late afternoon shade from an array of boulders while Augie paced and ranted.

"How could those heartless bastards just up and leave us out here frying our nuts off?" Augie said. "This is all your fault, Teddy. You and Al nail his ass at his hotel like you was supposed to, and all this shit don't happen. But, no, you guys gotta get cute and sit in his room in the dark like two blimpo raccoons. Shit, fucking Elmer Fudd would make a better hit man than you two horses' patoots."

Teddy reached over casually and picked up the nearby Henry rifle. He delicately brushed off the sand that clung to it from where Vince had flung it when he got shot. He examined it thoughtfully as Augie carried on.

"Here's another thing I just thought of." Augie said. "You move your ass a little faster out of that cabin last night and our best driver ain't dirt napping with Rattlin' Ramon and the Hiss Sisters. Yeah, I know Kyler tossed the damn snake at the guy and it got him in the neck, but you move faster and we get Kyler out so he don't play his nasty-ass games on folks. And here's something else you Dutch tulip snappers seem to like to do that irritates the fuckin' livin' piss outa me ..."

The sun was setting behind the peaceful mountains and the desert was crowned by a fantastic, multi-colored sky. It was a portent that night would soon be blacking out the beauty of the natural painting made by the dying light.

A single gunshot boomed and echoed across the desert twilight.

Then all was quiet.

* * *

An hour later, the searchlights of a multi-purpose vehicle panned across the desert night. The lights homed in on a distant object. It was the prone, bloody body of a man lying on the ground. A section of his head was missing.

The vehicle stopped and two EMTs jumped out of the idling truck. Their silhouettes in the truck's high beams scrambled to the body, crouched, and examined it.

"This must be that Vince Bartolo guy," one of them said.

Two gunshots flashed out from the darkness. The large caliber rounds ripped completely through both medics and they crumpled next to Vince's body.

* * *

A shadowy figure emerged from the black desert night into the wash of the truck's headlights. Two Ton Teddy De Groot balanced the Henry rifle in his hand. He clambered into the emergency vehicle and drove away, following tire tracks back the way the vehicle had come.

Chapter 62

Coll, Connie, Dina, and Jim sat around the dining room table at the Creeger home. Coffee cups and breakfast plates with dabs of uneaten eggs and toast crusts littered the table.

"They found two rescue workers dead out in the desert last night," Jim said.

"I sent them out there to get those morons out of trouble and look how they act," Coll said.

"Looks like Augie bought it out there too," Jim said. "Big hole in his chest."

"That leaves Teddy as the bad guy. Killed innocent, unarmed men in cold blood. Fixing his ass won't bring those rescue men back, but it'd be the right thing to do," Coll said. "I should've finished him at the hotel."

"They say when you go after someone out of revenge to dig two graves," Dina said.

"How's the World Series going?" Jim asked.

"I made my final playoff bets with the cashiers a little after midnight," Coll said. "The game today is the decider as to what teams will play in the series. You should've seen their faces when I upped the bets into seven digits a casino. Thought I'd be turned down flat, but they all keep giving their okay."

"They say okay because you could lose the farm and they could gain a hell of a lot, if not all, of their money back. Ever think about that?" Jim said.

"Today, it's all I'm going to think about," Coll said pointing upward. "I'll have it all riding on the series."

"Oh, yeah, your McFuggin."

"My winnings—"

"Should there be any," Jim said.

Coll reached into his pocket and withdrew a pack of betting tickets and pushed them across the table to Connie.

"Here are the tickets for my last bets. I hope you have something to collect at the casinos, but who knows?" Coll said. "I'll contact you so you know who and how much to bet on each series game. The casinos know you'll be my agent for the remaining bets. After the World Series, I want you to wire the money left in my account to that Swiss account we set up. If it amounts to anything, I want it converted to mostly bearer bonds and certified checks. Large denominations, but leave some in cash. I took some travel money out of the local account yesterday. What's left you send to Zurich."

"If you win, the total must amount to some piece of change," Dina said. "I saw what the paper said about your bets. Woowee, a girl could do some serious shopping with that kind of wampum."

"Dangerous shopping," Connie said.

"Newspapers know more than I do, I guess," Coll said.

"Newspapers will tell you how you're doing," Connie said.

Coll nodded at Connie and stroked her shoulder.

"Better get me to the airport, Jim," Coll said, getting up from the table. "You all know the plan, so 'til we meet again, I'll have good thoughts for everyone."

Jim stood and drank the last of his coffee. "Let's saddle up, partner," Jim said as he strode to the garage.

Connie rose and embraced Coll, Dina crossed to them and gave Coll a goodbye kiss on the cheek. Coll and Connie kissed long and hard, then eased their faces apart.

"I'll meet you at Kelly's Pub in Cong in three days, Angel," Coll said and took a sip of his coffee.

Connie picked up her cup and held it up to Coll.

"Here's to long life, and a merry one. A quick death, and an easy one," she said.

"Here's to a pretty girl, and an honest one. A cold beer, and another one," Coll said and tapped his cup against hers.

Coll put down his cup and tenderly touched her pretty face. He smiled at her blue-green eyes, kissed her lightly on her lips, then bolted from the room.

* * *

"All that money," Dina said. "Enough to make most men forget their promises."

Connie stared at the floor.

Dina took a small envelope from a drawer in the living room and faced Connie.

"Coll left this for you," Dina said, extending the envelope.

Connie opened the envelope, took out a card inside, and read its words.

If ever any beauty I did see,
Which I desired, and got,
'twas but a dream of thee.
— John Donne

Coll

"I'm dying here," Dina said. "What does it say?"
"It says he'll be waiting for me in Ireland."

Chapter 63

Once at the Las Vegas airport, Jim and Coll drove up to the main terminal building in Jim's vintage Mustang. Coll climbed out with a carry-on bag slung over his shoulder.

"I packed up my things at your place and left them in my suitcase in the clubroom," Coll said. "Have Connie take them with her when she heads for Ireland."

"Roger that. Got your tickets and passport?" Jim said.

"Yep, all there. Thanks for everything, Jim. I wouldn't have made it this far without you."

"Yeah, you would've. Got that McGuffanduck thing going on. *De nada, amigo.*"

"I had Connie hold back a few bucks for you guys. It can never repay the courage and kindness you've shown me, but it'll maybe buy you and Dina a vacation someplace nice. You really need to get out of Las Vegas sometime."

Coll reached into the carry-on bag, extracted a football-size pouch with a drawstring, and extended it to Jim.

"This isn't necessary, Coll. We did what we did out of friendship."

"So's this," Coll said as he placed the pouch on the passenger seat of the Mustang.

Jim looked down at the bag and shook his head.

"Call it a blessing to me, lad," Coll said.

Jim gave Coll a little salute and drove off.

Coll turned toward the terminal entrance and marched triumphantly to the door. It had been a summer of miracles. The baseball bets, the winning days, the discovery of a great friendship, and finally experiencing real love. He thought of Connie and how he'd left her that morning. He thought of all the times he'd flirted with love and tried to recall the women who were part of that failed pageant of his life. They were all now faded and faceless. All he could see was Connie. His dream of betting on the baseball games had come true and now, good or bad, it was almost over. In its place would be a new, brautiful dream, waiting to dream with him in on an Emerald Isle.

* * *

Signs inside the terminal indicated various ways to reach the airport's gates and arrival and departure areas. Coll consulted his ticket, then headed down a long corridor toward his boarding area. The corridor was empty except for occasional airport employees who passed him from the opposite direction. He turned his head toward his right shoulder and became aware of a second set of footsteps behind him, but didn't turn around to see the source. He walked on for several more steps when something hard was thrust into his back. He stiffened in pain, but kept silent.

"Men's room on the left. Go there," the all too familiar voice of Kyler Rotermund instructed.

The two men filed into the men's room. Once inside, Coll got shoved across the room hard. He stopped himself from ramming the far wall with his hands; his carry-on bag fell to the tile floor. Coll swung around to see a scowling Kyler Rotermund holding a revolver pointed at the bridge of his nose.

"And so we meet yet once more," Kyler said. "Strange how shit like that keeps happening."

Kyler checked the open spaces under the cubicle doors for any signs of occupancy. "Perhaps our last meeting, eh, Ratso?"

"You never know," Coll said.

"Before I kill you, I want to talk about baseball." Kyler said.

"Okay, let's talk about baseball."

"How much baseball money have you got in that bag?"

"Not much. Some travel money," Coll said.

"Let's see your plane ticket."

Coll handed him the ticket. Kyler studied it for a moment.

"Hmm, Miami. Nice this time of year," Kyler said. "Even nicer at the end of the baseball season." He threw the ticket on the floor. "Kick the bag over to me, then turn and face the wall."

Coll did as he was told. Kyler rooted through the bag and found a zippered pouch. He opened it and saw that it was filled with hundred-dollar bills. "Looks like maybe fifty grand here. You did okay, Nolan. Baseball's been good to you," he said as he crossed to Coll's back. "But my guys tell me you done better than this. Much, much better." Kyler jammed his pistol into Coll's ribs. Coll grimaced. "So where's the rest, McDago?"

"I give a lot at church," Coll said.

Kyler dropped the carry-on bag and put the gun barrel to the back of Coll's head. "Last chance to live, Nolan. Where's the rest of the bread?"

"Ask the IRS."

Kyler cocked the hammer on the pistol.

"I really wouldn't do that, Mr. Rotermund," Jim Creegers' voice said from behind Kyler.

Coll moved to the side and slued around.

Jim placed a pistol firmly against the nape of Kyler's neck. Kyler lowered his gun and Jim grabbed it around the cylinder, keeping it from rotating.

"Now step back ever so slowly. Put your hands behind your back," Jim ordered as he dropped the hammer gently on the Kyler's revolver and tucked it in his belt.

Kyler did as he was told and Jim handcuffed him.

"Coll, don't you have a plane to catch?" Jim said.

"You guys are like McDonalds. Everywhere you go you see them," Coll said as he picked up his airline ticket from the floor.

"I'm thorough. Now get your ride and fly out of here, partner. I'll take care of this dude," Jim said and pushed Kyler out of Coll's path to the men's room exit. Coll nodded, picked up his carry-on bag, and started to exit, but came back to face Kyler.

"Last chance to breath through your nose, Rotermund," Coll said and feigned a fast punch to the center of Kyler's face. Kyler reeled backward in reflex, hit his head hard on the tile wall behind him, and collapsed onto the men's room floor.

"Smooth reflexes," Jim said.

Coll smiled at Jim, punched him affectionately on the shoulder, and hurried out of the restroom.

Chapter 64

The jumbo jet landed with a screech of rubber at Miami International. The bright October sun exaggerated the colors of the airport's surrounding palms and flowering flora making it look like an impressionistic travel ad. The big airliner taxied off the main runway and rolled toward the docking stations at the main terminal.

Coll stared out the plane's window and wondered if he was doing the right thing in coming here, since Kyler now knew where he was headed. Kyler could still send men even if Jim got him taken into custody by the Vegas authorities. He figured that his stay, at minimum, would have to be brief and the reason for his visit would best be resolved in the next twenty-four hours, or else he'd have to abandon it.

Coll deplaned and headed down a long corridor with others arriving in Miami. He put his carry-on bag on his shoulder, donned some dark glasses, and wended his way to the warm outside. He climbed into a taxi and was driven away from the bustling airport activity.

"I see from your cover that you're a marine," the senior cabbie said.

"Former marine. You said 'cover' instead of baseball cap. You a jarhead?"

"Oh, yeah. Back in '52. Korea."

"Did mine in 'Nam. '70s. Semper Fi."

"Semper Fi," the cabbie said and twisted to look back at Coll. "We're a couple of lucky guys."

"What makes you say that?"

"We're back in America. Living in paradise. Lot of people weren't so fortunate."

"Amen to that, brother."

"Where we going today?" the cabbie asked.

"Hialeah running?"

"First race starts in about twenty minutes."

"Let's go there."

The cab left the busy Miami International complex and headed north. The car continued its northerly direction on Le Jeune Road for a few blocks. A couple of turns later, Coll arrived at the famed Hialeah racetrack. The driver deposited him at the track's entrance and Coll tossed a fifty on the passenger seat. Coll paid his track admission, jostled his way through the jam of racing fans to the paddock area, and panned the crowd. He saw no one who resembled his friend Eddie.

He found the track's main lounge, went inside, and pulled up a stool at the nearly empty bar. An affectionate young couple sat a few stools to his left, and a coughing man with his face buried in a racing newspaper sat around the bar's far corner to his right.

The bartender approached Coll with a napkin and placed it in front of him.

"What's your pleasure, friend?" the bartender said.

"Heineken, please"

"Coming up." The bartender got Coll his beer and set it up with a glass in front of him. Coll tossed a ten on the bar.

"Ever see a fella named Joey Geronimo?" Coll asked.

"Hmm, not at the moment." the bartender said. Coll noticed the man to his right had lowered his paper enough to get a peek at the inquisitor's face. More muffled, rasping coughs followed and the afflicted man raised his paper again.

"If you ever run into him, would you tell him I asked about him," Coll said.

"And you might be…?" the bartender asked.

"An old friend. Tell him Nightmare," Coll said.

The coughing man lowered his paper to the edge of the bar, then let it slide to the floor.

Coll turned to his left, smiled at the young lovers kissing, and took a sip of his beer.

The coughing man slid off his stool, crossed to Coll, and lingered behind him. Coll felt his presence, but didn't turn.

"Semper Fi, leatherneck," the man whispered in Coll's ear.

Coll wheeled around, removed his sunglasses, and stared at the man. Eddie Menning was older-looking now, with glasses, long hair, a beard and a mustache, but Coll saw through the changes.

"You old-looking geezer," Coll said as he jumped off the barstool and embraced Eddie for a long moment.

"I never thought I'd ever see you again, man," Eddie said with sad eyes.

"It's been a wild ride, buddy."

"Let's sit here, get drunk, and catch up on about thirteen years or so. Bennie, keep 'em coming 'til we can't stand up," Eddie said to the bartender.

"You've got it, J.G," Bennie replied.

"And he said he hadn't seen you," Coll said to Eddie.

"I said I didn't see him *at the moment*. He was behind his newspaper," Bennie said with a smile.

"A good bartender protects you like a loving mother," Eddie said.

Coll and Eddie gave each other the Reader's Digest versions of their past decade and, at Coll's prompting, left the bar. Coll was careful not to discuss his plans to go to Ireland while the bartender and others could overhear.

Eddie was reluctant at first to pick up and leave Miami and go along with Coll's itinerary for the day, but an onslaught of drinks took their toll on his resistance and soon he was sleeping like an asthmatic baby in a first class aisle seat next to Coll on a Delta wide-body.

Coll gazed fixedly out the window at the clouds and pondered the next phase of his plans while Eddie snored away next to him. An empty plastic cup was in Eddie's limp hand, but defied the gravity that tempted it to fall to the floor. A pretty flight attendant came down the aisle near the two men, pushing a refreshment cart filled with snacks, soft drinks, and liquor.

"Would anyone like a beverage? A snack?" she asked.

Eddie stirred, his eyelids fluttered, then stayed open. He dropped his plastic cup, looked around, and leaned across Coll to see out the window. He coughed deeply and lowered his head to near his knees for several moments before he raised up and looked at Coll.

"Where the hell are we?" Eddie slurred, followed by several hacks.

"That's a bad cough," Coll said.

"Yeah, I'm trying out for Doc Holiday at MGM," Eddie said. "Where the fuck are we?"

"You're going to really love Ireland," Coll said.

Eddie stared at Coll in disbelief, then turned his attention to the attendant patiently waiting in the aisle next to him.

"Sweetheart," Eddie said, "just leave the cart."

Chapter 65

World Series Game One. Coll read about the 200 or so protesters who marched around Minnesota's Metrodome with placards proclaiming the Atlanta Braves' use of the name, their fans dressing in Indian makeup, and using the "tomahawk chop," as offensive and racist. The unhappy group was reported to be orderly and caused no real problems for the playing of the game. Coll wondered what Amachee would think about these protest marches and smiled, knowing his friend would just shake his head and laugh.

The first game went well for Coll as his Minnesota Twins scored four runs in the fifth inning off Atlanta Braves pitcher Charlie Leibrandt en route to a big leadoff win. Atlanta 2, Minnesota 5. Rejoicing followed in the Coll Nolan camp.

In Game Two, Coll had a strange feeling that Atlanta would spring back to even the series. It was one of those hunches that don't go well. The Twins designated hitter, Chili Davis, banged a two-run homer in the first inning, but the Braves came back to tie the game in the fifth. Minnesota's third baseman Scott Leius hit a solo home run off Tom Glavine in the bottom of the eighth for the eventual game-winning run. Atlanta 2, Minnesota 3. A bad day for Coll, who'd given in to a hunch when the odds were stacked against him and had put a bundle on the Braves.

Game Three shifted to Fulton County Stadium in Atlanta. The Twins scored a run in the first inning, but the Braves scored one in the second to tie the score. The Braves took the lead on solo home runs by their right fielder, Dave Justice, in the fourth inning, and left fielder, Lonnie Smith, in the fifth. Minnesota tied the score with Kirby Puckett's homer in the sixth, and Chili Davis' 4-bagger in the seventh. The game remained tied through the eleventh inning. Coll, who'd bet heavily on the Twins, was running out of fingernails as the game went to the bottom of the twelfth. With two outs on Atlanta, Dave Justice legged in the game winning run from second base on a single rapped out by second baseman, Mark Levine. Minnesota 4, Atlanta 5. Coll had more than one drink that night.

Game Four. Twins third baseman, Mike Pagliarulo, knocked in one run with a single in the second inning, and another with a home run in the seventh. The Braves third baseman, Terry Pendleton, countered with a home run in the third, and left fielder, Lonnie Smith, hit a homer in the seventh to tie the score.

The Braves had two runners thrown out at home plate in the fifth inning: Lonnie Smith, who was on second base, got a bad jump on a ball that Terry Pendleton hit over Kirby Puckett's head in center field, but got thrown out at the plate. Pendleton was also thrown out at the plate later in that same inning.

    Braves second baseman, Mark Lemke, tripled with one out in the bottom of the ninth inning, and later scored the game winning run on a very close play at home: Braves back-up catcher Jerry Willard hit a medium-shallow fly to right field that was caught by Shane Mack. Mack, known for his strong arm, fired the ball home, but Lemke eluded the tag by banging shoulders with Twins' catcher, Brian Harper, in a very close play at the plate, and the Braves won the game. Minnesota 2, Atlanta 3. A squeaker, but Coll had correctly predicted the Atlanta win.

    Game Five. The Atlanta Braves unloaded for 17 hits against five Minnesota pitchers and won the game. Minnesota 5, Atlanta 14. Coll got that one right too.

    Game Six. The Twins scored twice in the bottom of the first inning. Twins center fielder, Kirby Puckett, made a crowd-stunning, leaping grab against the Plexiglass wall in left center on a long drive off the bat of Ron Gant, which saved a run in the third inning. Braves third baseman, Terry Pendleton, hit a two-run homer in the fifth to tie the score. The Twins took the lead on a Puckett sacrifice fly in the bottom of the inning, but Atlanta tied the game in the top of the seventh. In the bottom of the 11th inning, Minnesota's Kirby Puckett led off with a home run. The ball sailed over the outfield wall in almost the exact spot where he had robbed Ron Gant of extra bases earlier in the game. Atlanta 3, Minnesota 4. The MacGuffin was working and Coll was on a roll, but he had lost two high-stakes games which had to be offset by two of his four wins in the series. Game seven would tell the tale, a huge monetary tale.

On Sunday, October 27, 1991 the Minnesota Twins hosted the seventh game of the World Series for the year's finale of major league baseball. The series had been hard fought by both teams and the outcome, at this point, was anyone's guess.

Game Seven. The game was a pitching duel through seven innings. The Atlanta Braves had a chance to break the scoreless tie in the eighth inning when Lonnie Smith singled and Terry Pendleton followed him with a long double. Smith should've scored on Pendleton's two-bagger, but clever decoy play on the part of the Minnesota middle infielders delayed him from making the attempt for home. Later, a devastating double play turned by the Twins, ended Atlanta's hopes to get on the scoreboard. But there was still time to score as both teams entered the ninth inning.

As though the gods of suspense were controlling the game that day, the two teams were in a nothing-to-nothing tie at the end of nine complete innings. The seventh and deciding game was going into extra innings, another rarity in baseball history, having occurred only two other times since 1903.

Coll had instructed Connie to bet the largest sum ever bet on a sports game. The enormous amount was to be spread across the many casinos on Coll's list. The tension among heavy-betting gamblers would be unbearable. Their tranquilizer of choice for many wouldn't be alcohol this day. It would be Valium. Lots of it. For Coll, it was an uncertain look to the heavens.

Atlanta headed for the plate in the top of the tenth, while the stadium crowd and gamblers everywhere on Earth held their breath.

Chapter 66

Announcements and electronic signs requested pre-landing procedures to be performed by passengers as Coll's flight neared Maryland.

"We will be landing at Baltimore-Washington International in about ten minutes," the plane's captain said. "The temperature there is 72 degrees and the weather is clear and sunny. We hope you've enjoyed your flight, and thank you for flying with Atlantic Coast Airlines."

"We're going to Baltimore?" Eddie said. "What? To change planes?"

"I want to see my sister Kathy," Coll said. "She's going to meet us at the school where she teaches."

"She good looking? Got nice boobs?"

"Yeah, she picked up a cheap set at Walmart."

"Just asking. Haven't seen anyone worthwhile lately. I like a gal with a healthy rack."

"The only boobs you need to worry about are you and me," Coll said.

"Can't help it. I never forget great tits," Eddie said between coughs.

"You don't worry about tits. Worry about that cough."

"It's from these," Eddie said showing Coll his cigarette pack. "I gotta switch brands."

"Yeah, to no brands."

"You mean quit?"

"Cancer cures smoking, you know."

"You smoke."

"*Smoked*. I haven't had a cigarette since the last time I saw you," Coll said.

"That night on the roof?"

"Yep."

"So you quit, and now you're a reformed whore tryin' to get everyone to go straight, love peace, and accept the teachings of the Dalai Lama."

"Not everyone, just you."

"They got good pizza in Baltimore?" Eddie said.

"The best. In Little Italy."

"World's most perfect food."

"Thought that was milk."

"Nah, pizza, by a mile," Eddie said. "When I was a baby, if my mom's breasts gave out pizza I'd've never let go of her."

"We've got to get you into mammary rehab."

The airport van drove Coll and Eddie to Emmitsburg, Maryland, several miles northwest of Baltimore, and arrived at the Immaculate Conception Chapel on the campus of Mount St. Mary's College. Coll asked the driver to wait and slipped him a fifty-dollar bill as he and Eddie got out of the van.

The church stood on beautifully manicured grounds containing gardens of fall pansies in purple, yellow, and white; Endless Summer Hydrangeas in pinks and blues, and wooded areas with huge oaks and spreading maples. For a moment they both stopped and took in the scenery. It was far different from Las Vegas and Miami. The leaves on the trees were turning into their fall arrays of golds and reds, and a pleasant earthen smell wafted through the breezy air.

The church was a majestic stone building that directed the eye upward to a lofty bell tower on its right corner. Three tall, arched windows on the front of the church displayed antique glass that appeared to invite the sunlight to enter and illuminate the nave. On the left side of the building was a grand rosette with teardrop glass radials high on its stone wall, like a giant oculus ever-watching the heavens.

Beyond the church were the college campus buildings, and beyond them, the National Shrine to Our Lady of Lourdes Grotto with benches on a path that took one through depictions of the Stations of the Cross.

"This is Mount St. Mary's College," Coll said.
"Nice. Your sister teaches here?" Eddie said.
"She does."
"Is she Professor Kathy Nolan?"

"You'll see," Coll said as they walked over to the steps in front of the church and sat. A few minutes later a nun approached and stood before them. Both men stood and Coll reached out and hugged her.

"Hi, sis," He said and kissed her cheek.

"Been a while, little brother," she said. "Are you still Bob Smith?"

"Not any more."

"Good. I can scratch off lying in my next confession," Kathy said.

"This is my buddy, Eddie Menning, the fella I told you about. The man you sent the mail to."

"Glad to finally meet you, Eddie," she said.

Eddie stared at the nun in disbelief. "This is your sister? *Sister* Kathy Nolan?" Eddie said.

"Kathleen Margaret Mathias of the Sisters of Charity now," the nun said and gave Eddie a handshake. She took a step back and looked the two men over. "My Lord, look at you two. You look like poster boys for the '70s."

"Some things never change," Coll said and reached into his jacket pocket and took out a thick, letter-size envelope. "This is for you and the church," he said and handed it to Kathy.

"May God bless your kind heart, Coll."

She felt the weight of the envelope and looked sternly at Coll. "What's in here was earned honestly, wasn't it?"

"Quite honestly, Kath."

"When you called me from Las Vegas you said you were doing something with baseball. Does Las Vegas have a baseball team?" Kathy said.

"They have a whole bunch of them and they pay me very well to carefully monitor their progress," Coll said.

"Looks like they do, indeed."

"Yeah, but it may just be a one-season thing," Coll said.

"Well, you have to make it when you can," Kathy said. "We'll put it to good use and say a special prayer for you."

"Thanks, sis, I can use it," Coll said.

"Are you in trouble?" Kathy asked.

"When was I ever not in trouble?" Coll said.

"But not bad trouble," she said.

"Nothing Eddie and I can't handle."

"See how he drags me into his mess?" Eddie said. "By the way, thanks for your letters. They were a godsend ... um ... greatly appreciated."

"Coll, I have something for you as well." Kathy reached into her pocket and took out a small envelope and handed it to her brother.

Coll opened the envelope and removed a baseball card inside a plastic sleeve. He went slack-jawwed.

"It was the one baseball card that was missing from the set he gave you."

"Oh, my," Coll said. "It's the Mickey Mantle card. The rarest one of the 1952 Topps cards. Where did you get this?"

"It was in mother's things when she died. I have no explanation for it."

"A lot of that's going around," Coll said.

"Eddie, it's good to meet you. You take care of my baby brother, will you?" Kathy said. "Coll, I have to get to class, but give your old sis one more of those strong hugs of yours before you're off."

Coll hugged Kathy long and firmly, then kissed her goodbye. She turned and hurried away toward the classroom buildings a fair distance away. Coll and Eddie watched her go. As she reached the entry point of her building, she turned back to them and blew them a kiss. A second later she was gone.

"Her name's 'Mathias' now? She can't be married, can she?" Eddie said.

"Mathias is her saint's name. She's married to God."

"Saint Mathias? Never heard of him."

"Maybe going to church more would help," Coll said. "Mathias was the thirteenth disciple of Christ. The one who replaced Judas."

"Thirteen. Lucky for him, I'd say," Eddie said.

"He caught the biblical brass ring. And now we've got to catch a ride on a plane."

Chapter 67

Three plane flights, a train trip and a lengthy car ride brought Coll and Eddie to the front door of the Irish public house he'd been told was the place to get information about the ancient town of Cong, County Mayo, Ireland.

They entered the quaint establishment where the majority of the patrons clumped in groups around an antique oak bar. Some sat on stools, but most stood or leaned against the well worn wood. Others gathered about rickety tables lined against the walls of cream stucco with brown highlights from ages of heavy tobacco and fireplace smoke. Bare beams supported the sloped roof, and pegged oak floors went from wall to wall throughout the generous room. A blend of aromatic pipe smoke and stale brews hung in the air.

Faces turned to take in the two visitors. Coll and Eddie found an open spot at the rectangular bar and bellied-up to its rail.

A red-headed man, wearing a gray tweed flat cap, held up a shotgun and faced a short, squat fellow at the bar.

"Ya can't shoot a goose with a barrel this short," redhead said, pointing at the shotgun. "Ya need a long barrel, like this one." He leaned the gun in his hand against the short man's stool and took a much longer one from under the overhang of the bar. "See the length of the barrel on this one? It's for shooting geese. They fly high, don't ya know."

Several patrons took interest in the ballistics lesson.

Another man at the bar pulled a large caliber revolver from his belt and casually dumped it on the bar.

"Think I could get me a gander with this one?" he said to redhead.

"The only way you'll get a goose with that is if it's in a case at the butcher's," redhead said.

Guffaws and snickering surrounded the gun conversation.

A heavy-set, bearded man behind the bar approached the two newcomers.

"Lads," he said, and leaned on the bar, supported by timeworn hands.

"Two Heinekens," Coll said as every eye in the place frowned at him. "Uh ... make that two Guinnesses."

There was tacit approval of his modified choice, and most of the onlookers returned to their conversations.

"Two Guinnesses, aye. New in town, are ya?" the barkeep asked as he began to pull the dark stouts from a tap behind the bar.

"Yes ... aye. Came here for the waters," Eddie said.

"Begging your pardon?" The barkeep said with a knitted brow on his wrinkled face.

"A friend of ours was born here," Coll said, and glared at Eddie. "Her name is Hannigan. Connie Hannigan."

Some of the locals stifled their chatter and turned toward the strangers. The barkeep looked up, but waited for the brew's froth to cascade down a bit in the two glasses, then topped them off.

"Connie Hannigan, is it? Sure and it's been a while since we've seen the only daughter of Sean and Katy Hannigan, God rest their lovely souls."

"She's supposed to meet us here in Cong. Today. At this place. This *is* Kelly's, isn't it?" Coll said.

"Aye, it is, and I'd be Michael Kelly. And they call you ... ?

"Nolan, Coll Nolan. My friend here is Eddie Menning. We're from the States," Coll said, knowing his last comment was unnecessary.

"Coll, is it? Good name for a lad. Eddie and Coll. Are you two, you know... shall we say, more than friends?"

"Oh, no. Oh, *hell* no, nothing like that," Coll assured him. "We're old buddies from the service. The United States Marine Corps."

The locals stamped their feet and banged their glasses on the bar. Kelly grinned and set up the two stouts.

"What does that mean?" Coll asked, indicating the uproar.

"They think you're all like John Wayne. Did all those great war movies. He was here, you know, some time back. Great big fella. Made a movie here. Put old Cong on the map. 'Cept they called it Innisfree in the movie," Kelly said.

"*The Quiet Man*. I know. A great movie."

"John Wayne. One of only two men the town ever gave The Silence to," Kelly said with admiration in his tone.

"The S*ilence*?" Coll said.

"Aye, The Silence. The highest tribute we pay a person. Five minutes, in a row, mind you, of absolute silence in this pub. No mean feat, if you know this bunch of windbags."

"And who was the other one?" Eddie asked.

"Ah, His Holiness himself," Kelly said proudly, crossing himself.

An older local, perhaps seventy-five, came over to Coll.

"And might you be making a movie, as well?" he asked.

"Uh, no, I hadn't planned on it."

"I was in the John Wayne movie, you know," The old man said. "Was in the big fight that Mr. Ford filmed right in this very place. I won me fight. Knocked Liam Hogan on his duff right over there in that corner," he said pointing to the spot. "I'm in the film, you know. Paddy Yeats, that's me, right in the credits. Some of the lads was cut out of the picture, but not me. I would've knocked John Wayne himself on his arse, in them days."

"Then he'd've got up and put your lying self, Paddy Yeats, in a pine box with one swipe o' them cinder blocks he had for fists," one of the locals yelled from the far side of the bar.

The bar erupted in laughter.

"Your mother's dirty drawers, he would've," Paddy shot back.

"Paddy, stop pestering the paying customers," another local said.

"I pay, meself!" Paddy said, his face reddening.

"You haven't paid for a round since you got your confirmation money," another said.

"And the last time he bought a round, Beowulf and the fucking Vikings were in town," another shouted and the bar went into near hysterics.

"I'm damned if I'll be bandied about by the likes of them. Buy the house a round!" Paddy shouted above the din.

A roar went up from the patrons.

"This is a lot different than Albrecht's bar," Eddie said.

Kelly handed out foam-headed mugs, glasses were raised in good cheer, and Coll and Eddie were clapped on their backs by many of the locals.

"Glasses up for the two yanks who finally got us a drink from of that tight-ass Paddy Yeats," an elderly man toasted, to more exuberance from the bar's regulars.

* * *

The sounds of revelry carried out into the street as Connie Hannigan opened the pub door and stepped inside. Kelly saw her first, froze where he stood, and squinted at her long and hard. The locals saw his fixed stare and followed his gaze to Connie. The pub quieted. Coll and Eddie, their backs to the front door, continued to sip their stouts.

"Sure and it's the darling of the country come home to those who love her," Kelly said, arms spread, beaming.

Coll and Eddie turned toward the door. Coll put down his glass and rushed to her.

"Hi, baby," Coll said and kissed her. Connie pulled back from the kiss after a second and waved off his heavy breath.

"Looks like you've been in Kelly's good hands," she said.

"And now for something even rarer than Paddy's free round. *I'm* buying a round," Kelly said.

Deafening cheers rose to the rafters and bedlam broke out in the pub.

"Holy Mother of God. It's truly a day of miracles," one of the locals shouted over the noise and looked prayerfully to the heavens.

"Christ Almighty. Meself, Paddy Yeats, finally buys a round, and I'm bested by Kelly goin' over the top with a round of his own. Shite. No one's ever goin' to remember me most charitable gesture."

"Look on the bright side, Paddy," Kelly said. "You just might be able to whip Mr. Wayne today."

Chapter 68

Jack Morris and the Twins held the Atlanta Braves scoreless in the top of the tenth inning and the local Minnesota fans gave out a sigh of relief. The bottom of the tenth would be their turn to score, but Atlanta was throwing everything they had at them from the mound.

In the bottom of the tenth, Twins leftfielder, Dan Gladden, led off with a double and advanced to third on Chuck Knoblauch's sacrifice bunt. The Braves loaded the bases intentionally, and pinch hitter Gene Larkin came to the plate. Larkin hit a ball over the head of the Braves leftfielder Brian Hunter, who again had no choice but to play shallow in order to have a chance to throw the lead base runner out at home. Gladden scored the winning run on the play, and the Minnesota fans reveled in deafening approval, rocking the Hubert H. Humphrey Metrodome to its foundation. Atlanta 0, Minnesota 1.

There was one other, far-away heart that pumped euphoria that day. A heart owned by a man who had a MacGuffin. A gambler who'd made a deal with God, and now had to decide how he was going to complete his part of the bargain.

* * *

Jerry Cohen, along with several well-dressed management men and casino owners, sat around a large banquet table having coffee in the private dining room of the Hermosa Hotel. It was a quiet, reflective moment for Jerry as he stared at the blackness in his cup.

"Is it me, or have our customers gotten older?" a fat man said.

"Your whole clientele is old," a man with a red bow tie said. "Seniors on a mission."

"What's that supposed to mean?" the fat man asked.

"All those old widows you get. The dusters. You gotta vacuum them off before you buy them a drink," bow tie said.

"Them old broads got plenty of dough," a bald man at the end of the table said.

"Yeah, I went out with some of those old babes. Years ago," a man with thick eyeglasses said. "Thought I was gonna score me some heavy sugar momma to finance my first joint here."

"So, you gave her a little hide-the-salami and she came across with the moola?" the bald man said.

"Are you kidding?" eyeglasses said. "There was only one thing this old bitch was tighter with than her checkbook, and that was her muffie. Her gynecologist musta had to use the jaws of life to get her knees apart."

You didn't get nothing?" the bald man asked.

"I didn't get shit from that old bag," eyeglasses said. "Just a couple of spit-swapping sessions. The only thing she liked was getting oral sex. I coughed up blue hair balls for three months."

"Men ain't supposed to swallow," the fat man said.

"Now he tells me," eyeglasses said.

"Speaking of coughing up," Jerry said, "I wonder what ever happened to that fella who bet on all those baseball games."

"Right around the World Series, he split," bow tie said. "Never seen him since. Not sure I ever want to."

"Yeah, he nipped me for a bundle too," Charlie Mazio said.

"The guy hardly ever came up short, but I thought we had him at the end of the season. I'm tellin' ya, somebody up there's crazy about that sonofabitch," bow tie said.

"I got an idea," Jerry said. "Take your napkins there and write the figure on it that you think that guy got you for."

"Round figures?" the bald man asked.

"Best you can estimate," Jerry said. "The total stays in this room. Agreed?"

More than forty men nodded and wrote figures on their napkins. Afterward, they passed their napkins to Jerry. Jerry looked at each napkin and, on a separate piece of paper, he added them up. After a moment, he looked up at the anxious faces of his fellow businessmen.

"Gentlemen," Jerry began, "that Mr. Baseball took us for one hundred and thirty-five million dollars."

"Jiminy Freaking Cricket," the fat man said.

"Mama mia," bow tie said.

"This guy makes Pete Rose look like a bingo granny," Charlie Mazio said.

"On baseball, no less," the fat man said. "Not some Saudi Arabian sheik, not the head of Toyota, not even on a big progressive slot. But a goddamn baseball hustler? I'll be a sonofabitch. Go figure that one."

"I'll tell you one thing, boys," Jerry said. "I don't know what happened to that guy. And I'll likely never know where he is. But at this moment, I know one thing for sure. *Wherever* that guy is, he can afford to buy his own baseball franchise."

Chapter 69

A bucolic Irish cottage with its old fashioned, plaster walls and thatched roof stood in a peaceful glen amid gnarled oaks and tall chestnut trees. Inside, the moonlight streamed through the window, lighting the country bedroom where Coll and Connie lay braided together in an antique featherbed that billowed up from their slightest movement.

"Everything taken care of at the bank?" Coll asked as he fluffed up the covers creating a large linen mushroom. Connie giggled and nodded.

"Last of the money too?" Coll said refluffing the covers.

"Uh-huh, everything that was there. All done and tied up with a bow," Connie said. "Dina helped me with the paperwork, and an hour afterward, I was on the plane to New York, then here."

"How about Gibbs?" Coll said.

"Well, he had to make the final authorizations, but Dina double-checked everything he did."

"Dina? Not you?"

"She's the assistant manager. I'm just a teller."

Coll sat up abruptly.

"What's wrong, honey?" Connie asked.

"Nothing. I have to go to Zurich and get our money."

Coll got out of bed and started putting on his clothes.

"At this hour?"

"You sit tight here in Cong 'til I get back." Coll said and bolted from the bedroom.

A second later, Coll charged into the adjoining room where Eddie lay sound asleep.

"Eddie! Reveille, baby!" Coll yelled at his friend's prostrate body.

Eddie mumbled something unintelligible, rolled over and pushed his face into his pillow. Coll crossed to him and shook him until his body bounced on the squeaking bed springs.

"Get up, man. We've got an important date in Switzerland," Coll said. "It's payday."

Chapter 70

Zurich, Switzerland was beautiful and old-Europe quaint like its travel posters, but the last thing on Coll Nolan's mind was sightseeing as the taxi raced alongside the Limmat River down the city's streets. When the taxi pulled up to the tall, Bremenberger International Bank building on Hardturmstrasse, Coll handed a large denomination Swiss franc note to the driver, then he and Eddie leapt from the car and charged through the bank's front door. They marched up to an open teller window where Coll spoke with a young blond man.

"I need to speak with someone about my account," Coll said, trying hard to hide his excitement.

"Perhaps I can help you, sir," the teller said. "May I see your identification, please?"

Coll handed the man his passport.

"May I also have your account number, sir?"

"Yes, right here on this piece of paper," Coll said as he pulled a small paper from his pocket and handed it to the teller. The young man studied it for a moment, then keyed in some figures into a computer next to him. Coll looked on anxiously.

"I have your account on the screen, sir. What would you have me do?"

"Tell me my balance."

The teller wrote a figure on a piece of paper and slid it through the window. Coll picked it up and looked at it. His face went ashen and reflected abject horror. Written on the paper was a balance of 100 U.S. dollars.

"Will you please check this again?" Coll asked the teller.

"Certainly, sir." Again the teller consulted a computer screen and then handed Coll a piece of paper. And again Coll reacted like his best friend had just died in his arms.

"There must be some mistake here," Coll said raising his voice to the teller. "I had several ..." He looked around and lowered his voice. "I had a lot of American dollars in this account."

The teller again consulted the computer.

"Yes, sir, that's quite right," the teller said. "You had a *very* large sum in that account until about half an hour ago when everything was withdrawn except what you see on the papers I gave you."

"Who withdrew it?"

"Why, according to this computer, sir, you did."

"This account requires a picture as well as number for identification," Coll said. "Print out the picture please that's on this account." The teller did so, but looked puzzled at what he saw on the printout, then handed it to Coll. The picture on the printout was a picture of a smiling Jim Creeger. Coll felt his stomach hit the floor.

"Passport pictures are never very flattering," the teller said in an attempt to console his distraught customer.

Coll and Eddie exited the bank and went out onto the busy thoroughfare. Coll went over to a nearby parked car and slumped onto the car's roof.

"That sonofabitch Jim Creeger's screwed me good. I trusted him with my life," Coll said and pounded his fists on the car's roof. A man stepped out of the car and yelled something in French at Coll.

"Sorry," Coll said, pushing himself off the car. "Help me find my money and I'll buy you twenty of these little ..." He stepped to the rear of the car to read the make. "Vulvas."

"Volvos," Eddie said.

"Yeah, Volvos. Twenty of 'em. Something newer than this 1959 POS model."

The irate man shook his head, got back into his car, and started the engine. Coll and Eddie stood like two defeated football players after a brutal game. Their arms hung limp at their sides. Then, Coll wandered a few steps and saw something across the street that had been blocked from his view by a delivery van that had just pulled away. It was a small café-style restaurant.

Through its street-side picture window he saw something that nearly stopped his heart.

Chapter 71

Framed in the window of the café Coll saw the unmistakable profile of Jim Creeger. And to the left, was the equally unmistakable scowling puss of Kyler Rotermund.

Coll signaled to Eddie, who shot his gaze toward the café window. Eddie darted across the street, jogged down an alley alongside the restaurant, and disappeared behind the building. Coll went around to the street side of the idling Volvo and ripped open the driver's door. The surprised man began yapping at Coll in French. He yanked the driver from behind the wheel and escorted him forcefully onto the sidewalk where he stuffed a packet of large bills in the man's hand. The stunned man went silent and inspected the money with incredulous eyes.

Coll slipped into the car, put it in gear, and steered it across the street at full speed toward the restaurant. In a second, the restaurant's front window and part of its door imploded into the building as Coll rammed the Volvo directly into the table where Jim and Kyler sat. The two men were jolted to the floor. Everyone else in the restaurant escaped harm, but scurried for any exit out of the place. Coll jumped out of the car and darted to the stunned Jim Creeger lying on his back.

"You turncoat sonofabitch," Coll said. "Straight shooter, my ass." Coll picked up a steak knife from a nearby table and pressed it against Jim's throat, keeping him down.

"So long, *partner*," he said bitterly as he raised the knife high and took aim at Jim's heart.

"Coll, I had to," Jim said weakly. "They got to Dina."

"Bullshit."

"His buddy, the fat one, Teddy, is holding her someplace around here right now."

"Where's my money?" Coll said.

"There, on the floor. The bags under the car."

Coll saw two large sports-type duffel bags on the floor under the front of the Volvo. He went over to them, pulled one out, unzipped it and looked inside. It was full of bonds, checks, some United States paper currency, and a few Swiss bank notes. He was about to check the second bag when a somewhat disoriented Kyler Rotermund attacked him with a switchblade knife. Coll saw it coming at the last second and ducked to the side. The attack missed its target and left the knife rammed into the Volvo, puncturing its sheet metal hood to the knife's hilt. A wooden chair exploded on top of Kyler's head and shoulders and dropped him to the floor like someone switched him off. A smiling Eddie Menning stood over Kyler's crumpled body.

"I am always having to save your raggedy butt," Eddie said.

"We're out of here," Coll said as police sirens could be heard in the distance.

Coll yanked the two duffel bags from under the car and bolted for the back of the restaurant with Eddie on his heels.

* * *

The Volvo owner stared through the window of the café at what was left of his car. Gawkers began to advance on the scene. The Frenchman put on a bit of theatrics for the arriving audience. His face scowled and he managed to yell out a dozen French expletives for good effect. Then he shrugged and trudged away, his eyes downcast in feigned grief. When he reached the opposite side of the street, he patted his pocket with the protruding wad of hundred-dollar bills bulging out from his breast pocket. His demeanor changed dramatically. The slightest smile appeared on his face as he waved to attract the oncoming police vehicles.

* * *

"What about your buddy Jim?" Eddie said as they scrammed through the rear door of the café and into an alley.

"Damn him," Coll said, and then abruptly stopped.

Eddie halted a few strides farther, turned back, and stared at Coll.

"Sometimes I hate loyalty. Come on," Coll said. "They've got Jim's wife, Dina. Let's get him and go find her." They doubled back toward the restaurant and paused in the cover of a trash shed directly behind its kitchen.

"Look, no one connects you with this," Coll said to Eddie. "They all took off before you got to the restaurant."

"And when the other shoe fell, he said …"

"You go in and get Kyler so he can take us to Dina," Coll said.

"I'll see what I can do. Swiss cops are everywhere," Eddie said.

"I know. They should be out somewhere yodeling or making chocolate, but the bastards are here, so we've got to deal with them. I'll see if I can divert them. Give me a ten-count, then go in," Coll said.

Eddie nodded and Coll bolted from behind the shed with the two duffel bags swinging from his shoulders. He scrambled around to the street running in front of the restaurant and looked in several directions for a plan of action to divert the on-scene police. A crowd of chattering people gathered in front of the café rubbernecking at the Volvo and the damage inside. More police vehicles arrived and officers positioned themselves to control the crowd.

Unable to see anything he could use in the area, he unzipped one of the duffel bags, unstrapped some of the money packs and began hurling hundred-dollar U. S. bills into the air all over the middle of the street.

"Look, free money! Come and get it! It's free money!" Coll belted out his come-ons like a carney barker.

The curious crowd who'd been at the café scene, and even the police, began looking Coll's way and soon rushed to pick up the money. The thoroughfare soon became chaotic with people shoving and grabbing to get at the elusive, floating bills that now filled the air and drifted on the breeze down the street.

Coll watched as a fuel truck driver began connecting the fuel hose to the adjacent building's heating system fill pipe. When the driver spotted the money wafting in the air and down Hardturmstrasse, he abandoned his fueling connection and ran into the street to get his share of the bills. Coll watched as the hose fell to the ground, spewing fuel oil that gushed into the gutter along the curb.

A man came from around the corner of the bank building smoking a Churchill-size cigar. When he spied the activity in the street, he tossed the stogie and ran for the free money that now was drifting all over the block. The lit cigar, like in some Rube Goldberg gizmo sequence, slowly rolled off the sidewalk and into the gutter where it awaited the fuel oil rushing directly at it. The resultant fire began its rapid way back toward the fuel truck.

Coll had seen enough to know it was time to get out of there. He chucked a final clump of bills into the breeze and dashed for the alley side of the restaurant.

A few seconds into his flight, Coll stopped long enough to watch the flames race up to the source of the fuel and envelope the rear of the truck. People in the street, seeing the flaming truck, began to run for safety in all directions. Drivers trying to get through the blocked-up street leapt from their vehicles and ducked around the corners of buildings for cover. The street became devoid of activity except for the growing fire, now with huge flames leaping up onto the fuel truck's back and licking at the cab. Even the Swiss cops withdrew from their accident investigation in the café and headed elsewhere for refuge.

A tremendous fiery explosion erupted as the truck's fuel tank rocketed sky high. Glass doors and windows in nearby buildings shattered from the blast. The street became an inferno. Secondary blasts propelled truck parts and street signage through the smoke-filled air.

Eddie entered the café from the rear door and shot over to Jim Creeger who was crawling on the floor.

"Coll and I are going to help you get your wife," Eddie told Jim. "You able to help me a little bit, big fella?"

"Do what?" Jim asked.

Eddie pointed to the unconscious body of Kyler.

"Help me get his big ass up and outa here."

Eddie and Jim dragged Kyler's limp body outside and into the shed where Coll waited. Fire trucks with sirens blaring and bullhorns barking commands sounded in the background, coming from everywhere in front of the building. People yelled out panicked directions and warnings in French, Italian, German, and English. Thick smoke blocked out visibility in every direction in the area.

"You sure know how to pull off a diversion. I'll give you that," Eddie said as they laid Kyler down in the trash shed.

"It went a tad further than I expected," Coll said.

"We patted Kyler down. He's clean. I pulled his knife out of the Volvo," Eddie said and handed the knife to Coll who pulled over a wooden box next to Kyler and sat.

"He's coming to," Coll said. "Sit his uglyness here against this trash barrel."

They propped Kyler up. He rolled around his bloodied head and opened his eyes.

"Kyler, Danny Glover's right. We're getting too old for this shit. Now where've you got Dina stashed?"

"Fuck you," Kyler mumbled.

"Wrong answer, Kyler." Coll kicked Kyler hard in the shin. He moaned in pain.

"Where's Dina, Kyler?" Kyler spat at Coll. Coll stabbed Kyler in the thigh with the knife. Kyler screamed like a banshee.

"Where's Dina, Kyler?" Coll hammered on. Kyler grimaced and tried to spit at Coll again, but the spittle only drooled down his chin. Coll grabbed him by the crotch and squeezed. Kyler screamed like a mortally wounded howler monkey.

"Jesus, Coll," Jim said.

"You know, life can be hell, but if you're stupid, it's a muvva. Where's Dina, Kyler?" Kyler started whimpering like a child. Tears flowed down his face.

"She's at church down the street. Big steeple. Teddy's got her in the main sanctuary," Kyler said. "He sees you, he shoots the bitch."

Coll leaned over close to Kyler.

"Is it still not over between us?"

"It's still on, Nolan. And Bartel's coming to get you and your buddy, and he's bringing hell with him."

"I'll jot that down," Coll said. "Tie him up and gag him, Eddie, then meet us at the church. Bring these two bags. Take this knife. Guard those bags with your life."

Coll gathered up Jim and led the way toward the church's towering steeple by way of a back alley. They found an unlocked back entrance and slipped inside the church. They worked their way to the sanctuary and peeked into the great nave of the church through an open doorway. They saw Two Ton Teddy sitting next to Dina in the middle of the rows of pews off the central aisle.

"I can't see it, but I'm betting Teddy has a gun on her," Coll whispered.

"Coll, I want you to know it wasn't the money," Jim said. "They threatened to kill Dina."

"I know what happened. It's okay. Save your thoughts for the mission at hand." Jim nodded and patted Coll gratefully on the shoulder.

"Now that we know where he is, I'll go around front. You stay here. See if you can find something to use as a weapon. If I get close enough to him to grab him, you come running. If you see that I can't get near him, wait a couple of minutes, then create a disturbance behind the altar back here. Make it loud."

Coll pointed to a spot in back of the altar. Jim nodded and Coll exited the same way they had entered.

Chapter 72

Teddy De Groot watched Dina as she sat and stared straight ahead at the altar of the church. Her eyes were red with lids only half open. Teddy sat close with a small revolver under his jacket pointed at her ribs.

A couple entered from the back of the nave, genuflected, and took seats in a pew near the rear of the church. Teddy shifted his bulk and checked them out carefully, then returned his attention to Dina. A white-haired man entered the church and quick-stepped to the very front pew, genuflected, and sat facing the altar. An elderly woman limped in from the rear door of the sanctuary and moved laboriously down the aisle, aided by a cane. She was dressed in black and wore a widow's veil. She struggled into an aisle seat a few rows behind Teddy.

Teddy glanced at her, then returned his attention to his captive. He checked his watch and looked over his shoulder toward the entrance. He grasped Dina's wrist with his free hand and surveyed the rising church activity. More people continued to file into the church, which unnerved him, but he knew where his primary oversight needed to be, or risk the wrath of his boss, Kyler.

A loud crash shattered the quiet from the right side of the altar. Teddy jerked his head toward the noise and, for a moment, took his pistol off Dina and held it at his side to clear it for possible action elsewhere.

Then something jarred the back of his pew.

* * *

Coll sprang from the floor behind Teddy's pew and grappled with the huge man over control of the gun. Coll got a hand on Teddy's pistol and the men struggled furiously. Teddy heaved Coll over the back of the pew and slung him forward like he was a sack of flour. Coll managed to twist his body to face Teddy while he kept his hold on the gun that the big man waved from side to side, trying to shake Coll's iron grip.

Dina bolted from the pew and sprinted to the back of the church. Jim Creeger charged out from the altar to help Coll in his fight with Teddy. A gunshot rang out as Teddy squeezed off a round that embedded itself in the arched ceiling.

The parishioners shrunk their heads to their chests and ducked low. A priest rushed to the altar to investigate the disturbance. Teddy fired three more wild shots as he wrestled with Coll, and now with Jim who joined the fray. One of Teddy's bullets hit the priest in the shoulder, crumbling him to the altar floor.

A few parishioners peeked over their pew backs, horror in their eyes. The veiled woman in black stood in defiance, screaming in Italian, as others crouched and stumbled their way to the rear door.

Jim and Coll wrested the gun from Teddy, but in the process, Teddy managed to hurl both of his attackers to the narrow floor between the pews where they became wedged, unable to get right up. Teddy took advantage of their awkward situation and trundled down the wide aisle bee-lining for the entrance. Coll popped up over the back of the pew and fired two shots at Teddy as he fled from the church. The gun clicked twice more, but Coll knew it was empty.

"Snub-nose piece of crap," Coll said and tossed the revolver on the pew seat. "Can't even stop a whale from fifty feet."

* * *

Outside, Teddy huffed his way down the sidewalk, knocking people out of his way like a runaway freight train. He rubbed his shoulder where the two bullets were lodged as he charged across the street. In his agony, he failed to clear an onrushing truck that hit him squarely in the middle of its grille. His huge body was hurled onto the street and tumbled several yards onto streetcar tracks in a busy intersection. Still conscious, though barely, he looked to his left in time to see the fast-closing, blue and white streetcar that rolled over him, cutting his body in two.

* * *

Jim wriggled free from the tight space that had confined him, and Coll pulled him to his feet. A few remaining parishioners went to the aid of the wounded priest. Jim rushed to the trembling Dina and embraced her.

"Shit!" Coll shouted, then realized where he was and turned to face the Corpus Christi above the altar. "Damn... I'm sorry," Coll said and hung his head in disgust.

Eddie waddled into the church laden with the two duffel bags. He took in the scene in the church.

"I missed all the action?" Eddie asked.

"Let's get back to Ireland. This country's wearing me out," Coll said as he trudged to Eddie.

"I couldn't get here any quicker with these big bags. I'm not a llama, you know," Eddie said.

"What about Kyler?" Coll said.

"I stepped out to see the mess going on in the street and when I got back to the shed the bastard was gone."

"Just as well. We're done with him," Coll said.

A man burst into the church from the street outside.

"Get the priest! Get the priest!" he shouted with a British accent as he hurried up the aisle. "The big man that ran out of here just got run over by a streetcar!" Then he saw the people administering to the bloody wound on the priest. "Oh, my God."

"Was the man alive?" Coll asked the Englishman.

"I seriously doubt it. He was cut in half at the waist. Huge man. Blood everywhere."

"So now there're two, *One-Ton* Teddys?" Eddie said.

Coll went over to Jim and Dina and put his arms around them. "There's an upside to all this. You're finally out of Las Vegas."

Coll embraced Jim for a moment, then kissed Dina goodbye.

"Eddie, bring me the bags," Coll said.

Eddie made his way to Coll, who unzipped one of the bags, pulled out a wad of cash and jammed it into Jim's hand.

""That'll get you and Dina safely home," Coll said. "I'll send you some more later. You've earned a bonus."

"Jeez, Coll, I—"

"Zip it, marine," Coll said.

Coll picked up the money bag and hurriedly left the church with Eddie wheezing behind lugging the other bag. They hied it up the street away from the café.

"We need to find us a taxi, but we'd better keep a low profile while we're around here," Coll said.

"Because of the priest getting shot?" Eddie said.

"Because we assaulted a Swiss citizen, stole a Volvo, totaled it *and* a restaurant, blew up an entire street, tortured a man, and then got into a gun battle in a church," Coll said. "But there is good news. Teddy shot the priest."

"We could dial it back a shade," Eddie said, huffing.

"Ya think?"

"Upside number two: Teddy's out of our hair," Eddie said.

"That leaves Kyler and Bartel," Coll said.

"We're goin' to Ireland, for crissakes," Eddie said. "Whose gonna find us there? *Nobody*."

Chapter 73

Two weeks later, back in Cong, Connie and Coll sat in front of a dwindling fire in the small sitting room in their rented cottage. The cool fall night made the glowing embers a welcome asset as they sipped on glasses of a Chateau Margaux in the flickering light.

"Kelly says the deal to buy the town will be completed tomorrow at noon," Connie said, staring at the dying flames.

Coll held up his glass of claret so the waning light of the fire made the wine glow.

"Buy the town? Who buys ancient Irish towns?" Coll asked.

"Industrial speculators. They think there are mining possibilities here. Gold and other valuable metals."

"Who owns the town?"

"A board of elders maintains the town's finances, which are all but non-existant," Connie said. "Everyone's dirt poor here. The deal would provide jobs, and everyone would get a share in the money from the sale."

"How much is Cong worth?"

"Michael Kelly says the agreed price was 15 million dollars," Connie said and stoked the fire with a poker. "They plan to destroy what's left of an

Augustinian monastery that was built in 1128. I love that old ruin. I played in it as a child. They're going to take down the Ashford Castle as well, and many other ancient landmarks. It's not right to take away a country's history."

Coll looked at Connie with concern.

"Eddie says the climate here has cured his cough. I think it's his quitting cigarettes, but regardless, he wants to stay," Coll said.

"What'll he do here?"

"He's always wanted to breed race horses. Thoroughbreds and the like. What better place for horses than Ireland."

"And you'd sponsor him?" Connie asked.

"I'd lend him whatever he needs. Hell, I owe the guy my life."

"And you? What will you do here?"

"First of all, I'm marrying you," Coll said and gave her a peck on the lips.

"Out on the cliffs overlooking the sea?" Connie said.

"On the Sea of Copernicus on the moon, if you want. You make the arrangements and I'll show up."

"And what will you do in this boring place afterward? There's no Las Vegas and no baseball games here."

"I'll find something."

Chapter 74

The usual band of locals adorned the bar at Kelly's as Michael tended to their never-ending thirst, and listened to their constant prattle and bickering. Paddy Yeats walked over to Kelly and extended his glass to be refilled, while Eddie stood with some of his newly-found tippling pals at the bar.

"I hear the deal for the sale of the town was signed today this past noon," Paddy related with a bit of melancholy.

"You heard right," Kelly said.

"And meself being too old to work in the mines, I'll just take me share in the currency of the realm," Paddy said.

"What mining might you be referring to?" Kelly asked.

"Why, the mining for gold and the like that we sold out for to those Black and Tan Brit shits," Paddy said, then spat on the floor.

"Then you'd be wrong about that," Kelly said.

The others in the bar began to take interest in the conversation.

"About the gold part, or them being shits part," Paddy said.

"Neither."

"Did the town get sold today or not?" Paddy asked.

"Aye, but not to them bleedin' limeys," Kelly said, to partially clarify the issue, but mainly to prolong the tease.

"Well, *to whom*, pray?" one of the locals said.

"Lads, we've had a bit o' luck. A bit o' luck hard to believe for even the Irish. Our little town was bought by Connie Hannigan's yank this very day. He bested the Englishmen's offer by over ten million U.S. dollars," Kelly said, hammering his punch line with his fist on the bar.

"That Nolan fella?" Paddy said.

"*Mister* Nolan, to you, from here on," Kelly said. "We get our share of the sale and he turned right around and gave the town back to us. Have you ever heard the like? The man's a saint, he is."

"Well, I'll be shat upon and flushed," Paddy said.

"A round for the lads and a toast to Mr. Coll Nolan," Eddie said. "He says I saved his life once. Well, he saves mine every day."

The locals raised their glasses and toasted with loud voices as the front door opened and in strolled Coll. A quiet fell over the clamorous bar as all conversation stopped, and every glass was stilled. Coll didn't understand what was going on at first, but then the light went on. After several moments in the silence, Coll moved to the bar as others made room for him.

"Thank you," Coll said. "All of you."

Kelly came out from behind the bar and embraced Coll like a proud father to his son. The room broke from its silence and the regulars continued with their petty arguments. Kelly returned to behind the bar and started setting up drinks up all around.

"The drinks are on the house tonight, boys. For all except that skinflint Paddy Yeats, who pays," Kelly shouted then winked at Paddy, and handed him the first drink of the round.

The front door of the bar opened and into the festive room strode four extra-large men in tailored suits and long topcoats, followed by a tall man.

The patrons took notice and grew dead quiet. Coll and Eddie swiveled their heads toward the door to see the reason. Kelly carefully watched the two American lads as their eyes panned down the line of the four huge men, then halted their gaze on the sneering face of the tallest man.

Chapter 75

The jubilant mood Coll had enjoyed now turned into a sickening fear as he laid eyes on the menacing visitors.

"How do you guys keep doing it?" Coll said to the intruders. "It's like playing full-scale *Whack-A-Mole*."

"We do it. Only I've got an extra little surprise for you this time," Kyler said, as through the front door stepped Bartel Vandermeer, older and grayer, but still a striking presence.

"So good to see you, Coll," Bartel said. "And Eddie. What an added, if not *shocking*, surprise."

"So, you've come all this way, after all these years, to have Eddie and me killed," Coll said.

"It's all that's kept me alive," Bartel said.

"Me hand to Christ, there'll be no killing of these two lads, so long as I draw the sweet breath of Ireland," Kelly said.

"You don't understand what these men have done to my family," Bartel said.

"I know all about the likes of your family. I saw *The Godfather* three times," Kelly said.

Bartel smiled politely at Kelly. "We're not Italian, sir. We're Dutch," Bartel said.

"And you think that's better?" Kelly said.

Bartel moved over to one side and nodded to his men who drew pistols and took aim at Coll and Eddie.

The pub exploded in gunfire, almost all of it coming from the bar. Nearly every man at the bar had a rifle, shotgun, or pistol pointed and launching lead in the direction of Bartel's men, who reeled and collapsed against the front walls of the pub. Kyler was knocked out the door by the recoiling body of one of the jumbo men who had jumped in front to shield him. The heavy volley ended as quickly as it began, leaving the bar nearly silent and full of acrid gun smoke. Bartel's well-dressed henchmen lay bloody on the oaken floor, with Kyler sprawled outside the front door.

Bartel had dodged the onslaught from the bar patrons by ducking to the floor, but now swung upright, pulling a pistol from a shoulder holster. He took quick aim at the unarmed Coll. A single shot boomed in the frozen barroom tableau.

Eddie's pistol shot hit Bartel between his astounded, wide eyes, and he slowly spiraled down on dead legs to the floor; his unfired gun fell from his limp hand like Goliath's javelin.

"Enjoy hell, Bartel," Eddie said and lowered his pistol.

"Hmmph. Dutch, me arse. Try fucking with the I.R.A.," Kelly said.

Coll and the locals rushed outside in time to hold Kyler at bay on the ground. A dozen guns bore down on his cowering body.

"Kinda takes the sport out of it, eh, lads?" one of the locals said.

"Aye, it does," Kelly said as he picked up Kyler's pistol off the ground. "So what'll it be now? A duel to the death?"

"How about a nice fistfight between Mr. Nolan and this mongrel here on the dirt?" Paddy said.

"Yeah. It'll be like Trooper Thornton and Danaher in the John Wayne movie," a local said.

"I'll hold all the bets at the bar," Kelly said. "What do you say, Mr. Nolan?"

"A fistfight? Really?" Coll said.

"The last time this town was alive was when they shot that *Quiet Man* movie here in Cong," Kelly said. "It's been dead ever since. A chance to relive that fine moment in time would go a long way toward reviving us, Mr. Nolan."

"Can we do it tomorrow? When it's light out and I'm sober?" Coll asked.

"Aye, tomorrow at noon," Kelly said. "Take the asshole from Hans Brinkerville down to the local jail until fight time tomorrow. Use their fancy car here," he said pointing to the luxury limo rental next to the pub. "I doubt they'll be needin' it anymore."

"I suppose this little boxing arrangement will be okay with you?" Kelly said to Kyler.

"Can't think of anything I'd like more," Kyler said.

The locals yanked Kyler to his feet and took him away in the limo.

"I'll say one thing for you, Coll," Eddie said. "Hangin' with you sure ain't boring."

"Yeah, I'm a regular Butch Cassidy," Coll said.

Coll thought about how he was inching up on forty and had to get ready for a fist fight, like he was back in high school. What he'd just uttered triggered a memory from when he saw *Butch Cassidy and the Sundance Kid*. He was beginning to feel his age and wanted the fight tomorrow to be over fast. He understood why Paul Newman, instead of fists, had opted for kicking that seven-foot character, Harvey of the Hole in the Wall Gang, squarely in the nads.

But he knew that kind of ploy only worked in the movies.

Chapter 76

The sun was high in the sky as the entire town gathered to watch the great fight on the western high ground near the sea. Coll, Eddie, Kelly, and others from the pub all stood in a cleared area in the center of the crowd. Kyler Rotermund was brought to the clearing by two big Irishmen, who wasted no proper etiquette on his handling. The chilly and blustery sea air had both Kyler and Coll choosing sweat suits for their fighting apparel, along with athletic shoes.

"The lads donated some laboring clothes to the Dutch oaf," Kelly said. Wouldn't be nice to beat the shite out of him in his Sunday mass suit. Buryin' him in it is another matter. All right, let's get the rules straight and get on with this fight." The crowd quieted and the two combatants were brought face-to-face.

"There'll be no eye gougin', no bitin', no kickin' in the private parts, or pullin' at a man's twig and berries. Understood?" Kelly said.

Coll and Kyler nodded, then Kelly stepped back and motioned the crowd to give the fighters room.

"Have a good clean fight and may God protect the just," Kelly said, finishing up his referee's spiel. "Now get on with it."

Coll and Kyler maneuvered around each other looking for an opening. The crowd murmured and chanted boxing advice to the fighters.

"It goes on, Coll," Kyler said. "Killing you with my bare hands will be just as satisfying as doing you with a gun. Maybe more."

"More satisfying than lighter fluid?" Coll said.

"Why don't you run for it and save yourself a bad beating?" Kyler said.

"Five thousand Viet Cong soldiers couldn't make me run. What makes you think I'd run from your pathetic ass?"

"Ever fight for your life, Nolan?"

"Often."

"Prove it," Kyler said, circling around Coll in a wide arc.

"I'm afraid all my references are dead," Coll said, sluing to keep Kyler directly in view.

Kyler charged at Coll and attempted a volley of rapid punches, but Coll sidestepped him and landed a solid shot to the side of Kyler's face. The crowd cheered the blow. Kyler shook it off, recovered, and countered with a combination to Coll's body that had him doubling over. Coll worked through the ache in his gut and came back up with a flurry of punches that sent Kyler stumbling backward into the neighborhood trout stream onto his back. He sloshed about in the current of a deep pool, regained his footing, and trudged back to the bank, shaking off the coldness. Coll stalked Kyler and knocked him down again into the icy water. Kyler struggled to his feet, picked up a grapefruit-size rock from the stream bed, and hurled it at Coll. Coll ducked the rock, and the two men maneuvered the fight away from the stream.

They fought up the hill that led to the sea cliffs. Each got in his licks. Blood and reddened skin began to show on the two combatants' faces.

"Victor McLaglen had the decency to work the fight toward the pub," Paddy Yeats said.

"We'll be having a pint soon enough, you old goat," Kelly said. "So be minding the fight instead of your thirst."

The town priest, close on the sidelines, watched the battle intently, feinting and shadowboxing in time with the two fighters. The battle moved farther up the hill as both men scrambled and clawed their way upward, parrying and landing blows as they went. Soon the land ended and fell off into nothing but sky.

Coll and Kyler reached the summit of the highest cliff and breathlessly faced each other. Coll peered over the near edge to judge its closeness. The view from the cliffs was spectacular as the sea crashed against the ancient rocks far below. The crowd followed right behind them like a swarm of drones trailing a queen bee.

"How do you like Ireland so far?" Coll asked, in panted installments.

"Ain't exactly like in the brochures," Kyler said, between gasps.

Coll made a short charge and summoned a punch from his weary arm that struck a solid blow to Kyler's nose that staggered him backward and onto one knee.

"Tell you what, Kyler. Answer me this question and I'll go easy on you."

"Shit." Kyler said and spat some of the blood filling his mouth.

"All right, for a million dollars, then. It's a baseball question." Coll said, breathing hard for words.

"Shoot."

"When Babe Ruth hit 60 home runs in 1927, whose record did he break, and by how many home runs?"

Kyler stared at the ground for a moment, then slowly rose.

"Lou Gehrig, by at least twenty." Kyler said, standing on shaky legs.

"He beat his own record of 59 home runs from the year before," Coll said, then punched Kyler a solid shot to his jaw and moved in to lay on a couple more, but Kyler ducked low and body-checked Coll aside, then grunted up a rock slab the size of a sofa cushion. He trudged at Coll burdened with the heavy stone poised chest-high. Coll tried to sidestep the attack, but got his heel caught in a crevice in the rocky terrain. Kyler scuffed Coll with the rock, a glancing blow on his shoulder that battered him to the hard ground.

Kyler moved back a few steps and set up for a second run with the rock. Coll lay helpless on the ground, awaiting his fate as he desperately tried to free his trapped foot. Kyler charged again, the large rock held high, and came down with a blow aimed at Coll's head. At the last second, Coll managed to free his captive foot and brought both feet up to meet Kyler's charging body. The jolt to Kyler's gut made him release the slab, which thudded to the ground inches beyond Coll's head. Coll's raised feet, planted in the onrushing man's midsection, used his momentum to catapult him above Coll and dump his body just over the edge of the cliff.

Kyler's hands clawed at the cliff's rim and tried to pull him back to safety, but the weight of his lower body was losing its struggle with gravity. Coll scrambled to Kyler, grabbed the tops of his hands, and dug in his knees to anchor himself, but he felt the big man slipping downward, squeezing out of his grasp. Kyler's body tugged Coll's shoulders over the edge and downward. He now clung to Kyler only by the ends of his fingers. But Coll's sweaty palms could no longer hang on.

Kyler's screams were heard fading as he plummeted to the rocks far down at the sea. The stunned crowd rushed to the cliff's edge and peeked over, where a hundred feet below, lay the twisted and crushed body of Kyler Rotermund.

Connie rushed to Coll, still draped over the precipice. He was too exhausted to help himself as Kelly and others pulled him back from the cliff's edge.

"Get this man some first aid!" Kelly yelled.

"Should we take him to the clinic?" someone in the crowd asked.

"I said first aid, you dolt," Kelly said. "The pub. Get him to the pub. Can't you see the lad needs a whisky and a pint?"

"Could use a bit of first aid meself," Paddy Yeats said.

"Sweet Jaysus preserve us," Kelly said glaring at Paddy. "Do ya ever quit?"

"How's my man?" Connie asked Coll as she ran her hand over his sweaty and blood-smeared brow.

"If I'm still your man, I'm doing fabulous," Coll said.

"You were fighting right where I wanted to get married."

"Call the good father over," Coll said.

She looked at him suspiciously, then turned to Kelly. "Can you get Father Murphy over here?"

The priest pushed through the crowd gathered around Coll and Connie and knelt down next to Coll.

"Can you arrange a wedding for this fair maiden and me for tomorrow? Right here on this spot?"

"I can," said the priest. "And I will. Nothing would give me more pleasure, except for maybe the tremendous fight I just witnessed."

Connie looked far out beyond cliff's edge at the white-capped sea and smiled. Coll watched her beautiful face, and felt what it was like to have hopes realized. He'd thought that winning a huge amount of money in Las Vegas was the realization of a dream, but now he knew providence and a windy cliff in Ireland were sometimes all a wishful thought needed to be.

Tomorrow Coll would complete a young girl's dream. He would marry Connie Aileen Hannigan, north of Galway, between Lough Corrib and Lough Mask, and to the west where the Maumturks Mountains look down to the sea.

Chapter 77

Coll took a trip to the Augustinian Monastery and walked among its ancient ruins. He had come there to sort out how he should handle the fortune that had blessed him. His part of the deal was to use the money to do something that would be pleasing to God. *Was buying back the town for the people of Cong enough, Lord? Did that pay our debt in full?* Would that create a sweet sound in God's ear? Somehow he doubted it.

The well-worn little pamphlet that Coll got at the church in Las Vegas was still wedged in the sweat-stained creases of his wallet. He took it out, opened its tattered, tri-fold panels and looked it over. His eyes went to a small passage at the top of the center section. It was from Matthew 5:16 and read:

> **"Let your light shine before men in such a way that they may see your good works and glorify your Father who is in heaven."**

From that moment, Coll knew exactly what he was destined to do.

Chapter 78

The helicopter landed in a field on the huge Crow reservation south of Billings, Montana. Ron Darby, the local sheriff, jumped out and walked to the Office of Native American Affairs a hundred yards away. Inside, he asked the clerk there if he could see Amachee. The clerk got on the phone and made a short call.

"My son will get him," the clerk said. "Is there any trouble?"

"No, no trouble at all," Ron said and stepped outside.

After several minutes, Amachee approached and greeted the sheriff.

"What brings you down this way, Ron?" Amachee said. "Need to know where the cutthroats are hitting?"

"Nothing as much fun as that, I'm afraid. Can you take a ride with me?"

"In that?" Amachee said pointing to the helicopter.

"It'll get us there a lot faster than by horse," Ron said.

"I've made my peace with the spirits, so let's go," Amachee said.

The flight took less than a half hour, and before Ron and Amachee could catch up on the latest fishing news, they were landing in a clearing near a large ranch with fencing as far as the eye could see. A large number of horses inside the fence nibbled on patches of vegetation wherever they could find them, while others trotted and frolicked around a white water stream that rippled through the property.

Ron and Amachee left the helicopter and hiked uphill to the gate and driveway that led to a sprawling ranch house. A new model, heavy-duty pickup truck was parked in the driveway near the rancher, and several horse trailers were parked in front of a massive barn a hundred yards from the house.

"Pretty nice place," Ron said as he stopped at the fence and draped his arms over its top rail.

"It is beautiful. Who owns it?" Amachee said, joining Ron at the fence.

"You do," Ron said.

Amachee stared at Ron, his eyes narrowed.

"What do you mean?"

"I mean you are the new owner of everything you see here."

"Who died?" Amachee asked.

"No one died. Looks like a dog bought it for you. Named Collie, I think the realtor said."

"Collie is not a dog."

"Well this Collie, whatever he is, must be man's best friend 'cause this spread cost a whole lot of dog biscuits. More than I'll make in my lifetime."

"My friend is very special," Amachee said.

Ron took a large set of tagged keys from his pocket and handed them to Amachee. "These open everything on the ranch, plus that new truck you see there in the driveway," Ron said. "There's a briefcase inside the door of the house with all the papers you'll need to get this place legally signed over to you. The realtor's card is in there too. Call her and she'll answer any questions you have. I've got to go take some bad guys to the courthouse here in Bozeman, so, Amachee, you have yourself a nice life."

The sheriff walked back to the helicopter and signaled the pilot to spool up the aircraft.

"You're going to leave me here?" Amachee yelled after Ron.

"This is your new home," Ron said. "You're home now. And you've got a new truck to drive anywhere you want, plus horses. What more mobility do you need?"

"Okay. It's going to take some time for all this to sink in, I guess," Amachee said.

"By the way, the land on your deed includes a big part of the river south of here. There's even a real pretty waterfall upstream," Ron hollered over the din of the chopper blades.

Amachee waved goodbye to the helicopter as it ascended over the trees and flew off into the distance. He opened the gate and stepped onto the driveway inside the fence, then closed the gate behind him. He went up to the truck and ran his hand over the chrome hood ornament that depicted a hawk in flight.

He ascended the front steps of the porch and saw a greeting card thumb-tacked to the door frame. He removed it and read it.

Amachee,
>   ***My spirits want you to always be safe too — and happy.***

Coll

Amachee pressed the card to his chest and bowed his head for a long moment before he rose and stepped to the front door. He tried several keys Ron had given him and found one that unlocked it. He made his way into the house and took a look around the great room beyond the foyer. He saw fine leather upholstery and the most exquisite mahogany furniture. Bookcases rose from floor to ceiling on one large wall filled with hundreds of volumes. In the center of the main wall was a huge stone fireplace over which was a carved walnut mantelpiece. Above the mantel was an oil painting. It was an original oil of Edgar Samuel Paxon's depiction of *Custer's Last Stand*. Amachee looked at the painting for a long moment. He then returned to the porch and crossed to an oak swing suspended by chains and sat.

A young colt came around from behind the house, stood in front of the porch, and stared at his new owner. Amachee looked back at him and smiled. He smiled not because he'd been given a fortune in gifts.

Amachee smiled because he knew his friend had realized his dream.

Chapter 79

Through the mullioned window of The Pirouette Dance Studio, Connie Hannigan Nolan faced a row of young girls in leotards and led the group in a ballet exercise. She smiled and radiated delight as she put her young lasses through their work at the barre. To Connie, the girls' faces shone with hopes of being part of *Swan Lake* and *The Nutcracker*, and traveling to places like Radio City Music Hall, The Bolshoi, and The Royal to perform someday. The girls could dream of their tomorrows, but Connie had all she'd ever wanted in this present.

Her studio was nestled in a row of small shops on a quaint street in Cong, which comprised just about the entire commercial enterprise of the town. Cong's population had been dwindling for years, and while the current resident count was under 200, its estimated value, based on the recent bidding war for the place, had soared into double digit millions in U.S. dollars. Coll had put additional money into municipal improvements, and Connie had added to the aesthetic value of the town by opening her dance studio for the local female youth. It may not have been the saving grace for the tourism of Cong, but it was for Connie.

* * *

Michael Kelly and Paddy Yeats leaned on the construction barrier at the ancient Augustinian Monastery and Abbey and watched men on scaffolds, who worked on the restoration of the exterior of the historic monument. Tourists gathered to watch with them and got to see something they rarely witnessed: something built by man and still standing after over 800 years. Instead of eroding and falling down, it was going up before their amazed and joyful eyes.

"All that's missing," Paddy said, "is a pint."

"Sweet Jaysus," Kelly said.

* * *

Coll breathed in the air as he knelt in what had been an overgrown meadow weeks before. Across rolling hills and past copses of trees, there existed a flat green field issuing the most enchanting aroma of vanilla from the freshly-mown grass. A young lad listened intently as Coll coached him with throwing motions to an imaginary target. The student mimicked Coll's instructions and laughed when his coach raised his fists in victory, as if the lesson had been perfectly learned and well executed. The boy wore a black numeral 8 sewn on the back of his orange jersey, and produced a special smile that Coll believed only visits a child's face.

* * *

Eddie Menning, mounted on a fifteen-hand chestnut horse, wended his way through a gathering of kids of mixed ages, and headed for a fenced-in field. The faces of the children inside were bright and alive with enthusiasm. A noisy crowd of people congregated on two sides of the field and sat in seats within the new stadium's enclosure.

A group of uniformed children with baseball gloves and colorful hats ran onto the open grass and took various positions, most of them facing the crowd. Bases had been installed, and white lines had been drawn in lime from home plate to the extreme right and left outfield fences. A boy with a bat listened for a moment to an man who whispered in his ear before he approached the batter's box. The front of his uniform boldly displayed the words:

CONG KINGS

A black-clad umpire blew a loud whistle. The crowd quieted to a murmur. A baseball game was about to begin.

Coll Nolan beamed as he looked on from the stands like an expectant father. Coll's love of the game was no longer tied to winning money on its outcomes, but with its pure soul that provided kids of all ages a chance to play, whether big or small. He loved the fact that baseball was the only major sport where a person does the scoring, not a ball or a puck; a game whose only object is to bring your players safely home.

Coll pulled the feather and cross amulet up from under his neck and looked at the gift that Amachee had given him and knew in his heart that he too was, at last, safely home.

The construction of sky boxes, terrace boxes, bleacher seats, and dugouts were well underway. A ninety-foot steel pole supported an enormous beacon light in the shape of a regal crown at its top that could be seen for miles. Coll knew people from near and far would soon be attending the games played here. There was a new stadium under construction for his beloved Baltimore Orioles at a place called Camden Yards. The closer his park compared to that one, the better.

Below the light pole hung a sign, positioned at the entrance to the field, and printed at its top, the words:

MacGuffin Baseball Field

Movng down the sign, the next line read:

**Maintained by the People of Cong,
County Mayo, Ireland**

Farther down green shamrocks appeared below a celtic crucifix.

And the sign's final phrase:

BUILT BY GOD

About the Author

Paul Sekulich was a Hollywood television writer and script doctor for several years and has now trained his sights on novel writing. He teaches television and movie scriptwriting on the college level, and holds degrees with majors in Theatre and Communications.

Detective Frank Dugan will be his lead character in a series of books he has planned for the near future. His new Frank Dugan crime thriller, ***Resort Isle***, the Frank Dugan prequel, is currently available on Amazon, as is ***The Omega Formula***, book number two in the series. A third Frank Dugan thriller, ***Murder Comes to Paradise***, will be making its debut this summer.

If you'd care to email or share your thoughts about this book with Paul, or see upcoming works from the author, visit his website at:

http://mdnovelist.com

I can't adequately express, in these few lines, how important reviews are to authors. Please take a moment to leave me a review at Amazon.com.

It keeps writers writing. And it is appreciated beyond measure.

-- PBS

Made in the USA
Middletown, DE
26 September 2017